Gripping! A fiery young ~~~~~ ~~~~~~ home, compelled to undo a heart-twisting mistake. Layers of trouble meet her in a sultry North Carolina summer. Sara Johnson Allen delivers a pulsing, gorgeous debut novel full of schemes of survival, schemes of love.

—**Mary-Beth Hughes,** author of *The Ocean House*

This debut is a literary mic drop. From its propulsive start to its satisfying close, *Down Here We Come Up* captures the convergence of three women who must weigh what's unpalatable against what's best for their children. Maternal sacrifice beats at the heart of this book, but its blood courses through the evolving landscape of race and class in the American south, the expanding drug trade, and the exploitation and abuse of migrant workers. It's an origin story and an examination of belonging composed in vibrant detail, with tone and themes reminiscent of *Where the Crawdads Sing* and Netflix's *Ozark*. *Down Here We Come Up*, like the hospitality attributed to its setting, will draw you in and won't easily let you go.

—**Alena Dillon,** author of *Mercy House*
and *Eyes Turned Skyward*

Kate thought she'd escaped the poverty and shame of her childhood, but when the mistakes and betrayals of her past come calling, she's faced with the debts she owes to history, to blood, and must decide how much she is willing to risk to settle them. Tender, honest, and thought-provoking, *Down Here We Come Up* is an illuminating journey to the dark heart of forgiveness and self discovery. A daring debut from a writer to watch.

—**Meagan Lucas,** author of *Songbirds and Stray Dogs*
and *Here in the Dark*

From the moment Kate "borrows" her boyfriend's car and drives south to confront her past, nothing seemed more important than reading *Down Here We Come Up*. This is a mother-daughter story like no other: vivid, suspenseful and full of high stakes questions about love, money, sex, children and immigration. A fabulous debut.

—Margot Livesey, author of *The Boy in The Field*

Down Here We Come Up stings, and it stings good. A mother's love can be as real as it is transactional. A daughter's roots can endure even as they destroy. Sara Johnson Allen's North Carolina and larger American landscape are startlingly alive on the page. In the space between its scorched grass and freezer burned peas, the book sizzles and aches. A tenacious and moving work.

—Simon Han, author of *Nights When Nothing Happened*

In exquisite prose, Sara Johnson Allen explores motherhood in the face of wrenching economic and racial realities of the American south yet weaves moments of joy and exhilaration throughout. *Down Here We Come Up* is written with such empathy and grace that I felt I knew these women and will carry them with me for a long time.

—Ana Reyes, author of *The House in the Pines*

DOWN
HERE
WE
COME
UP

www.blacklawrence.com

Executive Editor: Diane Goettel

Cover and interior design: Zoe Norvell
Cover Artwork: *Mayapple* (study for Inhabit), 2022, ink on paper by
Joan Linder. Courtesy the Artist and Cristin Tierney Gallery

Published 2023 by Black Lawrence Press.
Printed in the United States.

DOWN HERE
WE COME UP

SARA JOHNSON ALLEN

BLACK LAWRENCE PRESS

For my mother, Phyllis Hacken Johnson, who gave me everything.

PROLOGUE

JACKIE JESSUP'S APOLOGY to her daughter Kate refused to get lost in the stagnant air of her death. It rustled the tobacco leaves in the field beside her bungalow. It snaked through silver turkey houses and ripe hog lagoons before traveling across the acreage being clear cut for subdivisions east of Fayetteville. From there, it moved way down south, under concrete overpasses caught by sinking bayous on one side and rising seas on the other. The apology skimmed the rubble of neighborhoods left ruined and rotting after last year's Category Five, when the levees broke and everything low was left to drown.

Jackie's apology moved west across a country split into ill-fitting parts, some of the divisions made by grey lines on a map, some by beliefs handed down. Other breaks were created by different angles on the same story because, as Jackie had said many times, "A person cannot stand in two places at once. Use that to your advantage."

Near Fort Worth, in the hot, dry middle, Jackie's apology lagged, barely moved at all, although the words were still there.

"I should not have kept you from your daughter, but you kept me from mine."

It was as close to an apology a stubborn con artist like Jackie could offer.

In the end, Kate heard none of it. She did not hear that which had travelled so far, so fast, too late. At the moment of her mother's death, Kate was driving over the Bridge of the Americas into Juárez. She was crossing a border so wide it could only be partially sewn shut with razor wire, surveillance cameras, and border police.

It was a divide not unlike the one between people who love each other in complicated ways but cannot hear what needs to be said.

ONE

KATE LEARNED FROM Jackie all the different ways to calculate a value. There was a thing's market value, the perceived value, the true value, the if-the-buyer-was-drunk value. There was the value of everything that fell between the cracks of the car seats of men staying over. Kate and her twin brother Luke had the job of reaching down into the tight spaces for escaped cash or jewelry. They could at least swipe a few CDs to sell, but not so many that the man, whoever he was this time, would notice he had been picked through.

Early on, Jackie insisted her children pocket food from the free lunch program at school for dinner. Two-for-one, she called it. She switched the price tags on items in the grocery store until the Food Lion introduced bar code scanners. She got away with it at the Piggly Wiggly for nearly another year, but eventually even the older grocery stores caught up.

She saw everything. Like the time she noticed from the back pew on a Sunday morning in March, when it was just starting to get good and hot, the preacher's wife sweating through the back of her shirt, unfortunately white, showing a series of bruises across her shoulder blades. That warranted Jackie's eyes narrowing slightly, the church bulletin flipped over and a note made in her formal, old-fashioned cursive. That was their short-lived period as Free Will Baptists before they had been Seventh Day, then just run-of-the-mill Southern Baptists. Jackie eventually gave it up altogether because time was money and unless she could pull something back from the little she put in the offering plates, she might as well focus her resources elsewhere.

The kind of value Jackie hunted for went far beyond monetary. A bird in the hand was worth two in the bush. A pack of smokes was more valuable on the bedside table than all the way in the living room. An envelope mailed to yourself and left unopened gave proof of the date you knew something and wrote it in a letter. The imprint of the postmark stood witness. A box of old photographs bought at a yard sale, copies of other people's rental agreements stolen from a dumpster behind the beach realty office. The yellow pages. Any scrap of information might prove to be worth *something*. Then again, it might not, but one could never know.

Kate was no good in school, but she was a fast learner. She watched Jackie add things up, subtract out costs, look for opportunities that would yield *more*, whether it was a carton of Kool 100's or a white envelope stuffed with cash. Jackie could con people into anything because she saw ahead of everyone else by several moves. In a different set of circumstances, Jackie might have been a great chess player, someone who could beat the fast strategies of the men playing outside the Au Bon Pain in Harvard Square where Kate later followed her twin brother Luke when he received enough merit and need-based scholarships plus loan money that it didn't matter he had no actual money.

Luke had their mother's sense of scope, a patience for making one move that led to another then another, eventually landing where he wanted.

"I'm getting out of here," he whispered to Kate in the darkness of the bedroom they shared.

"When? How?"

"Soon. College." He was not even ten years old.

Kate lacked her brother's patience. If Luke and Jackie were glaciers capable of steady, long-term calculation and grinding pressure, Kate was a volcano. She learned to spread sparks that eventually burned so fierce they devoured all the oxygen, leaving only black ash. Not every fire Kate set was intentional, but most were useful because another thing Jackie had taught her children was how to look for buried shine where everyone else saw rubble.

The morning Jackie called to drag up what her daughter had tried to put down, Kate was checking the roof vents at work in the university greenhouse. *87 degrees. 56 percent humidity. 8:21 a.m.* Kate recorded it all on the chart by the control panel. After a bad week avoiding her boyfriend Charlie, she was glad she was the first one on shift this Friday, alone with just the sound of the ventilation fans. Everyone else who worked at the greenhouse had a master's or PhD in botany. Kate only had a GED, but she knew what she was doing. She had worked in greenhouses since she was fourteen. She could effectively deadhead, pot, prune, graft, irrigate, and transplant, rarely consulting the databases other staff members used to see if something was full-sun or partial or how far one thing needed to be planted from another. Except for the other employees, Kate loved her work. She loved the invisible business of growing. She loved how at first, there was nothing but the blackness of the soil, some constellations of white fertilizer, but nothing visible, until the heat and light on the surface created enough pressure for something to push through.

Kate wound her dark brown hair on top of her head then

twisted in a pencil to secure it. The thick bangs she was trying to grow out fell across her forehead. She pushed them to the side as she lifted a limp habanera plant out of its plastic pot with her thumb. Root rot. All the anti-fungal soil in the world wouldn't help if the others who thought they were too good for that part of the job kept replanting seedlings too deep.

Kate was finishing recording the blossom yields for the habaneras when her phone vibrated in the front pocket of her khaki uniform shorts. She flipped it open to see a number with an unfamiliar 210 area code. She was about to clap it closed then realized it might be Luke from someone else's device.

"I thought you were already in Nantucket." Kate held the phone between her shoulder and cheek. Silence on the other end. "Hello?"

"I reckon you were expecting someone else."

Kate could not reconcile her mother's voice with the neat rows of plants or the lines on her graph paper. Her skin already damp from the greenhouse's humid heat, she felt a drip run between her shoulder blades.

"I know you're there, Katie. I can hear you breathing."

Kate drew a short breath. "What do you want, Mama?"

"So *that's* the way you say hello after all these years?"

"It's only been a few months, and you're the one who said you weren't going to call me again."

"I don't recall saying that."

Kate looked over her shoulder toward the window of the office. Staff were not allowed to use phones in the houses. Kate sank down on the concrete floor behind the plant table. She crossed her legs, her knees resting on her Timberland work boots. "Mama, I'm at work. What do you want?"

"Listen to you," Jackie said. "You might have forgot, but down here, we show respect for our elders. Anyway, what kind of work? I thought you were a kept woman of some Harvard professor."

Kate should have known better than to tell Jackie about Charlie. That last call, Jackie wanted Kate to invest in a new Cook Out franchise she claimed to be opening in Wilmington.

"Look, I need something."

"I figured."

"You say that like I've never done anything for you." Jackie made a whistling sound as she inhaled again.

Kate could smell the Kool 100.

"Katie, I need you to come back home for a while."

She heard the sound of someone punching the code into the keypad on the greenhouse door and pulled back smaller against the plant table. "Mama, that's not going to happen."

"I have something you want," Jackie said.

Here it comes, Kate thought. Never something for nothing. She had to give her mother credit for that. Every deal had two sides.

"I need you to get someone's children."

Whoever had come into the far end of the greenhouse was writing with a squeaky marker on the whiteboard used to track work flow. Kate was careful to keep her voice down. "Whose children?"

"It doesn't matter."

"What children do you even know?"

"That's what I need to talk to you about. In person."

Through the legs of the tables, Kate now saw her boss Prendi's blue Vans moving down the aisle toward her, his tapered jeans tight above his ankles. Kate pulled herself up onto the heels of her boots, but stayed crouched down.

"I have to go."

"Don't you hang up on me, Katie."

Kate clapped her phone shut.

Prendi stood at the end of the row, staring at her where she crouched on the floor.

"Were you talking to someone?" Prendi shoved his hands in the pockets of his hoodie. "You know we don't allow phones in the greenhouses."

"Family emergency." Kate stood but felt dizzy enough she might sink back to the floor.

Prendi stared at her, not the way other men did, something different. When she first started the job, Kate knew Prendi resented her the same way the other people who worked at the greenhouse did. No one else got three weeks off in a row like she was about to have. Just like getting Kate the job in the first place, a phone call from Charlie a few weeks ago left Prendi as a postdoc saying the only thing he felt he could to a tenure-track professor on the main campus where a building was named after his family. *Yes. Of course.*

"I wasn't able to find anyone to cover your shifts, so could you please do the PH tests on the hybrids before you leave?"

Kate ignored her phone vibrating in her shorts front pocket. "Yes, and I'll flush the irrigation system too."

Kate opened a metal drawer in House Three. She turned off the phone. She gathered the soil test packages. Tearing open the first test with her teeth, she scooped tiny spoonfuls into the plastic test tubes. Although the April morning was still cool and flat grey outside, the houses were warming up. Kate used the edge of her T-shirt to wipe the sweat away from her eyes.

Kate knew heat. She knew it up and down like the motion of a paper fan in a closed-window church. Blot-a-cloth-against-your-sweaty-forehead heat. Waving-up-from-the-asphalt-like-a-mirage heat. Wet heat. That was the kind she grew up with outside of Wilmington in the creaking, rotting bungalow with no air conditioning. Kate and Luke would steal the box fan from the living room, point it directly where they lay stuck to the sheets in the double bed. They pressed frozen wet washcloths like hard fossils into their armpits to bring their temperature down.

Crackling heat. "You've got a way of jumping out of the skillet and into the fire don't you?" their neighbor Ruby Newkirk said when Kate was seventeen and pregnant and about to run away from home the first time.

Kate knew heat well enough to know Jackie's call was a lit match dropped in kerosene.

She slipped into the women's changing room and turned her phone back on. She leaned her shoulder against the metal lockers waiting for the display to come back.

She pressed "1" to play the only message left out of fourteen missed calls.

"Katie, we need you. I wouldn't ask you to do something for nothing. I have something for you, something I know you still want." There were voices in the background, several people talking over each other making it hard to hear at first. "Katie, I found her."

Kate played the message again.

And again.

Katie, I found her.

Kate sat down on the lacquered wooden bench that divided the locker room. Jackie was probably lying. That's what her brother Luke would have said.

We need you. What kind of "we?"

She skipped out on the rest of her shift. The entire ride back on the 66 bus, Kate tried to stay above all that Jackie's call dredged up.

Usually when a memory rose up, Kate had the ability to remove it with fast, accurate scalpel incisions that could cut the memory right out before it could take her over. Cut. It was only forty-eight hours of her life. Cut. It was something that she had already decided and couldn't take back, like emptying a clip of ammunition that can't be reloaded. Cut. It was something that was better for everyone. Cut. That puzzle-piece-clicking feeling when she smelled her baby's skin. Cut. Running her bottom lip across the impossible petal softness of her daughter's head. Cut. Surgical precision.

That had worked for eight years. Cut it out before the loss could flow through her. Follow Luke to Boston. Cut. When Charlie asked her out five years ago and she knew already they were wrong together, she still said yes. Cut. Every time she saw a four-year-old, then a five-year-old, then this year, eight-year-olds, Kate searched them for the features that might have formed from that sweet new-born face she had briefly held against her own. Cut. Somewhere, that girl. Cut. Kate had cut and cut and cut.

TWO

HIS ADDRESS GAVE it away if you knew property values in the blocks west of Harvard Square. Back in Wilmington, the Victorian might only be an elegant house in a historic district. Anyone might own it. In Cambridge, the once colonial college town situated in a major biotech and financial hub, Charlie's house was a multi-million-dollar home, sold to him by his father for a dollar. Kate remembered the first time she walked behind him up the original granite stairs to the porch with its swing and oversized wicker furniture set with thick floral-print cushions. A porch like that was rare in New England, but something even the poorest homes had in the South.

Three months into their dating, Kate moved in. The house was part of Charlie's family inheritance. Everything about him was part of that handing down too. Charlie was tall. His dirty blond hair was cropped short, his large grey eyes rimmed with thick eyelashes. He moved with a confidence that made him easy to follow.

His father C.J. had the new money. Charlie's mother Jean brought the old. Charlie once explained to Kate what a Boston Brahmin family was, how the cash no longer flowed as it had in the eighteenth and nineteenth centuries in the form of Far East goods, opium, and enslaved people. Kate found it disconcerting how he said it all so casually. Now it was mostly a name, real estate, and decent annual payments from various century-old trusts. Between the lines of inheritance on both Jean and C.J.'s sides of the family, there were many houses, which promised to keep her brother busy. Luke was a restoration carpenter, currently benefitting greatly from Charlie's family's historic holdings.

When Kate first saw their oldest property on the island in Maine, she had only been dating Charlie a few weeks. Kate hadn't understood what she was looking at until later. Jackie would have called it a dump. The main house, old servants' cottage, and smaller cabins weren't even winterized. The kitchen hadn't been updated since the 1960s because through the 1980s hired help made the meals. There was no sand beach, just steep steps down a rocky cliff to a dock below. From the dock, miles of steep coastline were visible, much of which Charlie's family owned.

"I don't think we have anything like this in North Carolina," Kate said, starting to realize the depth of the history she was staring down the barrel of.

"That's because the Union troops burned your aristocracy to the ground in 1864," Charlie said. "That sets back wealth accumulation."

She didn't like when he used his professor voice with her.

The Nantucket house, where Charlie and her brother Luke were waiting for her right now, was different. It was newer, covered in silver shingles with a wall of windows facing the ocean. Most of the homes on Nantucket were that same grey shingle, designed to blend in with the natural landscape, Charlie had told her. There were only two other houses within sight of the property.

Had it been a North Carolina beach, the houses would be so close you could throw a can of beer from one deck to the next.

There would be mini-golf and bumper boats wafting exhaust. There would be waterslides, a Dairy Queen with long lines and dusty moths flying around in the flood lights. A surf shop with cheap foam boogie boards and oversized beach towels with close-ups of the faces of panthers and tigers and phrases like *Ride-Or-Die* airbrushed over Harleys. There would be weather-beaten piers like the one where she used to lean over the railing and watch the Portuguese man-of-wars tangle their purple tentacles in the barnacle-encrusted pilings.

None of that in Nantucket. Everything there was so fucking beautiful.

The layers of historic legacy nestled in the multiple properties unnerved Kate. She was sure she might be asked to leave at any given moment. Not Luke. He was fine with it. He acted like he would completely deny any memory of being born to a single mother in an old sharecroppers' bungalow with no central heat, or at least deftly skip over any question about his past. She had seen him do it before. And he had his reasons.

Jackie had used her children's identities to take out credit in different forms over the years until their scores were beyond repair. Kate attempted to explain this to Charlie when he asked why she had a pay-by-the-minute cellphone. Luke was the one to first find out what Jackie had done when a guidance counselor helped him fill out his FAFSA forms for college. After some digging, when he understood the financial disaster Jackie had created, that had been the moment, as far as Kate could tell, that he was done with their mother. The fact that she had tampered with his future, he would never forgive her for that.

Luke loved their life with Charlie's family. When someone threw out the *New York Times* crossword clue to the room, Luke was the first to offer an answer. He learned quickly how to pick a lobster and eat a steamer. He swirled his wine in long-stemmed glassware. Kate understood Luke had been looking for a better-suited family his entire life, especially one with a father.

The last time she had seen her brother was nearly a month ago at a Jewish deli. Lately, Luke had been thinking maybe their ancestry traced that way. He thought there might be something to the charoset and the smoked salmon. Before that, it was Middle Eastern. He told Kate he really felt something when he ate this one lamb couscous dish at Café Zerza in Kendall Square. But the restaurant closed down unexpectedly, and he told her he would keep conducting his research this way, stuffed grape leaf by grape leaf, gnocchi by gnocchi, kebab by kebab, and now Jewish food, food from regions that could explain them. Kate and Luke had thick, dark hair. Her skin was more olive than her brother's, but they were both tan again after the first few sunny days to end New England winter. They looked nothing like strawberry blonde Jackie with her bright blue eyes and translucent skin. Luke would keep going until something struck him, running from his taste buds all the way to the very core of his DNA. He was one to want answers.

Kate pushed her house key into the lock. She leaned into the heavy wooden door opening it into the dark, cool house. She knew she was alone. Charlie and Luke had caught the first ferry. She was expected on the last. She and Charlie had been avoiding each other effectively since the previous weekend after returning from his friend Anton's place in Brooklyn. She suspected that what they had done there after too many drinks had finally ended them, but neither had confirmed it yet.

By now, she guessed Luke and Charlie were busy in Nantucket becoming part of the frenetic motion of all the house guests lifting bikes and kayaks down from roof-top car racks, carrying overflowing grocery bags and coolers full of live lobsters and cherrystone clams. They would be lining cases of wine up by the sliding glass door of the living room, stacking towels on deck chairs.

Kate moved through the foyer, which was twice as big as the bedroom she and Luke had shared growing up. A hand-carved mahogany railing followed the staircase as it rose up above the marble mantled fireplace where three generations of Charlie's family had dried out galoshes and overcoats. She moved to the bottom of the staircase. Her palm against the smooth wood steadied her.

"Chickens always come home to roost," Kate's neighbor Mrs. Newkirk liked to say when someone had to face the damage they had done. Mrs. Newkirk had been both a grandmother and a mother in many of the ways in which Jackie was incapable. Her sturdy white farmhouse and the shade offered by the mature pecan trees that surrounded it had been one of Kate's favorite hiding places when she was young. Mrs. Newkirk had taught Kate how to make two small cuts at the base of a squirrel's tailbone to strip the fur off in one pull, how to make caramel frosting without burning the sugar, how to put up a bushel of peaches when they all came in at once. Kate swallowed hard against the memory of dropping flour-dusted meat into the bacon grease, which popped and spat onto her bare arms.

"Katie, get under that thigh before it sticks to my cast iron," Mrs. Newkirk said handing her a spatula. "Trick is to cook it through without it getting tough. That right there is the key to just about everything, Sugar."

Mrs. Newkirk had been like family, but in the eight years since she left North Carolina, Kate had not so much as placed a phone call or written a letter to the woman who had in large part raised her.

Jackie liked to lay out her blame more directly. She liked to say, "Katie, you could ruin a two-car funeral, couldn't you?"

The southern women who raised Kate had an endless language of judgmental wisdom accusing people of paddling with one oar, acting like a squirrel in a cage, staggering around like a chicken with its head cut off.

Kate started up the sweeping staircase to change out of her work clothes. She drew her phone from her pocket. At least Jackie had stopped calling. There was only one missed call from an unknown number she guessed was Prendi on the greenhouse line wondering why she disappeared mid-shift.

She listened to Jackie's voicemail just one more time.

Katie, we need you. Katie, I found her.

In the upstairs hall with the long Persian runner extending in front of her, she could hear what she had missed before in the background of the message. She turned up the speaker volume all the way and listened again to be sure. It was Smith, his voice familiar, the sound of him flowing deep and pulling at the earth of her, turning the soil to expose the roots. His voice raked away her ability to breathe.

She could make out: *not if I'm there.* Then he said something in Spanish.

It made no sense that Smith would be anywhere near Jackie. They hated each other. Also, he didn't speak Spanish. When Kate failed Spanish sophomore year, Smith was high in the desk right next to her failing it too, him for the second time.

From the top of the stairs, Kate headed straight for their bedroom, which at midday was full of light from the windows that faced the street. On her side of the unmade, antique four-poster bed, she found her duffle bag on the floor. Kate lifted it onto the rumpled white duvet. She riffled through what she had started packing for Nantucket. Her cosmetics bag. A linen cocoon dress. Her bikinis with the most coverage. Two long sundresses, one navy blue, one burgundy. She had been packing for the cocktail hours on the deck, the nodding, the smiling, the listening to Luke and Charlie make their plans to catch an early morning run of bluefish on C.J.'s Grady-White.

She thought again of the voicemail message. Thought of Luke, the way he was so woven into the family to the point she couldn't see him anymore. How Charlie made it clear in Brooklyn what her value was to him.

Suddenly, she wasn't just packing for the weekend. She was stuffing everything into the duffle bag. Her most expensive pair of jeans. Various neutral-colored tank tops. The black cashmere sweater wrap, a Christmas present from Charlie. She pulled everything from her drawers and the closets. The T-shirts she wore the most. Her black heels. The wooden hangers swung wildly in the aftershock of her pulling. She had not known how badly she wanted to leave until she was packing to go.

THREE

FOR THE FIRST couple hours after leaving Boston, Kate leaned forward almost touching the steering wheel, her shoulders tight. Driving west on the Mass Pike with the rest of the people getting an early afternoon jump on leaving the city, Kate kept Charlie's Audi in the right lane much slower than the rest of the traffic.

Charlie would not know his car was missing for a while. He was on Nantucket for two weeks then headed to the island off Maine for another two. This is what he had done every single summer of his life. Paddling, swimming, sailing. Shucking oysters for cocktail hour in various homes along the New England coast. He would return to the classroom in September, his dark blond hair burnt lighter, the freshman girls stunned into silence by their impossible luck of having him for U.S. & World Order.

Charlie and Kate had originally planned to drive with Luke from Hyannis to Rockland, both ferry ports, moving from one island to another without going back to Cambridge. If that plan held, she could have as much as a month before he really understood she was gone and not just avoiding vacation with him.

She had only driven this route once in her life, but she knew the way was to follow 95 forever to 40 in Benson. Just keep following the blue shields with 9 and 5 under the red "interstate" banner. She remembered there were variations on that main route that the truckers discussed with her mother, their favorite stopovers and short cuts. She remembered the names of the various parkways (Merritt and Palisades) but not which was best. There were cut arounds in places she had never been but remembered the names. Allentown over Harrisburg. Tappan Zee not George Washington.

The only time she had driven this way herself was when she was the passenger of a man praying over her as they moved south, his right hand on her thigh, his left on the steering wheel.

In Hartford, she moved into the middle lane increasing her speed, but it was short lived. North of New York, the traffic clogged. The highway lanes narrowed so much she was sure she would be forced into another vehicle. They seemed close enough to touch if she unrolled her window. The line of traffic slowed to a standstill on the George Washington Bridge. With the loss of speed and momentum, she couldn't help but reconsider things. She had flipped from telling her mother no way to apparently having walked out of her life in Boston.

When Kate finally made it south of the city and the traffic let up, she could breathe again. The bridges stretched over rivers that were lined factory after factory, their smoke stacks so tall they needed flashing lights to warn airplanes. Just past Trenton, she slammed on her brakes and barely missed rear-ending the minivan in front of her. All the cars funneled down to a single lane. In the stop and go, she kept leaning around to try to see how far the traffic went.

When Kate finally reached the front, she saw the police lights flashing. Where three cruisers were parked along the shoulder of the road, she braced herself for the accident. When it was her turn to pass by the officer waving them through one by one, Kate saw the problem. A dog paced back and forth across the lanes. Its tan fur twitched over ribs so defined, it was clear the dog was no one's pet. Two police officers crouched down with a white paper bag trying to lure the animal over to them.

As she passed slowly by, she heard one of the officers say, "Are we going to have to shoot this fucking thing?"

"That's the last thing we need." The other officer threw half a bagel to the dog cowering by the lane divider.

All the way through New Jersey, Pennsylvania, and Delaware, Kate couldn't erase the image of that dog up against the divider.

In the port of Baltimore, cranes lifted rectangular boxes from the decks of container ships down onto the backs of tractor trailers. Loaded trucks barreled by her, shaking the Audi with their weight. It was just past nine when Kate finally stopped at a convenience store in Columbia, Maryland. She needed gas. She had to pee. She was hungry, but also Luke had called her twice in a row near Laurel.

When she parked and called back, he answered half way through the first ring. He started right in, "Where were you? I'm sailing tomorrow morning, so you need to find another ride."

And this was the problem, Kate thought. She had fallen into the world of Charlie because, yeah, she had liked him, anyone would. He was incredibly charming, but he had never felt like home to her. She wasn't like Luke in this. He not only felt comfortable, he was choosing Charlie's family over her.

"Well, I'd hate to get in the way of your sailing."

"I thought we had a plan. I just drove from the house, and waited here for almost two hours. If you missed the ferry, you could have just called."

"I won't be on the next one either."

"Just get an island taxi when you get here," Luke said.

"I'm going back."

"To Cambridge?"

"No. Mama called."

She could hear the air coming through the open window of his truck. He had just purchased a new F-150 and painted the logo for his restoration company on the side. "Katie, what are you doing?"

"She wants me to come home."

"She's always wanted that."

"It's different this time."

"There's nothing different. You've forgotten what it's really like down there."

"Luke, you act like everything up there is ours. It isn't."

"You want to see my deed?"

This was something Luke was endlessly proud of. His new two-family gut job in Lowell. Luke paid a mortgage. Kate didn't. No rent either since she moved in with Charlie, though she paid in other ways.

Kate had seen people's reactions to her at different alumni receptions and Homecoming cocktail parties. Once they found out about Charlie's research, Playboy Enterprises as a force of cultural change in mid-century America, there was always some flash of recognition, some sort of new understanding of him...and her. Even the Women's Studies professors who argued with him about the effects of pornography did so standing a bit closer than Kate felt necessary. They looked at her like they knew what she was. She had been asked more times than she could count if she was a Bunny.

"Katie."

"Luke."

"I am afraid for you."

"Because I'm tired of pretending?"

"Because you can't stand it when things are normal." Luke sounded increasingly angry. "You are walking away from something for nothing." His voice softened when he said, "What we have right now might not come again."

Kate felt her jaw tighten as if by an unseen bolt. She was sick of how blind he was. "I don't think you and I have the same thing. You get business loans from Charlie's family, with no interest. You get all their contacts to keep you working."

"Yes, and you get a job you aren't qualified for without a degree. And you pay no rent to live in one of the finest examples of Classical Revival architecture in Cambridge."

Kate felt her anger rising up in her chest and her cheeks burned. "I don't want to be there anymore."

"Katie, what you want is usually dangerous. It always has been."

Kate took the phone away from her ear and pressed the red off button to hang up.

Luke had managed to weave himself right into the fabric of Charlie's family. They were his family now. He would never do anything to endanger his life in such proximity to wealth and legacy; he relished the invitations to Nantucket, to Maine. Not to mention the job connections. All on his own, Luke had completed his undergrad in applied mathematics with a minor in history at an elite university. He decimated the odds on that one given their origin. But the seed money to start his restoration carpentry business, that came from Charlie's father. Years in finance left Charlie's father with a taste for volatility and a flare for hospitality. He was always in motion, tying ropes, slapping backs, dealing cards, shaking all the beers in the cooler like a fraternity kid. And as soon as he returned to C.J.'s glass-and-shingle house, Luke would take his place next to Charlie's father at the poker table, ready to be dealt in.

The bathroom in the Maryland gas station was located at the end of a long line of glass coolers. The stall reeked of urine and the disinfectant trying to cover it up. Kate pulled her T-shirt up over her nose.

When she was done and opened the bathroom door, there was an older man with a grey ponytail and wire framed glasses waiting in the hall. The words under the Confederate flag on his shirt read: *We know you don't understand.* He nodded and watched her walk away as he continued to wait for the men's bathroom.

There were many moments like this in her life where she held the gaze of an older man and tried to figure out whether he was staring at her the way other people stared, or if the double take was one of Jackie's old boyfriends recognizing her. Her mother had known a lot of truckers.

She selected a Diet Coke and bag of pretzels. At the counter, she held out a twenty-dollar bill to the cashier, an overweight white man with a pink and green Hawaiian shirt who either didn't see the bill or was choosing to ignore it.

"A girl like you should be careful." He crossed his arms across the pattern of his shirt. "People are always looking to take advantage."

Kate tried pushing the bill closer so he would take it. It didn't work.

The man continued, "But *I* am always watching. That's how it has to be these days. Everyone for themselves. You have to look out for number one."

"Here you go," Kate said.

"You mess with the bulls, you get yourself a horn."

"You know what? Keep the change."

She was through the glass door when she heard him call out behind her, "Better watch out."

As Kate inserted Charlie's gas card into the slot at the pump, she saw the man with the Confederate flag shirt climb into an eighteen-wheeler parked on the side of the building where the semis lined up. From the cab, he watched her through the windshield.

She knew driving south would be like letting poison seep into the well. She could taste it, bitter and sharp on the sides of her tongue, the menthol smoke, the chemical air freshener, the aftershave of strange men. She squeezed the handle of the gas pump hard and thought of the trucker from California, the one with the boots stained from the slaughterhouses where he picked up his freight. Her skin prickled as she thought about those boots placed neatly by the front door. The way he smelled of burnt motor oil.

There would be no stopping it. Memory was what happened when you drove for hours, the blank screen of grey highway cut with white dashes, pine tree after pine tree on the side of the road like curtains for a stage.

It wasn't until Kate was south of DC that the cars thinned out. Everyone picked up ten or fifteen over the 70mph speed limit, weaving between the eighteen-wheelers. Kate kept up with them, liking the feeling of moving fast in the Audi. She made it to Emporia, Virginia before she was too tired to keep driving.

The kid behind the counter at the Hampton Inn had a sweet baby face, his medium brown skin was disrupted with acne across his round cheeks. He looked too young to be working a night shift at a hotel off I-95. His black hair was pressed flat on the left side of his head, like maybe he had fallen asleep on the desk before she came through the door. It took him a great deal of opening and shutting drawers and moving of papers to get her checked into the room.

"Where you from?" the kid asked wiping the back of his hand sleepily against his left eye. She wanted desperately to be in a bed, not talking to anyone, even this kid who seemed nice enough and was just doing his job, albeit sleepily and slowly. "New York City? You look like you would be from New York City."

"North Carolina."

He looked down at the computer and then passed back Charlie's credit card. "The address with this card is Massachusetts."

"That's where I live, not where I'm from." She hoped he wouldn't ask for a license. She had never gotten hers.

Jackie had little regard for rules that weren't her own, so when Kate skipped drivers' education classes, Jackie handed Kate the keys to the Ford Fairmont anyway and told her to pick up a two liter and a bag of ice on her way home. Later, when Kate followed Luke to Boston, she liked how someone else operated the T or the buses she rode, so she could put her head back on the glass and close her eyes. After she met Charlie, she didn't need to drive at all.

When someone asked for her ID, she always just lied, saying she had recently lost it. She had yet to meet a bouncer or doorman who wouldn't let her in, or a bartender who wouldn't serve her.

The kid handed her the plastic key. "It's room 114. This floor. Down the hall past the elevator."

In the room, the faint smell of bleached linens and air conditioning on high met her as she moved through the dark. The street lights outside lit the space between the curtains. She took off her clothes and left them on the other bed. Kate slid between the sheets. In the

, her face against the pillow case, Kate remembered the smell of the hospital eight years before. Kate had waited and waited for that space to close. It never had.

And what had happened last weekend with Charlie and his friend from undergrad, Anton, made things even more unstable and confused. She should have seen it coming. In a way she had.

She and Charlie had lasted longer than expected. She had met him on the steps of his campus while she was waiting for Luke to get out of the last exam of his senior year. Charlie had been in his first year of teaching. If she hadn't been there, at the front of that particular building on that particular campus, in a place he first assumed she had earned entry, it might have never started between them, at least not something he took seriously. By the time Kate disclosed to him the vaguest facts possible (she was not enrolled there, her brother was the student, she was a waitress, she was not "from" anything except for down south), they were enjoying the benefits each brought the other. She had always known it couldn't hold, but maybe for a while she had hoped it was possible.

"Anton is the one who streaked through the quad during a blizzard," Charlie had said when he pressed the doorbell on the brownstone in Carroll Gardens. "Another time he accidentally set one of the libraries' copy machines on fire. He made the most airtight fake IDs, truly works of art."

A deep, crackling voice came through the speaker, "State your business."

Charlie held down the button again and said, "Fuck you."

The interior door buzzed. Kate followed Charlie up two flights and waited in front of a door at the end of the dark hallway.

The apartment door swung open filling the hallway with light from the high-ceilinged room behind it. Anton brushed his dark hair from his face. It was longer in the front than the back, uneven like he had cut it himself. Even in the poor lighting where Kate stood behind Charlie in the hallway, she could see Anton's eyes were a startling, bright blue, although the skin around them was puffy and red. He wore a thin grey sweater with a tear in the crew-neck seam and a large hole at his left wrist. His sweatpants were a faded grey.

"Jesus." Anton stared at Kate. He rubbed his palm against his cheek. "You didn't tell me she was movie-star beautiful."

Kate was used to people's prolonged stares and their comments. (*Girl, you fine. Damn, where did you come from? Why are you walking away? Come back.*) But something about Anton made her feel shy like she had before she learned how to use her looks to her advantage.

"I'm a gentleman," Charlie said, walking past Anton into the apartment. "I don't talk about the physical attributes of my girlfriend to people like you, my brother."

Anton didn't move from the door or invite her in.

Kate held out her hand to him. It was a gesture she had learned was necessary in Charlie's world, but didn't feel like her. "I'm Kate."

"Anton." He shook her hand, still not moving. "It's like I'm actually standing here with Claudia Cardinale circa 1968. No. Claudia Cardinale meets Emmanuelle Béart."

Kate felt the warmth of his palm. She hadn't realized her own hands were so cold. "Yeah, so, I have no idea who those people are."

From somewhere inside the apartment Charlie said, "French actresses. Anton was a film minor."

"It was a film and video studies concentration. And Cardinale is Italian."

Kate pulled her hand away from Anton's and shifted her weight under her backpack.

"Are you going to let me in, or just stare are me all night? Because this could get weird."

"Maybe both," Anton said stepping out of the way and letting her into the apartment. "Maybe all of the above."

Charlie's friends were from all over the world. They were in finance on State Street or drilling wells for better sanitation in Ghana or lobbying for some legislation on Capitol Hill. They were all well-spoken and possessed the ability to move lightning fast through topics, easily vacillating between changes in U.S. environmental policy, the best roast for a stove top espresso maker, current events in the European Union, and crude humor. They were usually well-dressed, each in their own unassuming way. They all possessed something Kate could not put her finger on, but could now pick out across a crowded auditorium or subway car.

Anton was nothing like any of them.

In the back of the cab, he licked the glue on the paper of the joint he expertly rolled. Anton was taking them to a bar in Soho he said was the only place on Friday that wouldn't be overrun with tourists or craft beer enthusiasts.

At the door, the bouncer looked apathetic at first when Kate said she didn't have an ID.

"I'm twenty-six," she said.

"She's twenty-six," Charlie said.

She looked back at him. "I just said that."

He shrugged. "What? I'm just serving as your witness."

The bouncer was still unimpressed.

"She's with us," Anton said and slipped the bouncer a twenty.

The bouncer slid the folded bill back into his pocket and stepped aside.

Inside the bar, Anton handed Kate a large, half-filled shot glass that matched his.

"You seem like a kamikaze girl."

"I don't do shots," Kate said, taking the glass anyway.

He looked down at her, standing close enough that she had to tip her head back. "How did you get by without a license for so long?"

Kate shrugged. "They always let me in eventually."

"What about buying drinks?"

She smiled and took the shot.

"Yeah. I believe that. No shortage of suckers to buy someone like you drinks."

"I'll get around to it someday," Kate said.

Anton pointed to the back of the room. Kate turned to see Charlie playing darts with a man with a shaved head and salt and pepper stubble. The man wore navy blue mechanic's coveralls and had a dramatic posture for tossing the dart, his fingers flying open as he released.

"I guess he still spends all of his time talking to strangers?"

"Whenever he can." Kate handed Anton her empty shot glass. "I'll take a Captain and Diet next time."

"Alright, Captain."

The bar was getting busier and people were filling in behind them. There were some younger people like them, but mostly an older crowd, people who left hardhats and fluorescent yellow vests hanging on the backs of the chairs. Anton told her that the place was a union hangout, lots of tradesmen and municipal workers. He stood up on the brass rail under the bar and leaned way forward, both of his elbows on the lacquered wood, to order the next round.

When he turned around with her drink Kate asked, "Is it true what Charlie said? That you're some genius that could have taken over the world?"

"He likes to think the best of people. Until he doesn't."

"Then it's true."

"Kind of true in some contexts."

"So yes. You could have taken over the world but chose not to."

"True-ish."

Kate found herself being able to talk to Anton in a way she hadn't talked to anyone in a while. She didn't feel the need to think every word through to make sure it didn't reveal too much or fail to say enough. She just said what she wanted.

They both turned when they heard someone shout with excitement at the back of the bar. The man in blue coveralls was slapping Charlie on the back and reaching his hand out. Charlie reached into his pocket and turned over some amount of money.

Anton said, "You know he likes slumming it. That's part of his thing."

She did know. Kate liked having someone see it as clearly as she did and saying it out loud. Trying to convince her brother that Charlie adopted damaged people from the opposite end of the economic spectrum was pointless. Luke didn't care. He wanted to be taken in.

They watched Charlie walk up to the board to take the darts out of the cork. He moved with slow ease, his back straight, shoulders down, a learned posture of holding himself a certain way, even in a dive bar.

"He's constantly conducting an ethnography."

"What does that mean?" Kate tucked her free hand into the

back pocket of her jeans.

"It means he's always observing and analyzing, not really connecting, just looking for the next interesting subject."

Kate had to admit Charlie was distant, but that was a relief when she met him. Distance and safety were about all she craved then, and that was what Charlie offered.

"You're good with that?" Anton asked.

"With what?"

"That he likes you for the *kind* of person you are, not necessarily you specifically."

"People like me for a lot of reasons that aren't about me. That's how people are. They make up what they want. I let them."

"That's magnanimous of you."

She didn't know what that meant either. "What else can you do?"

"I'm just saying, it's one thing to be his friend when you know how he is. I'm guessing it's another to be his girlfriend."

"It usually *is* different, being friends and being more than that."

"You know what I see when I look at you?" Anton extended his pointer finger and pushed back the hair that fell forward over the front of her shoulder.

"I don't care what you see, but you're going to tell me anyway aren't you?" Kate reached up and pulled the hair he had moved back the way it was before.

"Yes, I'm going to tell you anyway."

"Of course you are." She couldn't hide her smile.

Anton held up a finger as he pronounced, "It's possible you have nowhere else to go."

Her smile gone, Kate turned away, catching a glimpse of them both in the mirror behind the bar. She could see them standing there, Anton much taller than her, the top of her head barely visible above the bottles of liquor that were lined up.

"What's your point?" Kate asked, noticing the older blonde woman on the stool next to them using the mirror to watch them both. She turned back to face Anton. "We're all trapped in one way or another. You are."

He looked amused, which bothered her. Kate looked down the bar to see Charlie bringing two beers back to the dart game and the waiting man in coveralls. The bar was so crowded now that people moved through holding their drinks overhead and pressing against each other. Kate had moved into the space between Anton's knees, his long legs making a V-shaped space.

"So you're telling me to be careful," she said.

"I'm just telling you what I see."

His face was only inches from hers as they stared at each other.

"I'm not blind. Order me another one. Please." She turned and pressed her belly to the bar.

"Aye, aye."

Their arms were still touching when Charlie reached them. He was out seventy-five dollars, drunk, and wanting dim sum.

"You know the one with the yellow walls and metal fans," Charlie said to Anton. "The original one from the 1920s."

"I do know the one, but we just got these."

"Down the hatch, kids." Charlie put a hand on each of their shoulders. Kate felt the pressing of his thumb on her collar bone. Here we go, she thought.

In Anton's dark kitchen, Kate was washing glasses for them to drink the sake Charlie brought back with them from Chinatown. He stood holding the remote right in front of the stereo flipping through tracks on a Yo La Tengo album. Kate knew he was watching her and Anton through the pass-through between the kitchen and the living room.

"If you leave this many dishes in the sink in an old building like this, you'll have mice." Kate pushed a pile of plates stained with a red sauce rousing a rotten smell.

"I already have them. And cockroaches. See?" Anton pointed to something dark that scuttled across the tile backsplash.

"Too small to be a real cockroach. That's like a baby beetle." She turned away from the sink to face him. The only light in the galley kitchen was from a lamp in the living room where Charlie was. Anton's blue eyes looked colorless now.

"You should kiss her," Charlie said.

Anton laughed but didn't move. "That sounds like a terrible idea."

"Don't you think she's beautiful?"

"That goes without saying." Anton walked back in the living room, sat down on the couch, and lit a cigarette.

"Kate, come in here," Charlie said.

She stood in the doorway drying her wet hands on the back of her jeans. She leaned against the frame.

Charlie walked over and stood close to her. She looked up at him. He had turned thirty-three over the winter and was starting to have slightly deeper lines mark his face. This only made him look more distinguished somehow.

"Do you like New York?" Charlie asked, a hand firmly gripping her waist.

"The people seem nicer than Boston."

"That's not saying much." Charlie leaned in and kissed her. When he pulled away, she put the back of her hand to the corner of her mouth where it was wet.

"You sure know how to make a brother jealous," Anton said from the couch.

"Brothers can share," Charlie said.

"You obviously don't have a brother," Anton said.

Kate felt her chest tighten as Charlie slid his hand down the front of her jeans. "What do you want?" he asked.

The question was more of a problem than the situation. She had been in burning houses before. She let out the breath she had been holding. She walked over and stood in front of Anton on the couch.

"Nothing good will come of this," he said.

She didn't need him to identify a bad idea for her. She was well aware of who Anton reminded her of. It wasn't the way he looked so much as the way he was. Kate knew the room was dark enough, the effect of the pot and alcohol strong enough. As she reached down for the bottom of her shirt and pulled it over her head, she felt an electric rush.

Anton whispered, "Fuck." He reached out and ran his hand from her bare stomach to her side where her tattoo of a tree was drawn, its roots entangled over her hip. He wasn't Smith, but the trace of fingers across those branches pulled up the space of that love's absence. What Charlie was walking the three of them into wasn't the same exact recklessness, but it knocked loose a similarly satisfying velocity.

"What's this for?" Anton asked.

Kate didn't answer. She didn't give up that part of herself.

"She likes plants." Charlie said from where he leaned against the wall watching them. "Especially trees."

She looked over her shoulder at Charlie, a flash of anger rushing through her. He knew nothing about her roots, what they meant needled there into her skin.

"That's not what it's about," Kate said.

"But you do like plants," Charlie said.

Just to make him pay for that misinterpretation, she lowered herself onto Anton's lap.

"Relationships are just a construct," Charlie said from across the room.

"Like the elephant in that Buddhist parable," Anton said.

"You're both full of shit," Kate said as she unhooked her bra. "It's a test. And I always fail those."

The next morning, Charlie woke Kate up where she had fallen asleep next to Anton on the pullout couch. He was turned toward the wall of windows. Charlie and Kate dressed quickly, closing the apartment door behind them quietly.

Charlie eased his Audi onto the BQE headed for 95 North. It was too early on a Sunday morning for there to be much traffic. Kate didn't try to bridge the silence. She couldn't look at him. They had let something out of a cage, something she couldn't recapture. She doubted he could either. Her head pounded.

As they crossed the state line into Connecticut, Charlie turned to her and asked, "Do you think we should get married?"

A bolt of electric panic shot through Kate. It was the opposite of what she thought he might say this morning. The exact opposite. "Why would you ask me that now?"

"Why not?"

"After what we did last night."

"What *you* did last night."

"What *you* started."

Charlie gripped the steering wheel and tightened his jaw so much she heard his teeth scrape under the pressure. He didn't look good. His usual healthy-looking, glowing skin had a greyish under-tone to it. He looked like he hadn't slept at all.

"I found the pregnancy test box," he said finally.

Kate's stomach felt like it was rising up into her throat. "You dug through the trash?"

"Why didn't you tell me?"

"You literally went through our trash?"

"I always do a double check. You're terrible at recycling."

She had pushed the box all the way to the bottom of the bin under Styrofoam meat trays and balled up paper towels soaked in grease.

"I didn't tell you because it was negative."

When Kate saw that single line showing she was not pregnant, she had never been so relieved. As she dropped the plastic stick wrapped in toilet paper into the trash can, she thought, *What am I doing here?*, then pushed away the doubt until now.

Charlie looked disappointed. "I thought maybe it was positive."

"It wasn't."

They drove in silence for a few miles until Kate felt the anger surge. "If you thought I was pregnant, why would you take me out drinking? Why would you stand there watching me with your friend?"

Charlie seemed to consider this for a moment. "I didn't think it would go that far."

"But you didn't stop me."

"You didn't look like you wanted to be stopped."

She heard the biting anger in his voice. "This should tell you what I mean to you."

She reached out and turned the radio up so loud it hurt her ears. If she had her own car, her own way back to Boston along with her own place to stay once she got there, it would have been much easier. She had none of those things.

Charlie reached out to turn down the volume, but neither of them said anything else for the long car ride back to his house. The thin threads of what they were doing with each other had finally frayed and snapped.

FOUR

AN HOUR AND a half south of Emporia, Kate stopped at a Bojangles and parked the Audi. She was hungry, but she was also stalling. The freedom she felt yesterday morning driving away from Massachusetts had been replaced with a nervous, haunted feeling.

Jackie had not called again. Not hearing from her mother gave Kate the unsettling feeling her mother already knew Kate was coming, like Jackie already knew she won the first battle.

The line for the drive-thru wrapped around the Bojangles building. Kate found a seat in the dining room and pushed the paper back on her chicken biscuit. Ruby Newkirk would have taken issue with the greasiness, but she would have approved of how the dough kept tender.

"Can't get a biscuit like that up north."

Kate looked up to see a white woman with grey hair cut pixie short under her brown Bojangles visor. She had a gold nose ring and small grey eyes. She was running a carpet sweeper under the table across from Kate.

"No, ma'am."

"I saw those Massachusetts plates. Just thought you should know that's about as good as it gets." She pushed her sweeper toward Kate's table.

"I'm actually from down here." Kate moved her feet out of the way.

"You don't look like it." The woman adjusted her visor down on her forehead.

Kate was wearing expensive jeans and a white T-shirt from Lord & Taylor, but she knew it was the tall leather boots and the black cashmere sweater that draped to her knees that looked most out of place.

"Where do you live up there?"

"Boston. Cambridge, actually." Kate shifted on the vinyl surface of the chair.

"Boston. You got the Red Sox up there?"

"They do." Kate said.

"What you doin' down this way?"

"Going to see my mother."

"Must be hard on your mama to have you so far away. You get a box of biscuits to take to her. She would appreciate that I'm sure, unless she's the type who only likes her own."

"She's not much of a cook."

"Well, people have they different talents."

Back on the road as she drove, Kate thought about how Jackie had plenty of talents, most were just problematic. For example, Jackie was an exceptional liar. Extremely skilled. At social services disputing the amount of her benefits check, the town clerk's office, or the utilities company, chances were, she was lying. Countless times, she and Luke had endured Jackie emptying out the contents of her purse on innumerable counters in search for the previous bill, the stolen checkbook, the EBT card that wasn't working right when they switched over from paper stamps, some official letter exempting her from paying property taxes. She could make a scene so embarrassing to everyone except herself, she usually got what she wanted in the end. Most people where they lived in a rural area between Burgaw and Wilmington knew how Jackie made at least some of her money, and she used that. At eight years old, Kate already knew her mother wasn't pretty. Not the way people constantly told her she was. Jackie *was* powerful and persuasive. Barely a hundred pounds, Jackie filled up a waiting room with her presence, the way she stood somehow taking up more space than people twice her size.

"Rupert Jones, you know you owe me a hundred fifty dollars," she'd say at the customer service window at Walmart or Jiffy Lube.

Rupert or Evan or Tom would stand behind the counter at the elementary school office, Kerr Drugs, or the public library having no idea what Jackie was talking about.

"You know that I know that you owe me from..." Jackie would pause and feign discretion. "Well, you know why you owe me that money. If you will just waive this lien from the propane company, we'll call it even. Rupert, *you know* how cold my house can get. *You know* that my poor children suffer from weak immune systems."

At this point, Jackie might pull Kate up to the counter to be presented as a person who required warmth. Karl or James or Terrance or whoever had the unfortunate task of dealing with Jackie would start to give in because his coworkers were leaning in to hear just how much money was owed and for what.

Jackie was a force in part because of how fast she could figure things. She easily passed the CPA exam she studied for when Kate and Luke were in fourth grade. When she was unable to get a job as an accountant at any of the firms in Wilmington because she had never graduated college and a few years of it didn't amount to anything, she just put the knowledge to keeping books (and keeping things off the books) for a marina in Hampstead and a deli in Carolina Beach.

Jackie knew the full name of every single employee at Town Hall. She spent a summer learning about the migration patterns of shrimp when she was dating a shrimp boat captain. She studied franchise recruitment packages for Hardee's, Golden Corral, and Dairy Queen, even though she didn't have the cash to invest in them.

Everywhere she went, Jackie soaked up knowledge and details to use to her advantage. It was what both Luke and Kate had known their entire lives. And it was why Luke was right in saying Kate should not go back. If there was an angle to exploit, Jackie would have a clear view of it. That was her endless expertise.

So Luke was right about the risk, but he had a way of being so single-minded, so driven to his goal he couldn't see anything from someone else's point of view. Just like Jackie.

Kate had seen how she was going to lose her brother early on, long before Charlie. But there was this time and space suspended between the hard edges of danger in their childhood and the unsteady comfort she couldn't trust when they were imbedded with Charlie's family.

The summer after Luke's freshman year, he got them jobs in P-town. His timing could not have been better. She'd been living near the Lechmere T stop in a sketchy situation that turned worse when she couldn't make rent and her ogling landlord suggested she might pay him in *creative* ways.

The opportunity Luke lined up offered employee housing in exchange for lousy pay and endless double shifts. When they arrived to work that summer, Kate was still hollowed out in some ways, a little over a year postpartum and exactly a year after running away north. Her time in Boston was spent working and waiting around for Luke who was always busy with school. He did make space for her then when he could, inviting her to parties, swiping her into events, bringing her pocketable food from the cafeteria.

At nineteen, a year was long enough to look up and see that for all that happened, you were free from the past, in most ways that mattered. She was glad she did not have a baby, relieved there was no Jackie up here. She was even okay, for the most part, with no Smith.

In P-town, even she could see they were starting over. Luke worked in a kitchen at an Italian restaurant. Kate cleaned hotel rooms at one of the nicer inns until the manager got a look at her and switched her to working at the front desk and bar.

That was the summer of swimming. In ponds in Wellfleet. On the bay side. On the ocean side. Out at Race Point on the very tip of this new state they inhabited, even though they were warned about sharks. No one was ever bitten although many people claimed to see fins and movement under the water more frequently than was probably possible. Mostly, they swam right in town, ending shifts then walking down Commercial Street to the beaches that appeared where the streets lined with shops and clubs dead ended.

At home the water was warm, sometimes near bathwater temperatures in the creek behind Jackie's house. The ocean at Wrightsville Beach felt cool at first, but within a minute you couldn't feel it against your skin. The water in this new place brought a numbing pain and shortness of breath…that's if you could make it up to your chest. Entering the sixty-five-degree water required an act of will that defied the body's natural responses. Luke adjusted faster than Kate, but he would still come out with his lips blue and teeth chattering.

One night in mid-August, they were tipped off about a bloom of bioluminescence. Kate had been feeling down all day, dreading the return to Boston where Luke would go back to his new roommate in his dorm, to his classes. Through a waiter at the inn's restaurant, she had scored a leaseless sublet in a place in South Boston with five roommates. Through a patron at the inn's bar, she landed part-time work at a florist near Copley Square. This had given her some hope. The bulk of her work would continue to be restaurants where the significant money was, but she had missed flowers and plants, taking care of them.

Kate, Luke, and their co-workers headed down to the beach sometime after two in the morning. Exhausted from work and sweating into the hot night air, they went into the water up to their knees. Luke ran his hand across the surface, which glowed. As he let the water run back into the bay, it looked like green molten lava flowing from his hand.

"But how?" she asked, mesmerized.

"They're schools of plankton. When they're agitated, they glow."

There was no moon at all, so every cupped hand they pulled from the sea brought a cascade of stars. Luke dove gracefully toward the deeper water, which exploded in light around him. She had been incapable of swimming for most of the summer, her sense of survival cutting her off when she reached her waist, her body not wanting to let her vital organs be submerged. At this point in August, it was becoming tolerable. She dipped under then swam toward the lit flame of her brother.

Just out of earshot of the other glowing swimmers, she told Luke she was afraid.

"There are no sharks here."

"I mean when we get back."

"Oh. Well." He trailed off not knowing what to say.

"I feel like you are going to leave me behind." As she treaded water in the otherwise black night, she looked down and saw her body as if she was radioactive. The light of millions of tiny plankton swirling around her.

"You already left me a long time ago," Luke said.

"What do you mean?"

"You and Smith. You met him, and you were gone."

Kate considered this. Having a boyfriend wasn't the same as leaving the state for college with the intention of never, ever returning.

"I was alone. With her." Luke ducked under the water creating a flash of light before reappearing again. "But we're here now. In the same place."

His words rang hollow in her ears. "We have to stick together."

Luke said, "We will."

The next summer, Luke had an internship at an architecture firm near Kendall Square and work-study on campus. Kate returned to P-town with many of the same people, the same swimming, but the bioluminescence didn't reappear. Nothing was the same without her brother.

FIVE

WHAT KATE REMEMBERED was an arrow-straight dirt drive connecting the county road to Ruby Newkirk's white farmhouse and the large expanse of fields that surrounded it. Jackie's house could only be seen a few acres to the north once you were almost all the way down that drive, at the very end where there was a loop that circled out in front of the larger house. Facing Mrs. Newkirk's home, Jackie's bungalow peeked out behind it like a sinking shadow amongst the fast-growing, loblolly pines. Growing unchecked and crowded, their trunks were tall and bare of branches until the tops that spread with vibrant green needles.

When they were together cooking, Kate avoiding going home, Mrs. Newkirk would proudly tell the story of her land. The Newkirk family had owned large parcels of rich farmland for more than two hundred and fifty years. Ruby had married into the Newkirks, but she was from an equally well-off, land-owning family closer to Clinton and thus Raleigh, which allowed her to adopt a debutante's air of superiority, at least in comparison.

The Newkirk farm was not enough for her husband. Shortly after they were married, he invested in land out west, buying up timber acreage. He took Ruby out to Colorado to a trailer at one of his acquisitions. Barely twenty-one, Mrs. Ruby Newkirk was not the sort of girl who cared for living in a trailer, even if it was temporary. On top of the insult of the aluminum living situation, she had not liked the dry air or the sounds of the forest coming down all around her. When Ruby became pregnant with their first son, she moved back to the Newkirk family farmhouse. She would not give birth to a child out there in the middle of nowhere with no kin to see to her. That was what she told him. He could come back with her or not, she said. That was up to him.

He did follow her back. Timber was lucrative, but so was the tobacco to be picked, dried, and hauled to auction from his family's land like it had been every summer for the last two centuries.

"There's gold in this soil right here," Ruby liked to say about the crop as its leaves turned color near harvest. "Don't need to go anywhere else."

Ruby Newkirk had one more son before her husband died at thirty-two from a lung embolism.

Now behind the wheel of Charlie's Audi, Kate sat motionless in the middle of the county road. Her left turn signal clicked like a rhythmic warning. Mrs. Newkirk's land, as Kate had known it, was gone. All of it unrecognizable. The fields she remembered were replaced by a subdivision of single-story, brick patio homes. She could no longer see Mrs. Newkirk's house in the distance. When a white sedan appeared in her rearview mirror, Kate finally turned in.

Kate struggled to triangulate what she was seeing with what she had known as she navigated the smooth, new asphalt road. The neighborhood was alive with activity. A man painted the bottom of a motorboat, a drop cloth spread out under him to protect the concrete of his driveway. Teenaged boys milled around under a basketball hoop. Children in swimsuits and even younger ones in diapers ran through sprinklers.

Three young mothers gathered around a mailbox watched suspiciously as Kate doubled back on a cul-de-sac she thought would take her to the far end of the subdivision but hadn't.

Eventually, as Kate found her way deeper into the neighborhood, the houses became less finished. Building materials were corded and stacked up in unpaved driveways. In one lot, sandy soil was exposed under the straw laid out to keep grass seed from scorching.

Between two houses framed but not filled in, Kate saw a dirt access road that led to the bank of pines that sheltered Jackie's house, low to the ground with the creek further down behind it.

The bungalow's clapboards varied in shades from sun-bleached, bare grey on one side of the house to spotty black on the shadier side where the wood was mildewed. In between there were places where an old coat of white paint still held fast. There was an uneven chimney with red bricks missing from its crumbling mortar, pushed slightly crooked in various hurricanes and tropical storms. Kate saw that the developers had planted a line of fast-growing privet hedge to block out the view of where her mother lived. Jackie's dilapidated house with the junk in the yard reminded Kate of an old, sleeping dog chained to a tree just waiting for someone to mess with it.

There wasn't a driveway. There never had been, just packed dirt that kicked up dust every time someone pulled in or out. Kate willed herself to pull forward toward the house with its sagging roof line.

She put the car in park in front of the house. Her mother's room was toward the back, so it was possible Jackie would not hear her. In the side yard, Kate noticed there were several black scorch marks in the grass. Behind that, the grass grew sparse because the pines along the creek blocked the light. At the edge of those pines were several old cars scattered with stray pine straw, none of which were Jackie's Ford Fairmont. There was a white station wagon and two more recent model Chevy sedans, one on cement blocks. Tires were stacked up like a tower of Oreos. Kate could see Pepsi bottles, rusting cans of WD-40 and spray paint scattered around the edge of the yard. None of it had been there eight years before when Kate left. With the amount of rust on the cars and grass growing up between the cement blocks, it looked like they could have been there forever.

Kate figured Jackie must have had a mechanic or gearhead boyfriend, at least for a while, who left all this. That was how Jackie's house had always been. It was theirs and not theirs. There were always men coming through. It was how Jackie, who had no other significant means of employment, paid their bills. There was always someone leaving a pile of Schlitz empties or a case of half used paint cans picked up from a job. Where Jackie found the men, Kate didn't know, but they always came with their own goods, their own interests that altered the space.

There was still no movement from inside the house. Kate stayed in the driver's seat of the car. She saw that someone had plugged the rips in the porch's screens with wads of paper towel. The old brown vinyl recliner was still on the front porch, nearly buried in a pile of empty cardboard boxes tossed on top of each other.

When Kate and Luke were twelve, Jackie pulled up next to that recliner in one of the nicer Wilmington neighborhoods they drove through on trash day. Jackie always had her eye out for things she could resell. It had seemed there was no way the overstuffed chair would fit in the back of Jackie's Fairmont, but oh yes, it would fit if Jackie had anything to do with it.

The recliner made it as far as their front porch before they realized it smelled vaguely of stale beer or pee or both. So the porch was where the recliner stayed, pushed up against the front of the house. It wasn't long before the field mice were pulling the white filling out where the vinyl was torn along the arms and seat back.

The Audi was heating up like an oven. Still, Kate sat motionless. She listened to the sounds from the neighborhood drift from one side of the house and the drone of cicadas coming from the other. A box fan in the window above the brown recliner was turned off, but the blades of the fan rotated slowly, coming almost to a complete stop before being pushed forward again by an invisible breeze.

As she got out of the car feeling like a stranger, Kate reminded herself, this was still her house. She knew how to turn off the main water valve, how to flip the circuit breakers. She knew that sometimes when a tropical storm came through and always when a hurricane hit, the roof leaked into Kate's closet and along the back wall of the bathroom.

Kate reached back into the car for the box of biscuits the woman at Bojangles had convinced her to buy. They were cold now, but it felt good to have something to offer.

She made her way toward the front door. On either side of the brick steps up to the porch, Kate saw strewn cigarette butts. A few nip bottles studded the straggly lilies Kate planted when Mrs. Newkirk divided hers. Underneath one was a white sneaker, its toe wrapped with duct tape. Against the foundation, Luke's old bike lay like a rusted skeleton in the overgrown crab grass.

The wood of the porch floor creaked under her boot soles as she knocked on her mother's door. There were three empty shotgun shells scattered between a worn out welcome mat and the siding of the house. A dank smell came from the things crowded together in the humidity on the porch. She knocked again then tried the doorknob. They never had keys for the house, but it was locked now. Kate lifted up on her toes and looked through one of the three small panels of glass at the top of the front door. She could see the long green sofa in the living room was still next to the kerosene stove venting up the small chimney.

Kate was about to knock a third time when she saw through the lowest glass pane a woman emerge from the front bedroom. She had dark wavy hair and a medium-brown complexion. In this part of North Carolina, Kate guessed she was Mexican but wasn't sure. As she turned to peer out at Kate, her brow was furrowed above wide-set brown eyes. She did not open the door.

Kate had not told her mother she was coming. Jackie had lived in this house her entire life, but that didn't necessarily mean she still did. She thought about the 210 area code she had not recognized when she took the call in the greenhouse. Maybe Jackie really had moved.

The front door opened slightly. The woman held a plastic laundry basket against her hip as she stared at Kate. She was only visible through the space allowed open by a gold chain lock. She was older than Kate, maybe early thirties, with a delicately sloped nose. Her eyebrows were beautifully arched and her loose lavender blouse hung almost to the bottom of a pair of jean shorts, tight against her muscular legs. She wore purple platform flip-flops with oversized silk flowers on the strap.

Kate said, "I'm looking for Jackie Jessup."

The woman stared back at Kate but didn't speak. Kate thought maybe she didn't understand.

"My mother. Jackie Jessup. She called me. She told me to come here." Kate shifted nervously. "Maybe she moved?"

The woman pushed the door shut. Kate heard the rattle and

metal sliding of the chain lock. The woman opened the door slightly. Her voice was deep and pretty when she asked, "Katie?"

Kate felt a wave of relief. "That's me."

Kate had forgotten this smell. Damp and mildewed, so different than the smell of orange wood polish at Charlie's house. There was something new here too, a bleach smell she recognized from when Luke had worked shifts at the slaughterhouse the summer before they left for Boston.

Kate carried her box of biscuits, following the woman through the house. The kitchen was smaller than Kate remembered. The aqua-blue Formica table sat in its center with the same four metal-framed kitchen chairs with their torn blue vinyl-covered seats. There were several new plastic folding chairs fitted in next to the old ones.

When Kate saw her mother's closed bedroom door, off the kitchen, she felt dread. The woman placed her palm against Jackie's door, leaning in to listen. Kate remembered doing just that with Luke when they were kids, listening for breathing, trying to guess if Jackie was asleep or awake, with someone or alone.

"Wait," Kate said her heart pounding. She was not ready.

The woman turned to face Kate her hand still on the doorknob. Kate had always been tall, and this woman was a full head shorter than she was. They stood close together. Kate had the sense this person knew things about her.

"I'm sorry. Who are you?"

The woman didn't answer and turned the doorknob.

Panicked, Kate said, "Hold on. I need a minute." She was backing away. "I'll be right back."

The woman looked frustrated, hefting up the full laundry basket against her side. Kate walked through the door that connected the kitchen to the back room where Jackie once kept her Singer and bolts of fabric. The front of the house looked almost exactly the same as Kate remembered. The back room was unrecognizable.

The two windows that looked out onto the rusting packhouse behind the house were closed and lined with sheets of newspaper. A double bed was pushed against the far end of the room. A bunkbed was perpendicular to it, the foot of one bed close enough the touch the head of another. The room smelled like body odor and sweat but also cologne, and something vaguely floral like scented body lotion. The room was full of boxes. So many boxes. Unlike the ones on the front porch, these were full, stacked on top of each other. A box of canned tomatoes, one marked corn meal, another opened at the top to reveal packs of Hanes bright white athletic socks.

The woman walked past Kate, taking her laundry to the washing machine on the back porch.

"I'll just be a second."

The woman shrugged like it made no difference, but it was clear she didn't like Kate surveying the room.

Kate went to the bathroom and closed to door. She balanced the box of Bojangles on the corner of the tub then looked at the other door, the one that connected to her mother's bedroom. Kate felt a flash of fear. She turned on the cold water tap and let it run, muffling the creak of the rusty hinges as she opened the medicine cabinet. It was filled with multiple cans of shaving cream, too many toothpastes, at least six deodorants. Softly closing the mirrored cabinet door, Kate realized that her mother was up to something that involved a lot of people.

As she splashed her face with the cold water, she couldn't shake that feeling of being watched. She turned off the tap and dried off with her shirt rather than use the dingy-looking towel hanging on the metal rod above the toilet.

Kate shuddered, feeling like the farm equipment technician from Tennessee was in the room with her again. That one never actually touched her. He sat on the closed toilet shirtless, a pair of Dickie's work pants around his ankles. He had thinning grey hair that he cropped military short, leaving tiny hairs all over their sink and the floor.

"Hush. I ain't gonna hurt you," he said the first time she pulled the shower curtain back to see him sitting there. "Just come on out of there, and get yourself dried off."

Kate was fourteen with the mildewed curtain pulled to her chest. She hadn't heard him come into the bathroom over the spray of the shower. He had taken her towel from the nail she hung it on and folded it neatly on the floor in front of him.

"Go ahead and get your towel," he said.

Kate judged the distance. Maybe if she stretched, maybe if she kind of took the curtain with her, she could reach it.

"Go on. Unless you want me to come over there and help you."

When she finally stepped over the edge of the bathtub onto the hand towel that they used as a bathmat, he reached into his underwear. She tried not to look as she picked up her towel from the floor in front of him and clutched it to her chest. Kate reached for the door knob trying to leave as quickly as possible.

He stood up and said, "Whoa now, take your time."

Kate tried not to look down at what he was doing with his hand.

"Just dry off nice and slow."

At fourteen, Kate was learning some things were best to get over with quickly. By the time he moaned, his face tensing like he was in pain, she was buttoning her jeans, denim sticking to her still damp skin. She had always suspected it, but now was learning it for sure. Everyone wanted something, and they would try to take it if you didn't offer it up yourself. Even in your own house. Even when you thought you were alone. Even with your mother on the other side of the door. For all you knew, she might even be in on the deal.

When the woman in the lavender shirt pushed Jackie's bedroom door open in front of Kate, cold escaped as if from a walk-in freezer. It was dark inside. A roller blind was pulled down to the top of a humming window unit. Jackie's room had always smelled of drug store perfume and cigarette smoke. Now it smelled like a hospital, rubbing alcohol and something earthy and foul Kate couldn't quite place.

The woman turned the knob at the base of the brass lamp by Jackie's bed. When light flooded the room, what Kate first noticed was the number of boxes in the bed. Most were shoeboxes, but on the far side against the wall there was a larger one tied closed with calico fabric strips. The open ones overflowed with newspaper clippings, old bills, and other papers curling out over the sides. There were three flat shirt boxes stacked on top of each other in place of a second pillow on the double bed. There was a scraped-up, blue vinyl vintage case with a cream-colored enamel handle. Lined up against the wooden footboard were a few larger cardboard boxes with their flaps folded against each other to keep them closed. Jackie always had reading and various paperwork lined up around her, research for some potential take or another, but this was way more than Kate remembered.

Jackie was asleep among it all, propped up on pillows and the faded chintz throws in peach and pink that matched a bedspread long ago ruined by a boyfriend who gave Jackie a bloody nose before she punctured the top of his shoulder with a high heel. The blood—his and hers—had ruined the fabric.

Seeing now the change in her mother, Kate covered her mouth with her hand. "What happened?"

The woman beside her didn't answer Kate. Instead, she spoke softly. "Jackie, wake up. Someone's here to see you."

Her mother was barely recognizable, her pale skin nearly see-through with a yellowish tint. Jackie was wearing a nylon beige nightgown that looked two sizes too big on her, the arm holes revealing pale, taut skin over her rib cage, the bones curved and prominent. Jackie had always been thin, but now her collar and cheekbones stuck out sharp as blades. The reddish tint of her straw-berry blonde hair was gone. It looked like dried out straw against the white pillow case. She had always seemed powerful in her tiny body, but now she was sunken, like one of the curled and yellowed pieces of paper in her boxes, brittle and ruined.

Jackie blinked her eyes open against the light. They were still the same icy blue. She held up her hand as she adjusted to the brightness. She had not penciled her blonde brows or put on eye-liner and mascara. Without her makeup, Jackie's eyes were rimmed in pink with short, sparse eyelashes. "Like a drowned possum," Jackie had always said applying layer after layer of mascara in the mirror before she would consider leaving the house.

"Maribel?"

"Yes, it's me. Your daughter is here too."

Jackie blinked and squinted, finding Kate. "Well, wonders never cease." Jackie cleared her throat. "Look who came home."

"Hi, Mama." Kate's voice sounded weak. "I brought biscuits." She realized she had left the box in the bathroom.

Jackie waved her hand in the air and made a face. "I can't eat that stuff anymore. Maribel will make me something that agrees with me." She pushed herself up higher against the pillows then ran her fingertips across the slack skin of her cheeks. "How long have you been here?"

"Not too long."

"How come you didn't call before you—"

When Jackie started coughing, her entire body convulsed like she was being shaken from the inside. The woman in the lavender shirt, Maribel apparently, moved quickly to the end of the bed and wheeled a heavy green oxygen tank next to where Kate stood. She reached down for a plastic mask and held it to Jackie's face. Jackie was only forty-six, but she looked much, much older. Maribel adjusted a strand of Jackie's hair under the elastic strap of the mask.

Jackie was starting to catch her breath, taking more even draws from the mask. Maribel reached out to open the bedside table drawer and took out a plastic bag. She replaced the mask with a coil of tubing that went around Jackie's head and set inside her nostrils.

Maribel moved to open the roller blind, letting more light into the room.

"Don't just stand there. It makes me nervous."

Kate reached to clear a box off the bed, but Jackie held up her hand and shook her head. Maribel pulled an upholstered chair from the corner of the room. Kate remembered that burnt yellow corduroy fabric Jackie used to refinish it. Kate had held the fabric in place when Jackie let Luke have a turn with the staple gun.

Maribel left for the kitchen, pulling the door shut behind her, leaving her alone with her mother.

Kate took the chair by the arm and pulled it closer to the bed. She couldn't imagine what Jackie might have told Maribel. A son who hated her. A daughter who left with no warning, then would not disclose her address. Jackie probably saw her children as the worst kind of people who leave rural communities, those who never come back to share the wealth with the people that gave them a beginning.

Kate felt her mother's eyes on her as precise and cutting as her shears when she still used to make most of their clothes.

"You look about the same," Jackie said. "You've gained some weight."

"Nice to see you too, Mama." Kate cleared her throat.

Jackie looked down at Kate's tall leather boots. "Have you taken up riding horses up there on your estate?"

"It's not an estate." Not exactly a lie. Not exactly true. Charlie had lighting fixtures worth more than Jackie's entire house.

"Well, you certainly look the part." Jackie adjusted the tubing. The oxygen tank made gentle sucking sounds with each breath she drew.

Jackie was trying to make her feel insecure, but Kate saw how her mother looked fragile and flammable as dry straw. Kate resisted the urge to ask what was wrong, what had wasted her mother this way to a skeletal, yellow-grey version of herself. That would come. To ask directly would mean that Jackie would withhold more.

"How's your brother? Construction still?"

"Restoration carpentry."

"How many people does he have working for him?" Jackie asked.

"Nine or ten," Kate lied giving the answer Luke would want her to.

Jackie nodded, begrudgingly impressed. "Thought he would do better up there than construction. The way he used to talk, you'd think he was going to work for NASA."

It had always upset Jackie that Luke had wanted to leave from such a young age. He learned early, from the television that Jackie parked them in front of, that he wanted a different kind of family, a different kind of life. *Leave It To Beaver* made him long for a father and resent his mother's rotating cast of characters. *Dallas* and *Diff'rent Strokes* showed him what wealth looked like, that it didn't come from the parade of schemes Jackie cooked up.

Kate knew that Luke's interpretation of Jackie was not wrong. But Kate could turn it another way. At least Jackie had never pretended to be someone she wasn't. Yes, sure, on the little cons, like pretending to work at a gas station or to own a green station wagon or to be married to a dentist, but she had never lied about the big things, the important things. Jackie had not said, your father was a good, kind man. She said, *you have no father*, which was true. She said, *you cannot trust people to do right by you. You cannot win a losing battle. No one will give you what you want or what you need, so you have to take it.* These things were all true.

Kate bit at the edge of her thumb cuticle, pressing her skin hard against the bone of her tooth. A bead of blood formed at the edge of her thumbnail.

"I can't believe you're still chewing on yourself like that, grown woman like you in those boots. And the boyfriend? No ring, I see."

"Always watching, aren't you, Mama?"

"Yes, that's my gift." Jackie gestured toward the front of the house. "Did you see what they've done out there? Those awful little houses. That's Mrs. Newkirk's sons. Sold the land to the developers. I never liked those boys anyway."

Kate was not surprised to hear the Newkirk boys were trying to unload the farm their mother loved. Once they graduated high school, they hardly came back at all, which left a lot of space on Mrs. Newkirk's porch for Kate. She thought about how Mrs. Newkirk's farm had been the largest for miles.

Jackie's bungalow was built on an acre of land her father bought from Mrs. Newkirk in the 1960s. Kate's grandmother's family had been sharecropping for the Newkirks as far back as anyone could remember. Once Jackie's father married in and bought it, the land was theirs, an acre sloped toward a slow-moving creek full of catfish with water moccasins nesting on the shore, not as good as the rest of Mrs. Newkirk's land, which was prime, Down East farmland.

Kate felt her heartbeat speed up. "Wait. Where is Mrs. Newkirk?"

Jackie reached for one of the shoeboxes. She set it on her lap and thumbed through a few curls of paper.

"Serves them right. Those boys thought there would be more money from their Daddy's timber business out west, but there was none. No land like they thought there would be."

"Mama, where's Mrs. Newkirk?"

Jackie's fingers held her place between the papers in her box. She looked into Kate's eyes. "That's one of the things I need to talk to you about. Mrs. Newkirk died."

"What do you mean?"

"She got sick."

Something like a fish hook pulled tight in the space where the bones of Kate's chest connected. "What kind of sick?"

"Heart failure. She died back in January."

"January? She died five months ago, and you didn't tell me?"

"I don't remember hearing that you bothered calling her too much after you left. She asked after you all the time, wanting to know where you were, how to reach you, what address to send something, but I never did really know, did I?"

Kate felt sorry for that truth, that she never spoke to

Mrs. Newkirk after leaving for Boston.

"Did her sons come home?" Kate asked, her voice catching.

"What do you think, Katie? For a couple days at the very end. They were gone as soon as they could be. Just like some other children I know." Jackie coughed. "She wasn't alone though. Maribel and I were there. That was before I got sick myself. So, yes, she was cared for."

She had left, and of course life went on without her. She was surprised though how it hurt to really understand that.

"Those boys have been selling her holdings off right under her for the last few years. Only about five acres left at this point. That's what's going on down here these days. Sell off the land to developers. Tanner Williams' place just sold for $1.2 million. Now he's got a condo up at Wrightsville Beach."

Jackie's mouth turned downward, the lines at the sides deepening. "The developer wanted mine too. I told him it wasn't for sale."

"You didn't name your price?"

Jackie looked genuinely shocked. "My father built this house."

"You always said, everyone has their number."

"There's such a thing as sacred too. I'm sorry, I didn't tell you, but I hadn't heard from you in so long."

A metal pan dropped in the kitchen, audible through the closed bedroom door.

They both looked toward the sound, then Jackie looked across the room. "Can you hand me my glasses? They're over there."

The tall bureau was covered in a clutter of costume jewelry, a dusty sewing box, and a wicker basket full of prescription bottles. Next to a pair of green plastic reading glasses, Kate noticed a plastic bag fat with marijuana.

"It's medical," Jackie said as Kate picked up the baggie.

"I didn't think that existed down here." Kate walked back and handed Jackie the green glasses. "Mama, are you going to tell me what's wrong with you or not?"

"Took you long enough to ask." Jackie put the glasses on. "It's Hepatitis C."

"What do you do for it?" Kate sat back down in the chair.

"You can't do anything. My liver's failing. Hand me those cigarettes there. I don't know why Maribel keeps putting everything just out of reach."

Kate paused before picking up the Kools of the far side of the nightstand. "What do you mean?"

Their fingertips brushed as they passed the pack, the first time they'd touched in almost a decade.

"They can't do anything for me." Jackie pulled her lighter out from inside the half empty pack. She struggled to light the cigarette, but finally seemed to find the strength. "Do you want to hear me say it? I'll be dead in a few months."

Kate reached down and slipped off her boots then curled her feet under her on her seat, stabilizing herself. "Are you sure?"

"You think I'd say something like that kind of guessing? I had a spell a few weeks ago. Maribel forced me to go to the hospital. I was too ill to fight her. That's when they told me. Complications from Hepatitis C. The infection caused a build up of fluid here." Jackie touched the right side of her stomach. "They drained me out, sent me home worse then when I started. I will not be going back there. I mean it. Do not let anyone take me back there. Meanwhile, they told me I've got COD or COPD or something with my lungs, but the other disease will get me first. Smith brought me that for pain management." Jackie gestured at the bag of marijuana on her dresser. "I don't touch the stuff. You can have it."

"They can't do anything for you?" Kate tried to keep her voice steady.

Jackie picked through the box in front of her, her cigarette hanging from the corner of her mouth. She held up an envelope like it was some kind of artifact, looking through the glasses sliding to the end of her nose. "No. They can't help me."

Kate waited until she was sure she wouldn't break into tears then said, "And what is all of this?"

"I'm sorting through my affairs trying to get things in order. That's what people do at the end." Jackie reached up and pulled the oxygen tube from her nose and let it rest around on her collarbone like a necklace. She held out an index card. "Could you put that in that garbage pail over there?"

Kate saw it was a recipe written in Mrs. Newkirk's handwriting, the ink faded to brown. She hesitated, but took it to throw in the trash basket by the window. Outside, waves of heat were rippling up from the fields. A flock of barn swallows were dipping down then rising up again. She watched the birds eventually land in the field, disappearing among the tobacco plants. She looked over to the packhouse's tin roof that was reflecting the sunlight back to her. She slipped the card into the back pocket of her jeans.

Kate walked back from the window. She sat down again in the soft chair and curled her fingers around the ends of its arms. "Are you seeing some kind of actual doctor at an actual medical facility?"

"You don't believe me? You need some lab results? They're in here somewhere," Jackie said fanning out some of the papers on her bed.

Besides a general practitioner who came around their house fairly regularly when Kate was a teenager, they never went to the doctor. Dr. Reeves had not primarily come for medical treatment. He often left behind paper prescriptions that Jackie filled at a constellation of pharmacies then sold off. Besides Dr. Reeves, she knew Jackie avoided doctors and hospitals to the extreme. She claimed her sewing kit, once sterilized, contained what you needed to give stitches, pull splinters, cut open boils. She believed that if you drank enough water, you could flush any virus or looming infection out of your system.

"I just don't understand."

"Well, now don't hurt yourself trying." Jackie set her cigarette in a notch of the ashtray on the bedside table. "It's liver failure. That's the end of the story."

Kate tried to push away the rising sorrow. "Okay, hold on. Let me make sure I'm keeping up here. Mrs. Newkirk passed away. Her farm is a subdivision. You are speaking to Smith. You are sick and…" Kate trailed off before continuing. "Some woman is doing your laundry and cleaning your kitchen."

"She is not *some woman*. Maribel is like a daughter to me."

Kate swallowed the knot in her throat. She had been gone eight years. She guessed that was long enough for someone to take her place.

"Does she work for you?"

"She has a name," Jackie said accusingly.

"Okay, then. Maribel. Did you hire her?" Kate knew if an arrangement involved Jackie, there was some kind of exchange. There was some resource flowing back and forth between her mother and this woman.

"What do you mean hire her? I told you, she is like family, the only family I have around here."

"Is she your cleaning woman?"

"Now you're just being ugly, assuming because she is Mexican she's a maid."

They could hear the clank of dishes through her mother's bedroom door. "But she is cleaning your kitchen. Right now."

Jackie let out a loud sigh like the conversation was exhausting her. "Maribel works for Walter Tate up at the Registry Agriculture plant. If you must know, even though it is certainly none of your business, I rent her a room. Your room. Not that it's yours anymore."

Jackie struggled again to light a new cigarette even though the other one still smoldered in the ashtray. Rolling the wheel seemed to require more pressure than she had to give.

Kate reached out and sparked the lighter for her mother. "Maybe if we went to a different hospital, maybe they would have different information."

Jackie drew on the cigarette until it illuminated orange and alive. She took a couple puffs, meeting Kate's eyes. "Look, I didn't call you down here to take care of me if that's what you're wondering. I have people I trust more to do that. I called you down here to do one thing, something I cannot do myself."

Kate was overwhelmed with it all. She undid her hair from its rubber band. She ran her fingers through it, letting it hang behind her shoulders. Jackie reached up to fluff her own hair. It was matted down on one side and sticking out in dry tufts on the other under the tubing. Kate knew her mother was jealous of her hair, although she would never admit it. When she was little Jackie complained that it was too hard to comb through, too much hair to do anything with. Kate had believed her until she got old enough to understand that she had the thick, glossy hair everyone else wanted.

Jackie said, "I need you to help me get three children."

Even with the air conditioning unit blowing into the room, Kate felt the heat inside her rising. Her heart beat faster as they finally came to the reason her mother had called, the main reason

Kate had returned before being sideswiped by things she hadn't known: finding her daughter and figuring out whatever Jackie was talking about with these other kids.

"Are you going to tell me what that means?"

"You know what it's like to lose a child," Jackie said in the dramatic voice she used when she was performing her way into getting someone to do something she wanted. "So, I know you will understand this situation."

Luke would have reminded Kate about their mother's various manipulation techniques.

"I didn't lose mine," Kate said. "I gave her up."

"It's the same thing."

"It's not."

"It is."

It wasn't, but it didn't matter. Jackie was just getting started. Kate had watched her do it so many times when she wanted something. Like gently conning the unassuming Walmart clerk at the returns desk. She'd start with cheap T-shirts and jeans with the tags still on accompanied by correlating receipts before having Luke push up a cart loaded with two or three microwaves, yes, in their original packaging, but definitely not purchased from the store. The clerk might look suspicious, because that was not a brand they usually sold, but what was that in the face of the easily exploitable store policy and Jackie who would never take no for an answer anyway?

Or how Jackie would spend a leisurely meal at various Red Lobsters as far as Rocky Mount, from beverage order through the Alaskan crab legs and surf-and-turf, peppering the waitress with compliments on her nails or earrings or frosted highlights, all the way through the free dessert, despite the fact that it was not Luke and Kate's birthday, to the end where she realized she had brought the wrong pocketbook and did not have her large velvet coin purse and thus no cash. Somehow she would then move from feigned confusion to shock to embarrassment to tears to having the wait-ress comforting her and calling in the manager to comp the meal.

In her more personal negotiations, those with men in the house from whom she wanted more money, she would first figure out their weakest point, the depth of their desire, and move from there in a series of steps to slowly get what she wanted from them.

Jackie put her second cigarette in a notch in the ashtray. "I know where your daughter is, but first we need to talk about the other children. Then we talk about your daughter."

Kate clenched her teeth, trying not to let her emotions play across her face. *Your daughter.* Those words. "You trying to hold that over my head isn't going to work. I'm not sure I want to know where she is."

"You wouldn't have come all this way if you didn't."

That was true. It was also true that she didn't know what she would do with the information. 17-year-old Kate had signed paper-work on a closed adoption, although Jackie had said shortly after it could not be legally binding because Kate was a minor. Still, Kate would not want to scare the little girl by showing up as a stranger saying, *I am your mother.* And yet, she had driven the eastern sea-board, primarily for her daughter's location. What else would she do with it?

"What are you talking about with these other children you want brought to you?" Kate asked.

"That's a complicated story, and I want to make sure we under-stand each other first."

"So too complicated to explain over the phone. And now I'm here, it's still to complicated."

Kate guessed her mother withholding meant Jackie was going to ask her to do something that was morally wrong or borderline impossible. She would build up to it.

"If you want to know where your girl is, we need to have an understanding."

"You're going to use me? Force me to do something—"

"I'm not forcing you to do anything," Jackie said. "I'm helping more than one person at once."

"You mean you're using a bunch of people at the same time." Kate felt a familiar pang of resentment, thinking of all the times she had felt like a moving part of one of her mother's plans and less like she imagined a daughter should feel.

She knew they would fight. She hadn't known it would escalate so quickly, but she should have.

"You owe me," Jackie's said louder, angrier. "An apology if nothing else. You take off eight years ago, after giving up that girl without telling anyone, not even Smith. After you didn't listen to me. I warned you that you were making mistake after mistake."

Kate felt her throat tighten with a hard pit.

Jackie kept going. "Then you show up here, only because I left a message saying I know where she is. You want to know where she is so bad, but you're the one who gave her away for nothing."

Kate's insides felt like they were vibrating, a shaking building up more and more intense.

"You don't sell babies, Mama. You let them go when you know they will have a better life without you."

"You didn't listen to me, and then exactly what I said would happen happened. Then it was too late, just like I knew it would be. And you did. You all but sold her. Sold her for a bus ticket and a few months of staying in those people's house up north so they could monitor your diet and make sure you weren't a druggie. Then they left you with nothing."

"So you really aren't going to tell me where she is?"

"First, I want an apology."

"Me too."

Kate left Jackie's house through the back door and moved across the yard past the old packhouse and its sloping roofed shed. She followed the line between the new housing development and Jackie's side of overgrown grass. She had nowhere to go, but she moved fast anyway.

SIX

WHEN KATE WAS growing up in the country outside of Wilmington, there was the Black church and the white church. There were the fourth-generation farmers and the newer people who couldn't figure out how to deal with the sandy soil. They all met on Ruby Newkirk's porch. You needed to get rid of the hornworms plaguing your tomatoes? Mrs. Newkirk would receive you from her rocker and tell you to spray some dish soap on the leaves then sprinkle cayenne pepper around the base of the plants. You had a problem with spots on your bean seedlings? Ruby could diagnose your plants with "dampen' off." Shaking her head, holding the tiny limp leaves out in front of her like they were contagious, she'd say, "Rip 'em out, and wait until the soil is warmer. Can't rush the weather."

Kate had grown up on Mrs. Newkirk's porch as much as she could. It was generally a good idea, especially as she got older, to stay out of her own house in order to avoid the gaze of whoever her mother had staying with them at the time.

One afternoon when she was thirteen, Kate sat on Mrs. Newkirk's porch floor rubbing thick silver polish onto a tarnished sugar dish.

"Pretty ain't it? That was my grandmother's," Mrs. Newkirk said looking down at the piece with the detailed engravings of delicate flowers. "Do it in a circle now."

"Like this?" Kate used more pressure to wipe away the rainbow-tinged tarnish.

Mrs. Newkirk nodded approval from her chair. "You can tell a lot about a person by how they take advice."

A car pulled in from the county road, dragging a cloud of dust along with it.

"Here comes someone." Mrs. Newkirk pushed back making the chair rock harder.

Kate turned and saw the gold VW bug, driven by a man whose head grazed the ceiling. "Mrs. Newkirk, it's Mr. James."

She clapped her arthritic hands together. "Seymour will have something good for us."

"Afternoon, Mrs. Newkirk," Seymour said, unfolding himself from the driver's seat while using a handkerchief to wipe the sweat from his creased brow. He was still wearing the white uniform from the barbecue restaurant where he was a cook. "You got any strawberries today?"

"You know I do," Mrs. Newkirk said. "You buying or trading? I reckon you didn't come empty handed."

Seymour laughed. "You do know me. I got some purple turnips, some collards, and something new for you."

He went to his passenger side and pulled out a cardboard tray of vegetables. As he walked slowly up the porch steps, he smiled down at Kate. Normally, Seymour was one of Kate's favorite people to see on Mrs. Newkirk's porch, but earlier that week, she had been in a fight with his daughter Leketha at school. She hoped he didn't know.

"You fixin' to have a tea party, Katie? Humidity's going to make it hard to keep that silver shining."

Kate smiled up at him. "No sir, but Mrs. Newkirk is."

"It's a luncheon," Mrs. Newkirk said rolling her eyes. "Those hoity-toity women from the garden club in Wilmington. Bunch of city slickers."

"Yeah, I know how they do." Seymour sat down heavily in the rocker next to Mrs. Newkirk balancing the tray on his knees.

Mrs. Newkirk waved her hand above her head like she was shooing away flies. "I don't know why I even bother with them, but we all have our obligations."

Kate began to gather up the stained rags and tea set. She would have to finish the silver tray later. She wanted to get Seymour some tea with the mint she had picked by Mrs. Newkirk's back steps when she first got off the school bus.

"What, no peas?" Mrs. Newkirk asked Seymour.

"There aren't enough hours in the day," he said and handed her his box of vegetables.

"That's the truth," Mrs. Newkirk said putting on her reading glasses to look closely at the harvest.

When Kate returned from the kitchen, Mrs. Newkirk was leaning toward Seymour's box of vegetables. Seymour nodded at Kate as she handed him the glass of tea, already wet with condensation, then found her place again on the floorboards.

"Now what in tarnation is that?"

"That's bok choy." Seymour lifted out the white and green plant.

"A bok what?"

"An Asian cabbage."

"Life isn't complicated enough?" Mrs. Newkirk asked.

"I like to experiment," Seymour said. "You just sauté them up in olive oil, or butter if you don't have oil. Pepper. Salt. Nothing complicated about it."

"I bet you learned that up in New York City," Mrs. Newkirk said. She sat back in her chair now having done an initial assessment of what Seymour had in his box.

"I did learn a whole lot up there."

Kate wasn't like Luke who was always talking about leaving, but she did like to hear Seymour talk about "up north."

Mrs. Newkirk dabbed at her forehead with the back of her hand. "I bet you miss it, being in the big city."

"I do." He took a long draw from his tea, draining half the glass. "They say it never sleeps, and I can tell you that's the truth."

"My husband always had fire under his feet that kept him wanting to wander. Dragged me off to Colorado. You'd think those trees on that parcel of land he bought out west were made of gold."

Seymour said, "Lots of money in timber, even round here."

"That man thought everything might be worth more than what it was. The way he acted, you'd think that big ole' sky was worth something."

Seymour finished off the last of his tea. "That's how some folks are. Always looking for something better. We can't help it."

Mrs. Newkirk turned to Kate. "Don't you go and get an idea going off like that."

"I don't know, Mrs. Newkirk, sometimes folks have to leave where they're from to do better." Seymour handed his glass containing only ice cubes back to Kate. She stood to get him more, but he shook his head and held out his hand to show he had enough.

"Shoot. I reckon moving around might be good for some people, but it wasn't for me. Now look here, Seymour, I don't want your bok-bok what-have-you, but give me them turnips, and I'll take those collards too."

"How you ask?"

Kate tensed. No matter who raised you, the number one rule was respect your elders. Then again, Mrs. Newkirk could take things for granted that most younger white people might not. Like saying please to someone who was black to show some respect, or at least to show you weren't a total, old South racist.

Mrs. Newkirk sighed. "I forgot you was so old fashioned. *Please*, may I have all those beautiful greens."

Seymour lifted the bunch of turnips and collards and handed them to Mrs. Newkirk. "Got to stay old fashioned. Teach these young people to act right."

"That's why people like me." Mrs. Newkirk brushed dried dirt off the turnips. "Because I know the old timey ways. I can't go changing now at my age. Katie, run and get a tray of strawberry pints for Seymour from the kitchen. Then we'll go round yonder and see what these collards are made of."

Around the side of the house was the claw foot tub Mrs. Newkirk kept filled with water.

"So it's going to be trial by tub to judge my pest control, huh?" Seymour leaned up against the house amused. "You know there's not a spider mite on those leaves."

"I got to make sure no one around here gets too big for their britches," Mrs. Newkirk said.

Kate noticed Seymour's head slide back slightly on his neck as his eyes narrowed.

Mrs. Newkirk must have noticed it too. "I just mean, nobody wants the hard work to do things right anymore. Even my own sons are too high falutin' to bother with their birthright." Mrs. Newkirk held her hand out to the fields beyond her house to indicated the wasted legacy her sons were walking away from. She handed the greens and turnips over to Kate, saying, "Get in there and wash those good for us."

Kate went down the stairs into the yard on the far end of the porch where the bathtub was. She got to work dunking the vegetables. From there, she was in Seymour's direct line of vision.

"You go to school with my daughter," he said.

"Yessir." Kate did not look up. She *really* hoped he didn't know about the fight.

"I bet you're as ready as my Leketha to be done with middle school. She and her mother have got her booked into every summer camp across the state including the governor's school for a week. They're bustin' up my checkbook pretty good." Seymour shook his head.

When Kate returned to the porch her arms full of wet greens and roots, Mrs. Newkirk opened up a clean dish towel to receive them. "You must be real proud."

"I am," he said smiling.

Leketha was one of the popular black girls in Kate's grade with her father's clear, dark complexion and height and her mother's eyes and long lashes. She was in all the academically gifted classes with Luke, and she hated Kate.

On the previous Monday, Leketha had stopped Kate in the hall. She pointed to the denim jacket Kate was wearing. "I think that's mine. I forgot it in the auditorium after the assembly last week."

"I bought this at the mall." Kate had taken the jacket in the lost and found.

Leketha laughed. "Yeah, right. Then what store is it from?" She stepped closer.

Kate had no idea what was on the tag, so she grabbed Leketha by the fabric of her T-shirt and pushed her back against a locker with a bang that echoed down the hall. Kate held Leketha there against the metal for just a second before Leketha's eyes flashed even brighter. She pushed Kate off as the chant began, *fight fight fight fight.*

Later that afternoon, when they were home, Luke asked, "How did you manage to get in a fight with Leketha James? She's better at algebra than anyone. Even me."

Kate shrugged, not wanting him to know about the jacket from the lost and found, a practice their mother encouraged. But Luke had given that up by then in favor of working local farms for his own money, which he kept well hidden somewhere in the packhouse out back. Kate had gone to get a bag of freezer burned peas from the back porch's deep freeze. It was usually the white girls who left her with the black eyes and scratches, at least until she learned the best way to win a fight was to start it yourself. It turned out though that National Junior Honor Society member Leketha James could throw a real mean punch when you stole her jean jacket then lied about it.

Seymour stayed to cut up the strawberries he had traded for. He sat on the porch steps, leaning against the stair rail across from Kate while Mrs. Newkirk rocked slightly in her chair, peeling the purple turnips.

"There isn't a single peck out of any of these," Seymour said holding up a bright red berry. "You're almost as good as me."

"I been around a season or two," Mrs. Newkirk said.

"I know it." Seymour moved his paring knife so fast Kate could barely focus her eyes on it before he had cut off the green top.

Mrs. Newkirk pointed her knife toward Seymour accusingly

and said, "Katie, this man makes the finest pulled pork in the state."

"Ain't nothing to it," Seymour said with false modesty, slicing through another berry. "Temperature control. After that, it's all in the sauce. White vinegar and red pepper flakes, that's the main thing. About a quarter cup of sugar, then I have my secret."

"Tell her the secret." Mrs. Newkirk said nodding at Kate.

"Can't tell no one the secret."

"Except me," Mrs. Newkirk smiled and pushed back, giving the chair a deeper rock.

"Well, now that don't count." Seymour looked at Kate. "Mrs. Newkirk is what they call a 'super taster' up there in New York City. She guessed it. I didn't tell her."

Seymour leaned back against the porch railing again, adjusting his legs under his weight. The sky lit up pink with lightning coming from behind the creek. It was too early to tell if it was just heat lighting or a storm coming in from the coast.

"You got a lot going for you, Seymour," Mrs. Newkirk said moving on to another turnip. "I kind of wish you could of stayed up there to show them how it's done."

"Well, that wasn't in the cards. But you never know what the future holds."

"Your mother was a fine woman," Mrs. Newkirk said. "She was my boys' chemistry teacher years ago."

They were quiet for a minute, just the sound of birds squabbling in the pecan tree limbs and the sound of a car speeding by on the county road. Kate thought she was hearing motorcycles in the distance before she realized it was the far away rumble of thunder.

"That dementia's a terrible thing," Mrs. Newkirk finally said.

"Thank you, Mrs. Newkirk," Seymour said, not looking up from his cutting. "You know, I was more at home than you'd think up there in New York. All that noise, all those people. It's like the entire city was a kitchen at the supper rush. I liked that about it."

Mrs. Newkirk flicked her little paring blade between the turnip's skin and flesh. "Katie, run and get those beans off my counter. We might as well shell those too while we're at it."

They were halfway through the beans when Seymour asked, "How's your mama, Kate?"

"Oh," Kate said trying to think what to say. Her mother was currently at their house with a mason who left so many sprayed down trowels and tools to dry on their back steps they had to jump over to the grass. "She's fine."

"I used to go to school with her," Seymour said.

"Her mama used to come here when she was a young 'un," Mrs. Newkirk said. "I couldn't get her to work like Katie does, but I kept an eye on her all the same. She used to read through my husband's books. After he was gone, it was nice that someone took an interest in them again."

"I do remember she always had her nose in a book," Seymour said. "I think she skipped a grade somewhere. I can't remember. Maybe it was two grades. And I remember she used to sell things before y'all came along. Half the girls in the high school had these little short dresses she used to make. She kept getting caught for selling things at school, and they'd shut her down, but she'd always find a way to start it up again."

Kate listened carefully for information because this was the kind of thing Jackie would never talk about.

"Lord yes, she could sew. I taught her how," Mrs. Newkirk said. "I just had it in mind to teach her to raise a hem and maybe make some curtains, but she was beyond me. She didn't even need patterns."

"She used to sell us stuff too that she got from her daddy's store once he opened it. People thought that he wouldn't make it. Coming up from sharecropping like that to own a business. Hardly anyone could do that. Your mama come to school with this whole mess of candy, Moon Pies, and whatnot and would sell them to us on the playground. Had to hide it all from the teachers. When we got older it was smokes and packs of Wrigley's. I never did know if her Daddy knew she was selling his stock, or if she was stealing it off the shelf."

"What about her mama?" Kate asked. She knew there was some map in these stories about family, some line from one point to another that could tell her what she had come from and how that measured up to where she was going.

Mrs. Newkirk looked at Kate. "Her mama died right after Jackie was born. That woman was out of her blessed mind. I tell you what though, she was something to look at."

Kate raked her hands across the shelled beans in the half-filled bowl. "Mama didn't get those looks."

Seymour looked at Mrs. Newkirk to see what she would say.

"No, I suppose not. She favors her daddy in more ways than one. Jackie's got a head for business like him."

"Sure do," Seymour said. "I remember her when she was big as a house working up at your granddaddy's store. He wouldn't hardly look at her but she worked the register with her head held high talking people into buying more things they didn't know they needed."

Kate pulled a green string out of the seam of the bean and felt a heat prickle under her skin thinking of her mother like that, the way Jackie seemed to have of never feeling embarrassment, always running some angle to talk people into something.

"She had gone off to that bible college for a while. A lot of the girls in those days didn't go off to school like her. It was different times wasn't it, Mrs. Newkirk?"

"Yes. Not like now where everybody's gone or going. Jackie's daddy didn't want her to go either, but she got herself scholarships. She was determined as she could be."

"She still is," Seymour said in a way that made Kate wonder what Jackie might have tried to pull on him over the years.

"Smart as she was having to drop out of college, and with only a year left to graduate. Came home pregnant and worked the store before she had y'all." Mrs. Newkirk shook her head. "Your mama got dealt a rough hand. A crazy mama, her daddy dropping dead right before y'all were born, losing the store, and then twins. How could the Lord above go and give her twins on top of all that?"

Kate's heart raced. Her blood rushed, causing a pounding current in her head. She had not made it fifteen minutes with her mother before leaving again. Just as she had when she was a kid, Kate was escaping from Jackie's house headed to Mrs. Newkirk's porch.

Kate walked fast along the edge of the new subdivision to the creek. On her right were the backyards with their kiddie pools and wilted tomato plants. Kate saw the developers had used sod with Bermuda grass, a poor choice. Bermuda liked full sun, which these back yards would never get. Kate remembered how the creek just beyond the trees frequently flooded its banks. The sod wouldn't last more than a season or two.

Kate could see the creek through the pine trees as she neared Mrs. Newkirk's house, running along the back edge of what had been farmland. There was a seldom-used dock before the creek took a sharp turn and flowed toward land that used to be owned by Mr. Knox. Beyond his land, the creek eventually joined with the

Cape Fear River then ran out to sea. Kate was in high school when Mr. Knox shot himself. She remembered him shortly before that staggering up to Mrs. Newkirk's porch.

"Now what should I do about these here?" He waved soggy, diseased plants.

"Stop trying to farm a swamp," Mrs. Newkirk said. "And go on and dry yourself out too while you're at it."

Kate was relieved that the pecan trees were still there. Last fall's pecans crushed under her boots on the ground. Their shells were still hard, although they would be no good for eating now. Kate could imagine Ruby Newkirk sucking her teeth if she was there to see it. "Waste ain't nothin' but laziness, and that's a sin. They call it 'sloth' in the Bible."

Mrs. Newkirk would hate that they were selling off her house, her land. Kate's chest hurt with missing her.

When Kate saw the two-story white farm house with the green shutters and pretty balusters around the porch, she took a deep breath. The years had left Mrs. Newkirk's wooden porch sagging in the middle at the steps. The paint peeled away from the clapboards leaving the dry wood splintered. The windows were lined from the inside with newspapers, the same as the back room at Jackie's house. Behind the house, Kate could see whoever was farming what used to be Mrs. Newkirk's land had planted soybeans right up to the back wall. Kate walked around to the side where the claw foot tub they used to wash vegetables was rusting, the back end sunk deeper than the front in the sandy soil. The clothesline Mrs. Newkirk hung her laundry on, even after her sons bought her an electric dryer, was tipped over, caught up in a row of blueberry bushes. The bushes had grown too close together, not letting in enough light. Those toward the back of the row looked like they had managed to set some fruit, but uncovered, the birds would take it. Kate took a spindly branch and wiped away the powdery mildew from the leaves.

It wasn't until Kate walked back to the front of the house that she noticed several folding chairs and a small grill surrounded by a dusting of black charcoal, all under the protective eave of the porch.

Kate tried the front door, but it was locked. She tried one of the windows, and it slid open. She gently reached inside and unstuck the newspaper where it was against the frame. It came loose, and she pushed it away to see inside. The furniture Kate remembered was gone. The dining room table with four leaves she often polished with Pledge was gone. The maple server and the glass curio case with the porcelain figures were no longer there. Even the light fixtures were missing, leaving black circles around the holes cut in the ceiling for wiring.

The furnishings were gone and the house was eerily empty, but it was clear people were squatting here. There were pallets on the floor, mattresses, sleeping bags like a sea of empty nests. It was like a recently abandoned ghost town, people's belongings laid out so closely that all the edges touched. There was laundry hanging on makeshift lines, men's shirts and underwear, most of it looking thin and worn. She could see the permanent stains at the armpits and in half-moons under the crewnecks of the T-shirts. There were empty shapes of people everywhere. Kate wondered why whoever was living here had not hung the laundry on the outdoor clothesline. She then understood whoever was here did not want to be seen.

The sound of children shouting and the shrill whir of a power saw drifted over from the new subdivision. The neighborhood was close by, but cut off from the house by the way the corner of the field intersected the property lines and a line of overgrown hedges.

Kate pulled the window shut and faced Mrs. Newkirk's front

yard, which was shaded just as it always had been by the pecan trees. Above Kate in the tree branches, cicadas threw their frenzied songs back and forth to each other. She remembered what Mrs. Newkirk had told her about the insects, how they lived underground for years before they climbed out from the roots of trees.

"What do they do when they come up?" Kate asked.

"They look for love." Mrs. Newkirk had smiled, showing her teeth.

Since leaving, Kate had been living underground in her own way, trying to hide within herself. She had come back to find out where her daughter was, in part, but also because this was the only place where she'd ever felt a sense of belonging. Though they were twins, she and Luke did not, as it turned out, belong to the same place. For all the relative ease and safety of the life she had in Cambridge, she didn't want to go back if it meant hiding her past, her secrets, herself.

Kate walked back along the line between the cultivated lawns and the creek, the path softened with pine straw. The sound of a motorboat engine grew louder as it moved upstream toward her. Through the trees, Kate saw a green aluminum skiff with a tiny motor cut through the black water. The boat's wake broke into an arch of shining ripples cutting across the creek's surface. She pulled herself behind the thick trunk of a pine tree to avoid being seen.

The boat driver's frame was instantly recognizable. He twisted back to steer the boat's tiller. She recognized the narrow cut of his shoulders and the muscular arms, apparent even from where she hid. His light brown hair grew shaggy under the black trucker hat he wore pulled down low, hiding his eyes.

Kate held herself motionless until Smith passed out of view at the sharp bend upstream. He had not seen her. She could tell by the way the sound carried that he was riding upcreek past Jackie's old dock. She realized she had been holding her breath. After all this time, after all that had happened, he could still make her forget to breathe.

For her, brushing off the past was harder than Luke made it look. Time didn't erase or diminish things. Kate knew time had the power to make things stronger. Once plants took root, it was relatively hard to kill them. House plants in a dark room would lean toward any suggestion of light. If a rose bush's roots hit a stone wall, they would grow through the foundation, finding the weak points to push through. Given time, a tree's roots could decimate a sidewalk. She reminded herself fiercer plants always rooted out the weaker ones. She had time. Her mother might not. Their negotiation could still go Kate's way without her having to do the impossible.

SEVEN

KATE STOPPED AT the edge of Jackie's yard when she saw the Ford Fairmont. Missing when she first arrived, Kate assumed it was dead and gone. It was a 1980 model, beat up even when she and Luke were fighting over who could have it. Back then there was plastic in the right rear window that sucked in and billowed out at high speeds. The front left light had been smashed in.

Now the car with a new paint job, more a pearled cream than the matte white it had once been, was parked in front of the house, pulled up so far the front fender almost touched the brick foundation. The lights and windows were all restored. The chrome was immaculate and free of rust.

As Kate walked closer to the car, she saw in the driver seat a man in his late forties. The top half of his chin-length black hair was pulled back in a ponytail, and he had a handgun tucked into a shoulder holster. The box of Bojangles Kate had brought her mother, then left behind in the bathroom, was on the seat next to him. He talked on his cell in a fast flow of Spanish, watching Kate pull her duffle from Charlie's Audi.

Inside, she put her bag on the floor next to the green couch. Maribel was gone. The dishes were put away, the table wiped down.

Kate sat down and pulled off the boots that were too hot and pulled on a leather flip flop. Charlie called them her Jesus shoes. He preferred her in heels, like the black ones nestled between her other clothes. They looked especially pointless now.

When the door from Kate's old bedroom creaked open, Kate jumped, dropping her second sandal. She hadn't realized anyone was in there. A young woman, maybe twenty, emerged from the bedroom. She had dark brown hair that flowed out behind her shoulders. She wore only a long peach T-shirt with a graphic of the Disney castle emblazoned in blue glitter. She rubbed her right eye with the heel of her hand. When she noticed Kate, her hand flew to her chest. "Dios mío, me asustaste!"

The young woman came to sit next to Kate on the couch. She put her hand on Kate's knee. She leaned in closer and dropped her voice, then spoke in Spanish.

"I'm sorry. I don't understand."

The woman looked confused for a moment before she pointed at Kate and said, "New?"

Kate shook her head. "This is my house."

The young woman looked worried. She pulled her hand back from Kate's knee. She stood. "Okay." She backed away before turning to the back of the house. She shut the bathroom door behind her.

Jackie was dealing in people. Whoever occupied the empty pallets on Mrs. Newkirk's floor at night, whoever these women were in the house, Jackie's current currency was human, in a different way than when Kate was growing up.

Kate went to the doorway of her old bedroom that the young women had left open behind her. It had always been the sunniest room in the house, especially in the afternoon. Now there were floral sheets hanging over the windows, tacked in under the sill.

They billowed in the hot breeze. The house had never known air conditioning, except now with the window unit in Jackie's room.

Particles of dust were suspended in the light over a double mattress on two box springs making it as high as an actual bed. Kate remembered that boyfriend of Jackie's who had worked at a mattress discounter. He had actually been nice, always bringing home bags of fried chicken and dinner rolls for Luke and Kate from a restaurant near his store. He had given them that bed setup leftover from a tent sale. By then, it had been her room. Luke had moved to the couch when Jackie said they were too old to be sharing.

The old wooden dresser that Jackie told Kate had been her grandmother's was still there, against the far wall, but there were also three wooden peach crates stacked up on top of each other sideways. One crate was stuffed with unfolded clothes, so many patterns and colors like one of the crazy quilts her mother used to make piecing together scraps of fabric. The second one held a few bottles of lotion and a philodendron whose stems were beginning to trail down. The top crate contained a stack of photographs and a worn leather bound bible. There were a couple prayer candles set in the crate as well, although the white wicks indicated they had never been lit.

The crates were being used as dividers between Kate's old mattress and a twin bed pushed up against the wall, blocking the door of a small closet. Kate remembered being pregnant and combing through the clothes in that closet trying to find things that would fit as her body expanded despite how little food she could keep down. Her mother often purchased brand names at one store on deep discount then tried to return those items to a different store with the retailer tags cut off, but the brand tags still intact. So Kate eventually had a small but useful collection resulting from the savvier clerks who refused Jackie's attempt at exchange.

The two bedrooms in the house were connected by a thin particle board door. Kate could hear her mother and Maribel talking.

"Her car is perfect," Jackie said.

"She will say no."

"She'll do it. I have what she wants."

"What if it's not enough?"

"It's enough."

Kate pushed the door open. Maribel was in the chair by the bed. She wore a long white cotton overcoat that might have looked like a doctor's in another context. Kate recognized it as the slaughterhouse uniform. Her hair was pulled back tight, no earrings, no watch, no rings, important absences in light of the machinery, which could catch on anything extra.

"Back already?" Jackie's voice sounded strong, but her head was laid back against the pillow as if holding it up was just too difficult.

"For the moment," Kate said although she had nowhere else to go.

To Maribel, Jackie said, "Juan is out front." She reached into her bedside table drawer and pulled out a fat church offering envelope. That was how Jackie had always stored cash. Kate wondered where she got them; she hadn't gone to church since Kate and Luke were ten.

Maribel looked over her shoulder at Kate leaning stubbornly against Jackie's tall bureau with her arms crossed over her chest. She did not want this woman in her house exchanging envelopes of money with her mother.

"I have to be more careful now," Maribel said.

Jackie reached out and took Maribel's hand, folded her fingers around the offering envelope.

"It's just for now."

Maribel took it. On her way out of Jackie's room, Maribel gave Kate a distasteful look, strong and clear.

Kate shut Jackie's bedroom door behind her. "Who's Juan? Your security detail?"

Jackie lifted a pile of papers from a Keds shoebox and laid them down on the blanket.

"He's a friend."

"What kind of friend?"

Jackie looked annoyed. "A friend friend. I've always had a lot of friends."

"Is that what you call them?"

"You never had many, did you?"

Kate felt the sting. Growing up, she had tried to keep the secrets of their house by avoiding anyone her own age. It had been lonely but effective.

"This friend carries a gun." Kate sat down in the yellow corduroy chair. It still felt warm from Maribel.

"Lots of people do. Most everyone down here. Don't you remember? It's an open carry state."

Through the wall, Kate heard the water running in the bathroom. "Who's that in our shower?"

"*My* shower? That's probably Valeria. Stay around after the second shift is over and you might meet Nina. They share the front room with Maribel."

"Does Juan live here too?" Kate asked and put the open toes of her sandals up on the wooden rail of the bed frame. "Or does he live at Mrs. Newkirk's house?"

Jackie looked up from her box. "Is that where you went?"

"Does that worry you?"

"Why should it?"

"You're not worried about what I might have seen?"

"What is it you think you saw?"

"People are living there. I'm guessing migrant workers. But you don't own that house, so you are trying to hide them."

Jackie sighed and pulled some of the paperwork into her lap. "I'm trying to buy Mrs. Newkirk's house from her sons. They're asking too much. Until I can talk some sense into them, I'm borrowing it for the growing season."

"Aren't they going to find out? Especially if they are trying to sell everything?"

"One's in Chicago. The other's in Atlanta."

Kate heard someone open a door and then close another a few seconds later. Kate felt a deep sense of invasion, one that was not unfamiliar. She was almost never alone in this house. There were always people moving through. In the past, they had been boyfriends or whatever her mother chose to call them. Visitors. Gentlemen. Fools. Fans. Sons-of-you-know-whats depending on the day.

Kate had never known who might come through any given door, who would be on the couch when she got home from school, who would be smoking on the toilet, or cleaning a catfish in the kitchen sink, leaving a trail of innards and blood splashed against the stainless steel, expecting her to clean up the mess.

There were times between the men where the house was gloriously empty, where Jackie didn't shoo Kate and Luke into their bedroom, or change the channel for some guy who wanted to watch NASCAR or the ECU game. In Kate's memory, those times between invasions were the exception rather than the rule.

She asked her mother the question she could have asked many times before. "Mama, what are you doing with all these the people in our house?"

"*My* house."

"Fine, *your* house, filled with these people who don't belong here."

Jackie was angry now, her face red as she spat out her answer. "*These* people? *These* people are willing to work the hogs and the turkeys and spray down the slaughterhouses and all sorts of things no one born here will do anymore. God forbid any white child stay here instead of moving off to better themselves. So who do you have? You have Maribel and Valeria and Juan."

"That's not what I meant."

"They know what family is."

Kate stared at her mother. "But they're not your family. You have them working for you."

"We work together."

"Doing what?"

"I help people," Jackie said with her chin slightly raised. "We help people."

"Help?" Kate was unable to keep the doubt out of her voice.

"You think you know me, don't you?"

"Well, Mama, I have spent some time with you over the years."

"A child doesn't know who her mother is. I could have been a lot of things if I hadn't been tied down here. Do you remember that man I dated?" Jackie asked. Despite her sallow skin and thin lips, Kate could still see the shadow of the woman Jackie had once been. She'd never been pretty, but she possessed a magnetism that drew men in, a crackling lightning-like energy.

"You'll have to be more specific."

"Don't be smart. Patrick Taylor. He was here one winter. You were maybe eleven. He and I talked about moving out to California and starting a real estate business."

"The one with the yippy dogs with all that matted down fur?"

Kate remembered a tall man with thinning blond hair who had six or seven little dogs who were always under foot nipping at ankles and filling the house with so much high-pitched barking Kate couldn't think.

"They were purebreds," Jackie said.

"They shit all over the floor."

"How many times do I need to tell you to watch your mouth in my house? We had a real plan. My plan, really, but he took it and went without me because I stayed with you. Do you know what he's worth now?"

Kate knew her mother was trying to snare her into a deeper, more tangled conversation. She took her feet off the bed, planted them on the floor for stability. Kate needed to at least try to be the one in charge.

"You have a history of using people, Mama."

Jackie sighed, flipping through the paperwork she had in her lap before returning her attention to Kate. "You know what people have to go through to cross the southern border?"

Kate did not answer. She did not. At least not specifics, although she remembered being in the room while Charlie watched a State of the Union with the second Bush talking about more funding for border patrol, more technologically advanced surveillance. No more "catch and release."

Jackie continued, her voice strong. "Getting here is just part of it. After that they need jobs, somewhere to live. If they have family here, they need help finding them. If they don't have family, they need even more help."

"And that's what you do?"

"I give people a chance at a life here."

"For a fee."

Her mother looked at her. She gestured for Kate to slide the chair closer. Kate hesitated but then did it.

"Maribel is my business partner. We move people to where they're needed. Believe me when I say we treat people well." When Kate looked doubtful, Jackie's mouth tightened. "Ask Maribel sometime. Ask her what happens to people who manage to cross the border but have no help waiting for them here on the other side."

Jackie's voice was dripping with a seething anger that Kate at first though was directed at her, but then realized was intended for someone or something else. Her lips were pressed tight together, the lines in her forehead cut deeper. "Think of it like the Underground Railroad."

Kate remembered a secret door between wooden panels in a house that Luke had been working on in Newton. He had pushed back the wood and shown her the tiny space against the hand-formed bricks of a chimney where six or seven people could hide waiting for the cover of night to move to the next safe space.

Kate said, "It's not like the Underground Railroad because you profit off them. Most those abolitionists were driven by religion, not money."

Jackie seemed surprised that Kate knew anything about it. "Look at you getting so educated about the world."

Even if the twentieth century was Charlie's area, by living with a history professor for four years, she had still learned more than she ever wanted about the triangle trade and how colonial indentured servants' court proceedings—and even their right to appear in court—differentiated them from the kidnapped people from Africa who would later replace them. She had been to more lectures than she could count, including official ones, and that was on top of experiencing Charlie's expertise on American history on a nearly daily basis.

Jackie pulled a photograph from the drawer of her bedside table. "I told Maribel I would get her children back."

When Kate took the photo from Jackie, she saw the three children, all with Maribel's large brown eyes, sitting in her lap. The oldest was a boy maybe nine or ten years old, then a girl several years younger, the littlest boy a toddler. The oldest had his arms around Maribel's neck, his hand on the side of her face, head tilted against hers, but Kate could see the worry in his eyes.

Maribel's smiling face was framed by a layered bob, not the longer hair she had now. She wore a blue button-down shirt dress with a tie around the waist. Kate could see they were on a bench in front of a plaster wall. There was part of a large window in the edge of the frame with children's drawings taped to it, facing the outside. Kate guessed it was a school.

"Where are they?" Kate asked.

"Juárez," Jackie searched Kate's face. "Did you fail geography too?"

"We didn't have geography."

"It's in Mexico. On the border with El Paso." Jackie shook her head. "El Paso. In Texas. I need you to drive down and get the children."

"Like pick them up after school?"

"This is serious."

"I agree. It sounds kind of like kidnapping.

"Don't be ridiculous. You are reuniting them with their mother."

"Why doesn't she go get them?"

Jackie shook her head. "Now you are just showing how little you know. That's not something she can do. But you can."

"I'm just confused. There has to be a process for this. Something that isn't illegal."

"Yes, there is," Jackie said, the annoyance in her voice clear. "Maribel applied for asylum. Now she gets to wait six or seven years for an interview. Her oldest will be grown by the time that happens."

Kate wasn't sure what to say. She had a sense of how quickly children grew and changed.

Jackie started in again. "No one is going to stop you, looking like you do, driving that expensive car you've got parked out there in my yard. What is that? A Saab?"

"An Audi. And it's not mine."

"It's not registered to you?"

"No, and the owner probably doesn't know it's gone, but he will in a couple weeks when he gets home."

"It's stolen?" This seemed to concern Jackie.

"Not exactly."

Jackie said to the ceiling more than Kate, "That could be a problem."

It didn't make sense. Kate could not see how Jackie benefitted from reuniting Maribel with her children. Maybe Maribel was paying. "Why do you need me to do it?"

"They're not U.S. citizens," Jackie said.

"But why me? I don't even have an ID."

"What do you mean?"

"I never got a license."

"Why didn't you get a license?"

"You never made me."

"That can't be true. Luke had one."

"I didn't." Kate felt a surge of frustration at all her mother didn't know and hadn't bothered to notice. She pushed the feeling back down, trying to focus on getting to the damn point of what her mother was laying out in front of her. "How am I supposed to get them back across the border?"

"You're going to say they're yours," Jackie said. "You'll pass. You're a little bit light as Mexicans go, but you're dark for being white."

Kate was having trouble processing this, all that her mother had formulated as a plan.

"I don't speak Spanish."

"It doesn't matter. It's easy. You smile at the guards. You say your children were staying with their grandmother in Juárez, that you are bringing them back home."

Kate glanced back down at the photo. "And the kids are just going to get in a car with a strange woman they have never met?"

"They speak English." Jackie pushed herself up on her elbows. She was getting animated again, speaking in the way she usually did when she had a good audience going in a doctor's waiting room or in line at the bank. "They know the plan. We've been working on this a long time. You just need to get three American passports made up. I guess four now that I know you don't have a license. I can't do this one myself."

Kate bit at the ragged place on her thumbnail as she studied the photo.

Jackie reached out and took hold of Kate's hand to stop her biting. She ran her thumb over Kate's nail. Kate could feel that her mother's skin was dry but warm before Jackie let go. "Call someone you know up there at Yale. They must have an entire office for all those students from all those foreign countries."

"Mama, it's Harvard, and I work at the greenhouse. I can't get people passports."

Jackie's face tightened as her mouth turned down. "What about your boyfriend?"

"He's in the History department. I don't think colleges actually issue visas or passports. I think you have to go to federal offices for that kind of thing." Kate laid the photo of the children on the bedside table. "Do you remember what you said when the Spanish grocery opened in the closed-down jewelry store in Burgaw?"

"What grocery store?" Jackie asked. "What are you talking about?"

Kate remembered it word for word. *What? Our beans and rice aren't good enough for them?* And when Jackie's church, the one she never went to anymore anyway, started offering a service in Spanish, she said, *They don't belong in our church unless they are cleaning it.*

Her mother had an angle with all of this. Kate just couldn't see it yet. "You used to complain about all the Mexicans moving in. About them not speaking the language. About them taking jobs, which honestly is funny since you have never really held down a real job."

Just for a flash of a second, Kate saw that she had hurt her mother, something rare but not impossible. Jackie tipped her chin up in the determined way Kate recognized. Now, Jackie would be an impenetrable wall. "Katie, you might not remember this, but down here we come up when we're called. We come up to the altar when we're moved by the spirit. We come up when folks need help. I don't know how they do it up there, but down here, we rise to the occasion. If you knew what happened along the border, you would do it."

Kate felt shaken, worried, but reminded herself to stay. "That's a great performance, but this is not a good plan."

"I need you for this one." A wave of worry washed over Jackie's face. "You know I wouldn't ask you if I didn't have to. You think I wanted to beg my own daughter to come back here? And then not even know if she would bother to show up?"

Kate felt a pang of guilt, but she remained deeply suspicious of Jackie's motives. Her mother was a swindler and, to make it worse, this most recent scheme seemed poorly-planned. Kate simply said, "How can I trust you?"

Jackie's oxygen tank hissed and clicked. "How can I trust *you*, Katie. You're the one who left me behind, remember? You just left with no warning, after I stood up for you when Lynette was coming for you. Remember? You lied to that Marine, what was his name?"

Kate had to think about it. "Mitchell."

"Yes, that was him. Saddest man I ever knew. He cried in his sleep. Don't you remember? It was you that left things a mess. Not me."

Kate did, although that period was hazy. She remembered Smith's mother, Lynette, kept showing up looking for her. Her son was in prison, and she had been blindsided by the adoption. Lynette wanted to know where her grandchild was. It had been nearly four months. Kate had physically recovered from having the baby, but she felt simultaneously dead and dangerous inside.

She remembered Lynette in Jackie's front yard screaming about kidnapping charges, Kate inside on the green couch smoking a joint with Mitchell. Through the front window, Kate heard Lynette say, "I've already called my lawyer," followed by Jackie saying, "I guess you have to be familiar with the law with a son like yours."

She passed the joint back to Mitchell.

Mitchell slowly shook his head back and forth where it rested against the high back of the sofa. "Baby Girl, you made yourself a big ole mess."

They heard Jackie tell Lynette she was dumber than a stump and always had been followed by Lynette unleashing a string of cussing and calling Jackie trash in multiple ways: trailer, white, nothing but.

They heard the sound of a car door slam and then the spin of tires in the dry dirt of the yard. Jackie, out of breath, came back inside. She looked at Kate on the couch and Kate exhaled a puff of smoke.

Jackie shook her head. "Don't say I never did anything for you. That woman was likely to kill you if I let her in here."

"Lynette's not going to do anything." Kate heard herself speak, but her voice sounded far away, not like it her own.

"I think she might." Jackie sat down in a kitchen chair they had pulled up to face the sofa. She picked up her lighter. She seemed to forget what she was doing for moment, an unlit cigarette hanging from her mouth, her thumb with its nail polished a bright coral against the metal of her lighter. Kate saw her mother was scared. Jackie's hand shook slightly as she finally flicked the metal and held the orange flame to the end of her cigarette.

Mitchell was one of the nice ones. That was why Kate had asked him for a ride to the bus station. She had made him promise not to tell her mother.

"She will have my hide, girl."

"I'll be back soon," she lied.

This, the second time she ran away from home, she wasn't a pregnant minor being ferried by an evangelical adoption service. She was eighteen. Before leaving, she pulled fourteen hundred in cash out of a mason jar where she hid it at the back of her closet. She would stay with Luke who had only called once since arriving at Harvard two weeks before, already sounding distant and swallowed up by his new life. She did not know yet that you couldn't move yourself into someone's dorm room.

"You better call her when you get there," Mitchell said when he dropped Kate at the Greyhound station in Wilmington.

"I promise." Another lie.

She started to shut his car door, but he called out to her.

"Hey. Here. Just so you don't become no Yankee." He had held out a black garbage bag duct taped closed at the top.

On the bus, Kate cut open the plastic with Smith's good pocket knife, the one he had given her before he was sentenced. Inside, she found a pair of tan cowboy boots with a carton of cigarettes tucked inside one and a fat bag of weed in the toe of the other. As the bus pulled out of the station, she ran her fingers over the blue threaded embroidery puckering the leather. Her fingertips felt numb like they were someone else's, running over soft skin.

Jackie reached down beside her for the oxygen. She arranged the tubing then said, "You told Mitchell you were coming back."

Kate saw a real moment of pain cross her mother's face. "People down here don't just leave their kin. They don't just walk away from their families like you and your brother did."

Jackie was very ill, possibly dying. Limited by a failing body, she would need Maribel and others to run whatever operation she had engineered here.

Maribel was separated from her children, and Jackie promised Kate could get them. Kate wanted the information Jackie had about her daughter. Jackie had created a triangle where the three of them were standing in each other's way while being each other's only path to what they wanted. Her mother might be ill, but she still had it in her to create a web between people where she pulled the strings.

"I wouldn't ask you to do something for nothing." Jackie reached into one of her boxes. She pulled out a piece of light green paper. She held it out for Kate to take.

Kate saw the embossed seal from the State of Massachusetts. She scanned down the page of information typed into the blanks "—seven pounds, six ounces—this day the sixth of April in the year nineteen ninety-eight—female." Kate saw her own signature, the shaky lines of the K, before the other letters became smoother and more certain in the loops of the rest of her name.

"There's this one too." Jackie gave Kate another sheet of paper. *Certificate of Adoption*. Kate saw the names of the adoptive parents, Toni Rossi and Daniel Williams and their address north of Boston. She already knew they weren't there anymore. Once, Kate had taken the commuter rail to the house where she had briefly stayed with them. There was an unfamiliar SUV in the driveway, two school-age boys riding bikes in circles around the house, no sign of a little girl who would have been the right age.

At the bottom of the certificate, Kate saw what she always wondered but never knew.

Name: Anna Dylanie Williams

Kate felt her mother search her face, assessing the measure of power this information held. She examined the form for her own name. It wasn't there. She was erased like she had never been there. Because she had *not* been there. She had not taken care of that baby who had become a girl. Anna. She had not held her cheek to hot forehead to test for a fever. She had not walked a floor over and over to create a rhythm that could put her baby back to sleep. She had not done those things that good parents did, the prices they paid for returned love.

Kate felt the absence of all of she had not had the opportunity to do, a pressure like being at the bottom of a deep pool. What she hadn't accounted for at seventeen was a sense of prolonged connection she never thought would matter. Kate had not known that it would mean something to be someone's origin. She had made the impulsive decisions, the swan dive of ignoring the basic laws of cause and effect that brought Anna into being. And now she couldn't break the longing. Kate wished with all her might that she could see Anna for even a moment.

"How did you get these?" Kate asked from somewhere outside of herself. She couldn't look directly at Jackie, but she could feel her mother's eyes on her.

"You listed yourself as Kate, not Kathryn or Katie. That held me up for a while. And trying to find people with the last name of Williams...nearly impossible."

"How long have you had it?"

"Only since last week," Jackie said, her voice quieter than usual, barely audible over the oxygen tank. "If you do what I'm asking, if you go to Juárez, just drive in and then right back out, if you do that, I will give you the address."

Kate leaned forward in the chair, putting her face into her hands. She managed to keep herself from crying.

Jackie's voice was quiet when she said, "We all make mistakes. Lord knows I have. But now you can go find her, if you want to."

"*If* I do what you want, which is impossible." Kate's hands shook as she folded the two certificates into a small rectangle.

"Don't get them all messed up now," Jackie said.

"I'm sure you made copies." Kate gestured to the overstuffed shoeboxes spread out on Jackie's bed. She slid the folded papers into the back pocket of her jeans. Kate would go through all the boxes until she found the address for her daughter.

She knew Jackie, a compulsive list maker and notetaker, would have written it somewhere. The more valuable Jackie thought the information, the closer she would keep it. Protected. Guarded. It was in there somewhere. Kate would find it.

Jackie reached for Kate's hand and said softly, "I know you can find a way to get what we need."

"I'm telling you, it's impossible." But then Kate looked at the bedside table to see the photograph of Maribel's three children. "I'll think about it."

She wouldn't, but she could imagine Maribel's pain. Kate had let go of her daughter after two days. And that baby, those two days, she knew must be nothing compared to losing three children old enough to know you were their mother.

"That's all I ask. That you think about it." Jackie closed her eyes and rested her head against the top of her pillow pile, indicating she'd said all that she planned to on the matter.

Kate left her mother and walked through to the room at the back of the house. She was startled to see someone asleep in the double bed pushed up against the wall. She had not heard anyone come in.

Kate stepped through the maze of cardboard boxes, moving closer to the bed as quietly as she could. It was a teenage boy, the skin on his nose and cheeks peeling from a recent sunburn. He must have shown up while she was at Mrs. Newkirk's house. He wore a pale blue Tarheels T-shirt that read, "*NCAA Champions 1993*" and a pair of oversized white gym shorts. Closer up, she could see the tear at the collar of the T-shirt.

She remembered the V-shape of that tear, the way she rubbed the worn jersey fabric between her fingers the day Smith broke into a municipal building to steal diesel. He was wiry and fast, able to scale just about anything. He had cleared the barbed wire fence with the grace of a pole vaulter. After several anxious minutes he returned, this time clambering over the fence with a full diesel can in tow, excited to fuel up his friend's ATV. She had pointed out they could just get it at the gas station, but he preferred the boost of adrenaline from stealing it.

Kate saw the cut before Smith felt it—under the tear in the shirt was a seam of blood on his collarbone.

The boy in the bed shifted. She was slowly backing up when she saw his eyes flash open. Kate realized he was just pretending to be asleep. Her breath caught in her throat as she turned for the back door.

In Jackie's back yard, the sun was sinking down just behind the pines, the air still humid. Kate walked toward the packhouse, the old tobacco barn where Luke once built his workshop. The corrugated metal sides were burnt orange with rust. The structure, which had once been used to store cured tobacco, leaned to the left.

A line of bluish light glowed under the eaves where the tin roof met the rusted sides, which made no sense. Packhouses weren't wired. She pulled back on the metal handle of the door, but it didn't open.

Kate walked to the corner of the packhouse where the light continued to seep out under the eaves. There was an old propane tank along the side. On the far end of it, she found the white marks Smith made when they were in high school. The letters almost glowed in the strange blue light escaping from overhead.

K.J. ♥ S.M. She had punched Smith in the arm after he scratched it with the metal tip of his lighter. "It should be the other way," Kate had said. She wondered then how that kind of equation was measured and which was the better end to be on of who loved whom. She still didn't know.

A car door slammed at the front of the house. Kate peeked out from behind the packhouse where she could stay mostly hidden

from view. The light in Jackie's kitchen turned on, followed by the
light in the back room where the kid pretended to sleep in Smith's
old Tarheels shirt.

Smith was everywhere down here. On her mother's dresser. In
a boat on the creek. In the tear on the T-shirt of the boy in the
back room. Engraved in the propane tank. She had heard his voice
in the background of Jackie's message. He would know what was
going on with the locked packhouse. Whether he would tell her
was another matter.

Kate stepped onto the front porch in a short jean skirt and off-the-
shoulder white T-shirt, her hair still wet from the shower. She had
moved the twin bed aside and found a box of her old clothes in the
bottom of the closet after Valeria left with Juan. As she had dressed
in her old room, she could hear her mother talking on the phone
through the shut door.

"I have the statement right here. I have the rest of the year's
statements too. I can read you the amount for each month. I'll start
with March. That's $43.44. April. $59.16. That's right. Yes. This is
for 1999. Yes, ma'am, seven years ago. But I know the benefits I am
entitled to, so you go ahead and get your supervisor if you need to."

The sky lit up with the flash of distant lightning. She remembered how she helped Mrs. Newkirk when hurricanes approached.
They pulled all the porch furniture in and taped up the windows.
Even Jackie, who listened to nothing, heeded those warnings, filling
the bathtub with water and filling the flashlights with fresh batter-
ies. That was what Kate wanted to do. Pull everything in close and
take account of what was still hers down here.

It was coming in fast now, the light turning a sickly yellow.
There was a smell of wet metal as the tops of the tall pecan trees in

the distance of Mrs. Newkirk's yard waved back and forth.

It had been too humid in the bathroom to apply makeup, so back in the Audi with the engine and air conditioning running, Kate used the rearview mirror to put on eyeliner.

After showering and dressing, Kate had slipped the birth and adoption certificates into the back pocket of her skirt. Anna. Now, she tucked the paper carefully behind the Audi's visor. Anna.

As Kate put the car in reverse, she felt what she always had, the magnetic pull north to south and south to north, she and Smith, magnets dead set on finding the ends of each other no matter which way they were turned.

When they were in high school, Luke had to distance himself.

"What? Are you too good for us now?" Kate had asked one night when Luke said he would rather stay at home than ride to Wrightsville Beach with them.

"I'm just trying to keep my criminal record in check. I'm applying to colleges next year."

Luke was probably right. Kate and Smith got in trouble. They got in trouble all the time.

Before the arrests, before the last one where Smith received a thirty-six-month sentence for intent to distribute, it was all small-time stuff: riding into town, or to Fort Bragg in Fayetteville, sometimes all the way to Raleigh to pick up an ounce or two if Wilmington was dry. Smith would divide it up and sell it mostly in dimes, occasionally a quarter to a Registry Agriculture exec's kid who had that kind of money.

"We need a plan, Katie," Smith had said one afternoon in the Hardee's parking lot where they were waiting to sell off their last bag.

"I guess," she watched for Max Thornton's CRX. She usually heard him before she saw him with his modified exhaust system and the way his bass pumped Busta Rhymes or Naughty by Nature.

"My dad wastes all of his time on the little shit." Smith held his cigarette out the window. "Floral arrangements, being the middle-man for annuals and perennials. It's a waste of time."

Kate was listening, but she wasn't thinking about the greenhouse. She was thinking that soon, Luke would take all the money he had been saving since he was thirteen and leave for one of those places in the college catalogues he kept hidden under the couch like precious road maps out of their life. She had seen the pages he dog-eared, kids sitting in grassy courtyards, course listings in engineering. She knew her brother well enough to know they were stacked in order of preference: MIT, Virginia Tech, Carnegie Mellon, Columbia, Harvard, Rensselaer Polytechnic, N.C. State, UNC, UNC-G. Luke would eventually only receive offers from Harvard and the state schools, which would years later lead him to say, he surely had benefitted from pure luck in the admissions process. He said he'd put money on the fact that it helped that his essay detailed his self-made workshop in a dilapidated tobacco barn in a rural setting. He believed the implied poverty in the essay and the evident need on the nearly blank FAFSA form had played a major role. He didn't care what the reason was. Luke understood he had been given a one-way ticket to a tightly locked kingdom. He knew you only needed one of those shots in your life to transform it.

"If I started growing, we could make way more money." Smith bounced his knee up and down, a habit that irritated her.

"Your dad would know."

Smith nodded. "The other option is pills. Sell enough to get my own place."

"Maybe," Kate said. That would be easier. It required no water, no light, no space. Percocet, Vicodin, and something new called Oxy were showing up all the time lately in shirt pockets and out-stretched palms. Several times Smith and his friends had crushed them into lines because boys were always at least partially about doing things for show. She preferred the mellow floating of just swallowing a pill or two with some Boone's Farm.

"There's that doctor in Clinton," Smith said. "Even after you pay him a grand to write the scripts, you can sell them for good profit."

"Maybe." Pills would be easy to move. Still, none of Smith's ideas sounded to Kate like the long game he claimed he wanted. Jackie taught Kate that nothing goes unseen for very long. Someone will eventually expose what you are trying to hide.

It was Luke who understood the real long game, something so powerful it would make you unrecognizable to the people who used to know you. There were only a few ways to run a real long game. Kate just wasn't good at any of them.

When the deputy sheriff came through the drive-thru, he took one look at Kate and Smith and shook his head. He eased his cruiser half way into the parking space next to them.

"Come on now." He unrolled his window. "You're starting to make this too easy."

"Just getting some dinner like you are, Sir," Smith said.

The Deputy eased out. He was a big man, slow in his move-ments. The door shut gently behind him.

This worried Kate. He rarely left his cruiser. It was just a dime bag, but she wished they had not left it sitting on the seat between them. Smith slid his hand over to cover it.

The Deputy reached his arm in through the truck's window right across Smith's chest. He took the little plastic baggy out from under Smith's hand and tucked it into his waistband just under his gun holster.

"Son, I believe you turned eighteen a few months ago."

"Yes sir, but a dime is possession, not intent to sell."

"I'm very aware of that, Smith, but it's still a charge."

"Possession of a dime with no previous offense?"

"You're moving more, selling to more people. This is the last warning."

"Actually, it's mine, Bobby," Kate said. She was seventeen and still a minor with no priors.

Smith's head jerked as he turned to her. His hazel eyes flashed worry. Kate knew the Deputy because he had been to her house before. On several occasions. Not as frequently as other men, but enough for Kate to know a few things about him, not the least of which was that when he did visit, the smoke billowed out from underneath her mother's door. He wasn't turning in what he repossessed. That she knew.

"Think you better call me Deputy, Katie."

"Oh, sorry, Deputy, Sir. I've just been so stressed lately, and I know you know how a little smoke here and there can really help."

She pulled her hair back away from her neck and wrapped it around her hand. She had learned a thing or two from her mother. She leaned forward to see Bobby through Smith's window and watched his eyes follow the hand full of hair to her chest where her tank top was now hanging open as she leaned over to see him.

"I wonder what your mama would say about that, Katie. You claiming you're selling drugs."

Kate laughed and let the weight of her hair drop. "She wouldn't like me cutting in on her business. Although she mostly sells pills, doesn't she? Honestly, I'd hate to think what she would say about a lot of things. I wouldn't trust her at all, if I was engaged in illegal activities, Sir."

Smith took in a strained breath next to her and said, "Katie, stop."

As the Deputy walked slowly around to her side of Smith's truck, she saw Max's CRX slow down to turn into the Hardee's, then speed up again when he saw them, a pop-pop loudly escaping his exhaust as he accelerated. The Deputy leaned into her window resting his forearms on the door. He was calm and soft-spoken when he said, "Be careful what you say."

"I'm just saying my mother has been known to say all sorts of things about people. I'd hate to think what she would say about you. Especially because of her…'job' and well, your job."

The Deputy's jaw tensed. "There's nothing illegal going on in your house."

"Maybe not, but it sure ain't right."

The Deputy reached in and grabbed Kate's chin hard in between his thumb and fingers. "I don't much like how you're turning out. Sort of a disappointment if you ask me." He pushed her head away hard.

As they watched the Deputy walk back across the front of the truck, Smith muttered, "What the fuck?"

She reached up to rub where she could still feel his grip.

When he reached Smith's window, the Deputy rested his fists on the top of the truck.

"I have been more than generous," he said. "Y'all better watch yourselves now, hear?"

Back in the driver seat of his cruiser, he put a few fries in his mouth before pulling out of the parking lot.

"What did you do that for?" Smith asked.

"You say you want a long game, you better start acting like it."

"How does making the cops angry help?"

"He doesn't want people hearing about what he does outside of work. I'm just letting him know I know."

But nothing changed, no long game crystalized. A few weeks later, Kate, Smith, and Max Thornton broke into the big high school in Wilmington. They were stoned out of their minds, trying to get the light board in the theater working and didn't hear the officers coming through the auditorium doors. They got off that time. Max Thornton's dad paid the lawyer who saved them from the breaking and entering charges. When Smith was picked up twice in the next month for possession, each time under an ounce, his mother Lynette paid the legal fees and fines.

But a year later, when they were both arrested in the parking lot of the movie theater, the charges were too much for anyone to evade. Through the windshield, Kate could see Smith's face against the hood, his hands cuffed behind him. She was already in the back seat of the cruiser. Two of the officers had argued about what to do with her. One said, "She's pregnant." The other, "So?" They met in the middle at cuffing her hands at her front, before the indifferent one pushed her hard and fast enough that she hit her head against the top of the cruiser.

Luke had taken Jackie's Fairmont to visit Virginia Tech that weekend, so Jackie had to beg a ride to come collect Kate from the station. Percy, Smith's father, provided that ride.

"Aren't you going to get Smith?" Kate asked as she followed Jackie and Percy out to the parking lot.

Percy shook his head and pushed the glass door of the station with a hard shove. "This time it looks like he is staying where he seems dead set on being."

Kate sat on the floor in the back of Percy's van. The seats had been taken out to make room for the floral deliveries.

They drove in silence for a few minutes before Jackie said, "It might have been a misdemeanor without those scales."

Percy swallowed hard and looked out at the road in front of him. "He's looking at three years."

"He won't serve the entire sentence," Jackie said softly.

A wave of nauseating heat washed over Kate as the baby kicked, as if it really wanted to hammer the point home. Smith had said everything was his in the car, the weed, the paraphernalia. She would probably just get another lesser charge. Percy took a curve in the road causing Kate to brace herself.

"What were you thinking?" Jackie asked looking back. "That movie theater parking lot is about the best lit place I can think of. Crowds of people moving through every two hours like clockwork. Just waves of witnesses coming through there."

Percy glanced at Kate in the van's rearview mirror. Kate avoided them both by examining the crush of browned petals pressed into the metal grooves of the van's floor.

EIGHT

THERE WAS NO telling what would happen. This was the South. They might invite her in and ask her to recount the last eight years while refilling her sweet tea over and over. Then again, they might run her off with Percy's old .22, the one he used to shoot rabbits behind the greenhouses. There was only one way to find out. Kate pulled into the driveway that separated the brick ranch from the greenhouses Smith's family had owned for more than seventy-five years. Their place was halfway between Jackie's and Wilmington, much closer to the town than Mrs. Newkirk's land.

Kate didn't recognize any of the cars parked on the business's side of the driveway. Still, she didn't want to walk through the storefront where Smith's mother Lynette would probably be on her stool behind the register. There would no doubt be a group of women, their arms full of silk flowers and green floral foam, buying something just to have a front seat at the news desk of town gossip.

Kate parked toward the far end of the driveway. She walked around the back of the long glass buildings where the grass was nearly waist high. In the distance, she could see where kudzu was growing up, softening the line of trees at the edge of their property into shapes like giant swamp creatures. The storm was still holding out, but the flashes of lavender kept lighting a darkening sky. The heat trapped between the glass buildings made the air look alive, rising up in waves. The glass was streaked and grimy, and now an opaque plastic lined the inside of the biggest house. She found the door she used in high school, but the handle didn't budge.

"You lookin' to steal something?"

He stood at the end of the space between the greenhouses, a wrench in one hand, a rag in the other.

She tried to draw a breath, but she couldn't fill her lungs the way she wanted to. They stood staring at each other, the sound of the cicadas almost drowning out the traffic on the street out front.

"You got a leak?" she finally asked pointing at the wrench.

"Most days I've got a few...same ancient irrigation system." Shaggy hair aside, he looked mostly the same. He was wearing a pair of heavy beige Carhartt's and a brown T-shirt with *Tidewater Florist* printed on the front pocket. "Most customers come in the front door."

The heat swelled and pulsed, making Kate's head pound when she said, "I should have called."

"It's been a long time since you've called. Why are you here?" He walked toward her slowly.

"I came to see my mother."

"Then why aren't you there?"

All the things she'd wanted to say to him since she had left were stuck in her throat. As they walked toward each other, she sensed how much had changed. Kate used to be able to look at Smith's face and know just what he was thinking. Now, with his clenched jaw and slightly narrowed eyes, he was mostly inscrutable.

They were just a few feet apart when she said, "I came to see what you know."

Smith stopped and looked down to wipe grease from the wrench. "I haven't talked to your mama in years."

Kate had always been the better liar. She kept walking toward him. "She dragged me down here, asking a favor. But now I see she's doing something bigger than usual, more illegal than usual."

"I still don't know what that has to do with you being here."

She caught him following the line of her neck down to her bare shoulder where her shirt sloped off. Her hair hung down her back, still wet from the shower. A quick pulse of satisfaction lit up under her ribs when he made himself look away.

"I know you've been over there," Kate said. "I know you gave her a bag of weed. *Medicinal*, she says, like she would ever smoke any of it. And that means you probably know what she's up to."

He asked, "How long have you been back here?"

Now Kate was close enough to see the gold flecks in his hazel irises. "A couple hours."

"It took you that long?"

"What do you mean?"

"It took you that long to be over here acting like you deserve an explanation for all sorts of things that aren't any of your business."

Kate put her hands down into the back pockets of her skirt. She tipped her head to the side and asked, "Why are you blocking the light with plastic on the sides of this greenhouse?"

"We had to spray the geranium crop for wholesale."

"So you closed the houses off and lined them with plastic to spray?"

"Mmm-hmm."

She stepped forward another foot closer to him. He was about her height. "You are the worst liar."

"Not everyone can be as good as you."

Smith was growing pot. He had to be. The opaque lining here at the greenhouses. Something was going on with lights in her mother's packhouse, which meant Jackie was also involved in whatever Smith was doing.

"Listen, my mother has something I want, but she wants me to do something for it."

"Sounds like her." He tucked the wrench in his back pocket.

She could smell the combination of his sweat and the laundry detergent in his clothes, both exactly the same as always.

He said, "I'm not going to get between you and your mama anytime soon."

"And you're not going to tell me what you're doing in the greenhouse?"

"Nope."

"Or why my mother's packhouse is sealed up?"

"Nope."

"Or how much my mother is making off these people in her house?

"Nope. Don't know anything about it, but I'm sure you're going to kick around here long enough to find out yourself."

Kate said, "Might have to."

Smith started back toward the end of the greenhouse, but Kate didn't move. He turned to look at her. "You remember about manners down here, don't you? If you're going to stay around, better come visit with my Mama. I wonder what she would think about you out here sneaking around the property. I wonder what she would tell her friends about that one. There's a bunch of them in there right now, up in arms about something. I'd like to see the look on her face if you walked in there."

"Not sure that's a good idea. Last time she saw me she wanted me arrested for kidnapping." Kate caught up with him at the end of the greenhouse.

"I couldn't say. I was at New Hanover Correctional the time. No one was telling me shit."

Kate felt the sharp guilt of changing her mind about their baby, for not waiting like she said she would. She had not told him that she had chosen adoption when she learned it was too late for an abortion. He had expected her to be there with their toddler when he got out, but she had run away instead. Kate had changed course so quickly, so drastically, that she herself had never fully recovered from all that happened after.

Kate followed Smith out front near the main road. There were racks full of planters and blooming pots with mixed annuals, velvety Martha Washington geraniums and pink and white begonias. Kate noticed a row of yellow million bells starting to droop against their hanging green plastic pots.

When they reached the door to Lynette's florist shop, he held the door open for her and said, "This should be fun."

"For who?"

"Me."

A loud rumble of thunder came as she stepped into shop. Lynette was perched on her stool, tapping a pencil against the counter to emphasize her point. Her blonde hair was blown out in the same style she had always worn. She had gained a little weight, but her cheek bones were still high and defined, dusted with a coral blush. She wore a heavy swipe of blue eyeshadow that made her hazel eyes look almost golden.

Kate was relieved she didn't recognize the four women sitting on stools at Lynette's counter. They looked more like they were at a bar with Lynette as their bartender than at the register where you paid for your fertilizer and perennials.

Lynette tipped her head forward and said, "You can't tell me that she didn't know exactly what she was doing when she stood up in Sunday school with her skirt hiked up to high heaven to make that comment about Mary Ann's daughter."

"Mama, have you even started making those centerpieces for the Sanders' wedding?" Smith asked, leaning a hand up against the glass front of the cooler where they kept the cut flowers.

Lynette pointed her pen at Smith as she said, "Boy, how many times do I have to tell you to not get prints on my glass—" Her pen froze midair as her eyes met Kate's. "Well, I declare! That cannot be Katie Jessup."

Kate stuck her hands into the back pockets of her skirt again. "Yes ma'am, it's me."

The women at the counter looked Kate up and down, pausing on her bare legs, her exposed tan shoulder.

Lynette cleared her throat. "Don't you, *yes, ma'am* me. Get over here and give me some sugar." She walked out from behind the counter. "Let me look at you! You haven't changed a bit. Well, maybe you've gotten prettier. I didn't think that would be possible. But Lord, it is."

Kate walked forward slowly until they met by a table full of favors for baby showers, ceramic teddy bears and pastel letter blocks ready to be filled with fresh flowers. Lynette held Kate by the elbows and shot a look at Smith, but he just shrugged. Kate could feel the pressure of Lynette's fingertips pressing into the back of her arm, her thumbs against her biceps. Kate's heart beat faster having to face Lynette like this, having to look her in the eye, not being able to turn her head to avoid Lynette's searching gaze and the heavy pressure of her grip while other people watched.

"Come on now. You better sit down and tell us everything," Lynette said. "I hear you married a rich Yankee."

The women shifted down the counter, making room.

"No, ma'am. I'm not married.

"Your mother said you had gone off and bettered yourself."

Living in New England for eight years, Kate had learned it was considered rude to interrogate your guests. There, interrogation might include asking them if they went to church or had travelled to Europe. To ask directly was breaking the boundaries that kept everyone safe from the fierce danger of being too personal. In the South, it was the opposite. Volunteering the information was rude. You waited to be asked. And you did not have to wait too long. In the South, people would ask you anything. Voices sweet as pie and questions seemingly innocuous, but it wouldn't take them long to start digging for where you buried the bodies.

Kate picked at the edge of a piece of tape holding down a circular about spring bulbs on the counter. "She exaggerates."

The women looked back and forth from Smith to Kate trying to put it together. Smith went to the metal door that led inside the cooler. Through the glass, she could see him checking the water levels in the buckets of cut flowers.

"I'm sorry your mother hasn't been well," Lynette said. "I checked in with her last week."

Kate nodded but found that to be another impossibility, that Lynette and Jackie would be civil enough to occupy the same space for longer than it took to pass each other in opposite lanes on the road without trying to run each other off.

Kate admitted, "She doesn't look good. And I'm worried that she isn't seeing a doctor."

The women at the counter let out a soft chorus of, "Bless your heart!" and "What a shame."

Lynette reached out and removed the stack of receipts pierced together on a stand by the register. She slipped them inside in the register drawer and slammed it shut. "Well, maybe now you can see to her. That's usually what a daughter does."

Kate had not faced this level of disapproval in a while.

Smith emerged then from the cooler, "Mama, we really need to get the Sanders' arrangements done so I can deliver them first thing."

"Son, I will get to it. Katie, you're going to stay for dinner. I've got that chicken I need to use up. You two go ahead into the house, and let me finish up here."

"Oh, I should probably be getting back." Kate was not sure if she was ready to handle sitting down at a table with Lynette and Smith.

"You're here now, you might as well stay. We can make up something for you to take back," Lynette said. Her voice dropped lower and grew colder. "Seems like staying for dinner is the least you can do."

The women at the counter heard the shift too and looked at each other. It confirmed whatever was going on was a story worth hearing.

Outside the sky had opened up, so Kate and Smith broke into a run across the driveway. They got soaked anyway.

Inside, the blast of central air made the house almost feel like the floral cooler. The kitchen looked the same. The walls were hung with the dusty silk floral arrangements too outdated for the shop that Lynette couldn't bear to throw away. The porcelain plate collection still bordered the perimeter of the room on a wooden rail.

"What can I get you?" Smith asked wiping his wet arms on his T-shirt once they were inside.

"Water would be great."

"How about tea?"

"Sure." She stood awkwardly in the doorway. "Can I use your bathroom?"

"Help yourself," he said opening the cabinet with the glasses.

The bathroom was filled with the hum of the clothes dryer. Lynette had always complained about how much laundry she did every day, washing three or four loads between Percy and Smith changing clothes multiple times, washing out soil, pesticide, sweat. Kate breathed in the smell of Irish Spring and the scent from a large bowl of potpourri that smelled like Lynette's shop.

Kate used a lime green hand towel to dry her face, neck, and arms. She leaned toward the mirror and used toilet paper to wipe away the eye make-up that had smudged in the rain.

She looked at herself in the mirror and remembered standing there in high school, usually in a baggy T-shirt from the green-house, dirty with soil from potting planters. It seemed impossible that she was standing here again, but there was the proof reflecting back at her.

Once, this house was home for her, made warm with Smith's parents teasing each other, the sweet embraces you could catch them in, if they didn't hear you coming. The refrigerator was stocked with a casserole or crock pot full or something Lynette made in advance to get them through a busy retail weekend. Kate was always wel-come there, especially when her own house felt menacing. She worked her shifts at the greenhouse for money but stayed after for meals and protection and the comfort of the couch where the big-gest argument anyone was going to get into was over who had most recently lost the remote.

That sense of safety was gone now because in Lynette and

Smith's view, she had crossed them. They had not forgiven her. She could feel the difference even alone in the bathroom. The question whispered in the walls around her, *what in the hell do you think you're doing here?*

Water poured down the outside of the bathroom window. Another flash of lightning struck at the same time as a loud thunder clap made her jump.

Kate sat at the maple kitchen table stained with drink rings and pocked with cigarette burns. Smith riffled through a drawer by the stove.

"You still smoke?" he said taking a cigarette from a pack in the drawer and putting it between his lips.

"No," she said. "Do you?"

"Nope. I quit a few years ago." He lit the long cigarette dangling from his mouth then came back to the table with the pack, a lighter, and a large scallop shell ashtray. She saw the shell had "Myrtle Beach" and a silhouette of a palm tree airbrushed on its pink inside.

"Is that from our trip?" she asked.

"No, from my honeymoon."

He pushed the pack of cigarettes to her side of the table. She didn't take one.

On one of their calls that Kate was careful never to tell Luke about, Jackie made sure to let Kate know when Smith finished out his sentence, he immediately married Jenny Collins.

"I didn't want to go there, but Jenny had her mind set." Smith ashed into the shell. "We're divorced now."

"I'm sorry. I didn't know that."

"Oh, it's fine. The only thing good that came out of that was our girls."

Kate, who learned early to keep a blank face when she was surprised or upset, could not prevent the wave of shock from surfacing. This her mother had not told her.

"Haley's five. Kylee is almost six-and-a-half."

Kate swallowed. "I bet they're beautiful."

"Sure are." He pointed to the refrigerator. "They're up there."

Kate went to the refrigerator. Looking at the pictures, a collage of Smith's girls at a water park, at the beach, surrounded by presents next to a Christmas tree, she saw his girls had Jenny's blue eyes. Eye color. That was just one of countless unknown things Kate never let herself think about. The last time she'd seen Anna, hers were the dark blue of all newborns, a color undecided. The girls displayed in a mosaic of apple cheeks and bright eyes on the refrigerator door were Anna's half-sisters. The girl would never know they existed if Kate didn't find her.

"Where do they live?" Kate asked.

"In Wilmington with Jenny and her boyfriend. They're here most weekends, except the big ones."

"Valentine's week. Mother's Day. Memorial Day weekend."

"You remember." Smith put out his cigarette in the shell ashtray. "Then sometimes I have them for longer depending. Sunday they'll be here and staying a week."

Kate cleared her throat. "They look like you. Except for the eyes."

Smith's hands instinctively went to his shorts pocket for his pack even though it was lying on the table in front of him.

"Are you going to smoke another?" Kate asked, coming back to the table. He had always been a chain smoker when he was nervous.

"Why? You want one?"

"Maybe." She slid one out of the package.

"Thought you quit."

"So did you."

Charlie hated smoking, so she kept trying to quit, sort of. Now, as Kate held her hair back away from the flame and leaned in for Smith to light her cigarette, she remembered how she had always liked that gesture that somehow said, I create the fire you breathe.

She took a deep drag then tipped her head back and blew the smoke to the ceiling.

"Has she told you where the baby is yet?"

Kate felt an electric shock of betrayal in her gut. *Anna.* "You know about that?"

"She told me, and I told her to call you. I didn't need to know about it."

"Why?"

"Because I have two daughters." Smith nervously shook his knee up and down .

Kate saw how much he wanted to land that blow. Her heart pounded. "Did she tell you where she is?"

He shook his head and ashed his cigarette. "I didn't ask."

Kate was silent for a moment, taking everything in.

"How long are you staying?" he asked.

"As long as it takes, I guess."

"As long as it takes to do what?"

"To get the truth."

"That's likely to take a while," Smith said. "Truth's like a greased pig."

"Pigs tire out eventually." The language they spoke was coming back to her. Kate liked the back and forth. It went fast, like a metronome, smooth in its trajectory: you're a liar, *no, you're a liar,* you're the one making the mistake, *no, you fucked things up.*

It was a fair fight.

"I don't remember you being too big on the truth."

Lynette pushed open the door holding a plastic shopping bag over her head to protect her hair from the rain. "Lord have mercy, those ladies will talk your ear off if you let them. I'm sorry to keep y'all waiting and hungry."

Kate had offered to help, but Lynette refused to let her. Now that she was sitting at the kitchen table watching Lynette trim the fat off chicken thighs with a sharp paring knife, Kate realized she should have offered several more times. She had forgotten the rate of southern negotiation, offer three times, be denied three, then make a final demand so the host can give in seeming reluctant.

"It's not like it used to be," Lynette said. "Hardly anyone is on payroll anymore. We're doing it all ourselves."

"That's not true, we have help." Smith leaned against the doorway to the living room. He had moved there from the table after Lynette came in, away from Kate.

"Not on an actual payroll," Lynette said then glanced at Kate, as if she realized she shouldn't have admitted to it so easily.

Kate knew she was talking about the undocumented workers. By the time she and Smith were in high school, people from Mexico and Central America came for the seasonal picking, and even more, the industrial hog and turkey operations. Big companies paid farmers to supersize their operations with long silver houses and lagoons full of waste connected to irrigation systems to spray as fertilizer on what was left of the tobacco, corn, and pepper crops. The migrants worked the jobs in the fields at the slaughterhouses or processing plant. Some worked all three. Many of them stayed.

Lynette reached up into the cabinet, getting down bowls to

bread her chicken. "When Percy was still alive, things were so much easier."

"I was sorry to hear he passed away," Kate said. Her mother had told her that one.

"Four years ago this September," Lynette said, her voice breaking as she cracked an egg into one of the bowls. "He went in for lunch, and I knew something was wrong. He used to make a ham sandwich, then walk around eating it. He never sat down for lunch in his life."

"Mama," Smith said softly moving from the doorway to the sink next to Lynette.

"It's just harder now than it used to be." Lynette dropped the chicken meat in a bowl of egg before dredging it in flour. "Oil prices are through the roof, and half the town drives into Wilmington to get plants at the Home Depot. Even the Piggly Wiggly carries hanging baskets now. They won't live for more than a couple weeks, but they can sell them for half as much as we can. Smith's out there sixteen hours a day. It's harder than ever to break even."

"Mama, we do alright."

Lynette sighed. "We'll make it, God willing. Of course, last month we had someone break into the shop and steal everything in the register. I always used to make the bank deposit on Fridays, left the week's money in the register, never had to lock the doors. And now I can't leave it alone for one night even—"

"Mama," Smith said. "Kate doesn't want to hear all about our problems."

"Well, that's probably true." Lynette dropped dusted chicken into the sizzling oil. "But with the way things are going, I have to wonder how much longer any of us family-owned operations will be around."

"There's always a way to make it work," Smith said. "You just have to think about it a different way."

Lynette looked up at her son from her fry pan. "Yeah, I know about your way." Then she turned to Kate. "Enough of all this business talk. How long are you down here for, Sugar?"

Before Kate could answer, Smith said, "Long as it takes to catch a greased pig." Smith reached into the cabinet above the refrigerator and handed his mother a plate.

"So then a long while," Lynette said.

Lynette and Smith exchanged a glance.

"Maybe you'll get to meet my grand babies."

They all felt the weight of that one, so no one said a thing.

After dinner, Smith walked Kate out to the car. Kate listened to the sounds, the field behind the greenhouses alive with crickets and cicadas. In the gathering dusk, three bats swooped around the floodlight that was at the back of the driveway where the asphalt ended. Their erratic flying always mesmerized her. It was hard to track them, the way they moved, jagged back and forth across her line of vision, not like the straight dives of birds.

Smith carried the casserole Lynette assembled and the chicken they hadn't finished. When Lynette said, "Tell Maribel to put it in for forty-five minutes at 325," Kate felt another flare of something like jealousy recognizing the familiarity of people who exchanged daily favors.

"Nice car," Smith said looking at the Audi.

"It's not really mine." Kate pulled her key from the front pocket of her skirt and pressed the button to unlock the doors.

Smith laughed when the car beeped.

"What?"

"We don't lock our cars down here."

"Maybe you should if the shop is getting broken into." She opened the passenger door so he could put the casserole on the floor mat.

They stood with the car door between them. He ran his hand through his light brown hair and looked at her like he was about to say something. The streetlight in the dark driveway flickered on.

"You're growing weed. I'm guessing a lot of it. In the greenhouses," she said. The whir of the central air motor kicked up from the machine on the side of Lynette's house.

He tried not to react, but the corner of his mouth turned up slightly in a smile. "Told you you'd figure it all out, smart as you are."

"Luke's the smart one."

Smith's eyes did not leave hers. Being around him made her feel like herself. It was as if she had been held underwater for the last eight years, her pockets weighted with stones. Now she was letting those stones drop to the riverbed. Her body was rising up, light to the surface.

"How many?

"How many what?"

"How many plants? How much are you yielding?"

Smith reached out and pulled the wide neck of her shirt back onto her shoulder, but it slid back off. "I haven't seen you in years. You think I'm going to let you in on everything just like that?"

Kate looked over to the dark greenhouses. The glass of the nearest one reflected the light from Lynette's kitchen.

"You might. Come on. Let me see it."

After Kate's shifts working at Smith's family's greenhouse in high school, they would move through the closed florist shop just like this. They passed the stools tucked under Lynette's counter. She followed Smith past the rolls of ribbon hanging on dowels, past the wall of dusty silk flower arrangements, the white buckets of carnations and lilies in the walk-in cooler, past the boiler room to the door of the longest house.

"Is there still a ghost?" she asked.

"There never was one," Smith said. "That was just something my father made up to keep us out of here."

"It didn't work."

Smith pressed buttons on a keypad above a new industrial-looking door handle. When the door opened, a current of greenhouse air escaped, heavy with the smell of a new kind of crop. It was hard to breathe for a moment, the pungent smell in her lungs, as she walked through the door he held for her. It was the same, more or less, except the changeover in crop. He walked slowly down the aisle in the dark house between the planter tables.

"Mama was lying when she said you looked the same."

"People change. They're supposed to." Kate's heart seemed to open wider, stronger, making more room for blood and oxygen to pump through hard and fast.

She moved through the house, slowly taking in the sheets of opaque plastic hung along the glass walls.

"Some people change more than others," he said. "You even walk different."

The old ventilation fan spun, filling the long building with its humming sound and slight vibration. The house was almost as long as the ones where she worked in Boston, but it was narrower. Smith had five tables on each side, covered in tiny plants. Thin black tubes ran down from a railway of metal irrigation framework.

Kate's mind moved fast, making connections between the stars of her favorite kind of constellation. She picked up a black plastic pot small enough to balance on her palm. Even in the faint light, she could make out the seedling, its tiny leaves spread like bony fingers.

"They look healthy." She pressed her finger into the soil. Moist, but not too wet.

"You've always known this business, just as good as the rest of us." Smith walked up beside her, nudged her shoulder with his. He reached out and ran his hand between the weight of her hair and her neck. His hand was rough with the calluses from the shoveling, stringing irrigation, reglazing, all the other things that he had done like his father before him to keep the glass house filled with growing crops. More than anything, she knew, it was the soil itself that dried the skin.

Kate set the plastic pot back on the table. "If I can figure this out as fast as I did, you've got a problem."

"My father used to say how quick you were." Smith pulled his hand away from her and tapped his temple with his index finger.

Kate felt the warmth of the compliment across her cheeks and neck. "It doesn't take much to figure this out. If you get caught, this is like fifteen to twenty." She walked farther down the row away from him. "Is this your first grow?" she asked.

He laughed. "You remember my first grow."

She did. In one way or another Smith had been at this for as long as she had known him. Back when she first met him, he had a miniature grow house in his bedroom closet that smelled of old sneakers. It only lasted until his father noticed the extension cord running under the door. Percy had taken those two plants outside and doused them in gasoline by the dumpster. Smith and Kate first smelled then saw the smoke that day as they were out front moving annuals to the pallets in front of the florist shop. Smith had sworn under his breath then found Percy smoking around the back of the building, watching the plants burn, the two plastic pots he had emptied under his arm.

"What's the difference between what you're smoking and this?" Smith had shouted pointing at his burning plants.

"A federal offense, Son."

"That's bullshit."

"Watch your mouth. You're putting us all at risk with this nonsense. Your mother. Me. Your sister." Percy looked at Kate but didn't include her.

After that, Smith tucked a plant at the back of the largest house in an overgrowth of ferns. It was well disguised, but eventually eaten by grasshoppers; one day just as the plant was getting strong, Smith found the leaves chewed up, delicate as lace. Next, he tried the back edge of the land that went from field to forest, but Percy found that too and dumped a can of white paint over the plants leaving them like limp, snow-covered Christmas trees.

Smith tried the swamp, but between insects, his father, early frosts, and poachers he never had been able to make it work.

Kate stood at the end of the row and turned to face him. "I'm talking about this crop." She extended her hand to the plants to her left. "Is this the first?"

"No. We just harvested."

Kate looked up to see the stars through the pollen-dusted glass above her. "The DEA can fly over this place and look right in at what you're growing. What are there? Two hundred plants?"

"One forty-five."

"Don't you still get inspected by N.C.D.A.?"

"I'm not worried about the Ag department. You remember

Tammy Winston?" Smith asked.

Kate remembered the woman from Mrs. Newkirk's porch as one of Lynette's best friends. She was "hoity-toity" as Mrs. Newkirk liked to say, but Tammy always had exceptional corn and peaches.

"Tammy's up at the headquarters in Raleigh now and tips Mama off," Smith said.

Kate stood in front of him. "So Tammy tips you off and what? You smoke it all."

"Funny." He hesitated before saying, "We move it."

"To Mama's packhouse?"

"Sometimes. Sometimes other places."

"You aren't going to be able to move all of these when they get full grown. And not this many. How big was your last grow?"

"About twenty."

"Oh my God." She walked away from him and back into the center aisle.

"I have to get bigger. I need the money."

"That's too big a jump, from twenty to one fifty. You've got customers coming in and out of this place all day. They're going to smell it when these things flower."

"That's why we lined everything with plastic."

For a while she had grown a few plants in Charlie's attic. He had liked her doing it because he got free pot, but even with a carbon filter she took from work, she couldn't control the smell. And that was just for three plants.

"I don't think the plastic will be enough."

"It has to be," he said.

"It doesn't have to be. Smith, just because you want something doesn't mean it will work."

The heaviness in the silence between them crackled for

a moment. For a while, they had both wanted each other more than anything else in the world. They had even wanted that baby, Anna, once she and Smith realized they had in fact accidentally created her, no matter how bad an idea it was. Yet, they had not ended up with her. They had lost their grip on each other. Kate pushed through the sinking feeling that came with remembering those few months of shared intention.

"Your mother said you work at a greenhouse. Harvard's greenhouse."

Kate brushed a dusting of potting soil off the edge of the table. "We don't grow pot."

"I've sunk a lot of money in this," Smith said. "Daddy's money, or what's left of it."

"Percy would hate this."

She saw him tense. He crossed his arms over his chest and leaned back slightly onto his heels. "I'm not letting this place go under. I need someone who's blood, or close to it. Mama thinks it's just the register getting robbed, but it's been more than that."

Kate could hear the tightness in Smith's voice, the familiar way it got higher pitched, electric when he was angry. "You can't trust anyone."

"You don't trust me."

"Well. Not entirely, but we are rooted together, in a way."

She thought of her tattoo, the same exact design as his, only his larger, lined up along his spine, the same branches as hers growing into his shoulder blades. The same roots etched across skin. The same swearing that they belonged to each other.

Kate nodded. She had locked everything away as hard as she could, but like the packhouse with the bolted door, it didn't matter. Light still escaped through the smallest cracks. She felt her heart race again, the idea of being tied to him again.

She belonged here. What an important thing that turned out to be. She felt herself shedding layer after layer as she remembered who she really was. Someone who could help with this crop. Someone who did better operating under the radar than being on the surface at on-campus world music concerts and trustee dinners populated by an affluent community of world-renowned scholars and the people who funded them. She had no place up there.

Still. She could not entirely dismiss the voice of her twin warning her over and over about her own volatility. She said, "This is not small-time high school shit, Smith."

"That's the idea. If this grow works, it could bring a quarter of a million."

"It doesn't matter if you're in prison."

"Shit's changing," Smith said. "It's legal out west."

"With a medical card. You don't have any way to become part of that."

This was something Kate had heard Charlie debate with his friends, one who was a lawyer in the Attorney General's office and another who was a psychologist. States like California and Oregon legalized marijuana for medical use almost a decade before in the late 90s. Charlie believed it would not be long before the liberal states in the northeast caught up. The lawyer pointed out the only thing with any hope of being passed at the state house in the foreseeable future was maybe decriminalization, and that was a big "maybe." The psychologist said pharmaceutical corporations would lobby against any kind of legalization. However, if it ever was legalized, they would be the first to rush in to develop. Kate did something she rarely did in that sort of back and forth. She spoke. She suggested that maybe that would mean a chance for other people to start growing, to create a new economy. The lawyer shook his head and said if they ever legalized it, and that was a big "if," the war on drugs had left many potential entrepreneurs with felony charges that would surely be used against them in the regulations for opening dispensaries.

Kate moved closer to Smith. She kicked the front edge of her flip flop at the tip of his boot. When they stood this close, she didn't have to look up the way she did at Charlie because of his height. Smith was right at her level.

"The longer you do this, the more likely it is you get caught. There are a million things you would have to think about."

"That's why I'm showing you," he said.

"There has to be something else you can do."

"You say that because you left."

"What does that mean?"

"It means you think it's easy."

"I didn't say that."

"But it is for you, I bet, living up there. For me, it's not. If I don't want to go work for someone else, this is how it is."

"Might be better to work for someone else then to get caught with this."

"You're not hearing me."

"Well, then what about something easier, like pills, like you said forever ago."

"I've done that."

"That's why I said it. You don't need light or water. You can hide them way easier."

"See there? This. This is exactly how anyone could tell you haven't been around in a while. You've missed a lot. I did sell pills. And I made a lot of money. That's its own system with people filling scripts, hitting up crooked doctors, dropping a dollar a milligram on oxys. That's the flush full of money part.

"But then there's the next part. There's people running out of money, or a pill mill getting busted, and then you're up in Charlotte hitting up these Mexican dudes from Jalisco, distributing black tar down east. And it's not like you're on top. It's not like you're making a bunch of money all at once. You're dealing with ten-dollar baggies.

"That's an entirely depressing system. I'm trying to avoid that. I watched my sister get caught up in that. My mama had her kids for a while, but she's doing better. Pills and all that wiped out a lot of people, Katie. A lot. Mrs. Parry, the science teacher? A junkie. Leslie Barnes, Crystal Johnson, all of those girls, them too, except Mary Beth Rose. She overdosed. You know that house over between the crossroads and that new gas station?"

"Christopher Rhoades' place?" These were all people they had gone to high school with.

"It's trap house. Get yourself killed walking in there if you're not careful. So, yes, easy money, but that is some dirty shit. Marijuana is clean, natural. If we can grow enough of it, we could really be starting something, not just going down the hole that other stuff sends you down. We can start by selling bud, but there is more we can do with it. I've been reading on it."

Kate tried to take in all Smith was saying. She'd seen a lot of cocaine and ecstasy since being with Charlie. It was always within arm's reach, if one wanted it. She didn't see a lot of pills. There was one accountant friend of Charlie's who always had a bottle of prescribed Xanax she was willing to offer up with hand-mixed cocktails. But Kate hadn't seen anything like what Smith was describing.

She knew he believed in the plant. Kate did too, but the laws didn't care. "I just wish there was something K-9 dogs couldn't smell, something that didn't need a place to grow and process." She expressed her doubt, but she was becoming convinced, Maybe he had thought this through more than she initially thought.

"I need this crop," he said. "I need more cash to keep all of this going. If you help me, I know it will work."

Then, like it was nothing, like she hadn't left him behind, like he hadn't been married then divorced and had two more girls in the time their daughter had celebrated eight birthdays, he pulled her into him and kissed her. She had forgotten how good he was at that.

"Where did you go? For all that time?" he asked. "I thought we had a plan."

"I don't know. You were gone too. Once you weren't there, it didn't feel like it would work."

"So you followed your brother up north and got yourself a rich boyfriend and a new life."

"And you got yourself a new family."

Then, just as they had always done, sweating under the hum of the fans that moved air through the tops of the greenhouses, they found their way forward. They stood in the same place, but everything was different. When they pressed into each other, they were in less of a hurry. No one was looking for them. They weren't hiding from his parents. Her mother wasn't after her. They barely moved their lips at first. The harder they pressed, the more she thought, this is what was missing. He pulled her skirt up to her waist. She undid the button on his pants.

At first, only slight movements of muscle and the grip of fingers on sweaty legs and damp clothing. He put his arm between her back and the high table careful not to knock any of the plants. She hooked her hands onto the back of his shoulders.

"I shouldn't have left," she said.

"I guess we didn't have a lot of options then."

"I should have come to see you, to tell you myself."

He changed the subject. "I missed you."

After that they didn't speak.

When it was over and they were pulling clothes back on, Kate looked down the length of the house. "Lord have mercy. What have y'all gotten yourselves into?"

And just like that, she knew for absolute sure she wasn't going back.

NINE

IT STARTED AS a pickup for a batch of triple-dipped acid, but shifted into something else. Shortly after Smith graduated high school, he and Kate went to Myrtle Beach to meet a kid they knew from Chapel Hill. Smith had been going west more and more, meeting up with people at the Cat's Cradle, Duke Coffeehouse, the Ritz, Local 506, all the places the thriving local band scene was blowing up. Smith was into the music, the harder sounding stuff that came through—White Octave, Stations of the Cross, Bloodmobile—but he was also into the connections, and being able to deal to the bands brought him to the back rooms of those Triangle area clubs. She had never seen Smith look so happy as he did sitting on the arm of a couch, head moving slowly back and forth with a bassist warming up. He'd take the cash they gave him, tuck it in the back of his jeans, and buy a band T-shirt after the show.

His main connection in Chapel Hill had moved to Myrtle Beach, so now they were there waiting for him at the Sea Dunes Motel. They had already been waiting two days. Kate loved it there, just her and Smith. She loved the lobby with its complimentary coffee. She never drank coffee, but since checking in, she had been mixing in five or six sugars and a few creamers, drinking cup after free cup. With her fingers wrapped around the hot Styrofoam, she felt like an adult in the lobby, turning the heads of the manager, the men checking in, a group of college girls from New Hampshire.

Outside on the beach, Kate said, "Let's not go back." They sprawled on a patchwork of bath towels from the motel, the ones guests weren't supposed to bring outside. She adjusted the towel beneath her before reaching back to undo her bikini top to avoid tan lines.

"We'll have to get some food soon."

"No, I mean back home."

Smith was on his back, his Corrosion of Conformity T-shirt laid over his face.

Kate rested her chin on a balled up hand towel. She studied the free paper from the lobby, brushing away the grains of sand as they blew across the newsprint. The open jobs were mostly at hotels and golf resorts. Kate was qualified for most of them, waiting tables, cleaning hotel rooms. She was ready to collect paychecks, start something real. More than anything, she was tired of the waiting, waiting for people to show up so Smith could sell to them. She was sick of watching her mother wait for some guy to knock on the back screen door and then wait for him to leave in time for someone else to show up at the front. It irritated her how Luke had been waiting his entire life for the application packages from admissions offices that were starting to arrive in their mailbox.

Envelopes for Luke. Dosed tabs of acid for Smith. The bulge of a wallet fat with cash in the back of a man's sagging jeans for Jackie. Everyone waiting on something. Kate could not be more tired of waiting.

"If this comes in, we could make nearly a grand." Smith sat up on his towel, his forearms resting on his knees to keep his hands steady as he started to roll a joint. The mirrored sunglasses he'd bought on the boardwalk the night before reflected back his moving hands.

"*If* it comes in."

"If I'm going to buy my dad out, I need to save some serious money."

Kate had worked in the greenhouse under Percy and next to Smith long enough to know that Percy was not going to sell his business to Smith. The greenhouse was Percy's life, and he didn't trust his son. Kate couldn't blame him for that. Smith had a dangerous kind of tunnel vision. He saw what he wanted to and blocked out what didn't suit him.

"Why would you buy it? He pays you well." It just didn't make good business sense to Kate. Smith wanted to traffic pot, acid, and ecstasy in order to get the cash together to buy a business he already had a stake in.

"But he wants to run it his way," Smith said. "I have all these ideas, and he's not going to listen to any of them."

"Maybe he knows what he's doing."

"The discount stores in Wilmington are taking our business."

Kate listened to Smith talk, but she was seeing clearly now for the first time in her life what *she* might want next. She wanted to leave for good, but not the same way Luke did. She was about to start her last year of high school, but she could've cared less about graduating. She didn't want to go to college. She just wanted to go somewhere else, to a place that wasn't Jackie's house, to a place of her own.

She held the front of her bikini to her chest, flipped over, and sat up. The surf was big, crashing so hard it made a sound like someone dragging furniture across an upstairs floor. Kate watched a couple walk by, a toddler between them. She couldn't tell if they were the grandparents or the parents, but the man, heavyset and sunburned, was a great deal older than the woman. Between them, they swung the little boy who squealed with delight.

The woman, who wore an expensive-looking wrap dress and had her hair tied back in a short ponytail, looked over and frowned at them. Smoke from Smith's joint traveled down the beach.

"If you're serious about making money, you'll have to stop using so much of what you're trying to sell." Kate wished he would go back to the room to smoke.

"I am very serious." With the joint still between his lips, he pulled her to him with the hook of his arm. Kate felt the weight of Smith next to her, his fingertips brushing against her stomach. She took the joint and put out the end in the sand. He buried his head against her neck, the skin of his lips rough against her collar bone.

Percy, Smith's father, was waiting for them when they returned to the Sea Dunes Motel lobby. Percy offered to buy them lunch, an easy sell since they were running low on money with still no word from the kid they were supposed to meet.

"Max's father got him to tell us where you were," Percy said.

As they sat in the Waffle House, Smith devoured two pecan waffles and a pile of eggs and grits. Kate had been starving when they walked in the door, but now the eggs and sausage in front of her made her feel sick. The one piece of sausage she put in her mouth made her gag. She nibbled on the raisin toast and listened to Smith's father.

"Katie, your mother has been threatening to call the police," Percy said. "She could press charges because you're only seventeen." He tented his fingertips over his coffee mug. The edges of his nails were permanently brown from soil. "Do you understand?"

Smith leaned back in the faux wood booth and crossed his tanned arms over the white undershirt he had thrown on because of the *No shirt, No shoes, No service* sign.

"Listen to me, son," Percy said. "The last thing you need is any more legal trouble. If you love each other so damn much, get married. Then she can't say anything."

Percy left them sitting in the booth with a fifty from his wallet to pay the twelve-dollar bill. Kate and Smith sat in silence on the same side of the booth, arms touching. He ate the rest of her sausage.

"Think she means it?" Smith asked, his mouth full.

"I don't know. I doubt it." She pushed her plate towards him so he didn't have to reach over her.

"Do you want to get married?" Smith asked, shoveling in the last bit of eggs and sausage. The smell of the sausage turned her stomach again. She realized that she had been feeling that way more and more.

"I don't know." She would have married him, but she didn't like the idea that somehow her mother was messing that up too, that they would get married to deal with Jackie.

Smith shrugged. "It might solve some problems. You could come live with me and get out of her house."

"She won't press charges," Kate said.

"That's easy for you to say. You won't be in jail."

Smith took the fifty his father had left and picked up the check from where the waitress had tucked it between the napkin holder and the salt and pepper shakers.

They returned to their spot on the beach. It seemed hotter with less of a breeze. They laid on their stomachs, each looking through the salty haze to different fragments of the dark blue horizon.

"What's wrong?" he asked when she pulled herself up to kneel on her towel.

"I guess the heat." She stood up wavering slightly and walked into the dunes to throw up.

She asked the motel clerk for the closest drug store. She brought the box back to the lobby bathroom along with a six pack of warm Mountain Dew for the ice bucket. She didn't want Smith there when she found out.

She told him that night in the dark of the cab of his truck, after they used the rest of Percy's fifty to go to an all-you-can-eat Calabash buffet Smith had been talking about since they arrived. Smith had eaten plates of fried flounder, jumbo shrimp, and alien-like crab legs. The only thing that appealed to Kate was banana pudding, which was only $1.99 for a dish. It was clear by then that the kid they were waiting on was not going to show up, and that meant there was nothing to do but go back.

He looked out of his window for a second, then back to her.

"Are you sure?" he asked.

She nodded again feeling a knot in her throat.

A slight smile formed on his lips before he stopped it with another drag from his cigarette. "Are you happy?"

"Are you?"

"You go first," he said, placing his hand on her knee.

"Ok, I'm happy if you're happy," Kate said.

"That's cheating. I'm asking if you're happy."

"Ok, then. I'm happy," she said, knowing as she felt a new sense of warmth flowing through her, it was true.

It was late when Kate returned to Jackie's house from seeing Smith's crop in the greenhouse. She was relieved to find no strangers sleeping in the beds in the back room, but the space felt too strange to sleep there herself. Jackie had made it clear, Kate's room was rented, and crowded for that matter. It had been tight for her and Luke, much less three people.

She took a top sheet and a quilt from the linen closet, which was stuffed with folded towels and jumbo packs of toilet paper. She laid the sheet out on the hard green couch. Kate matched her fingertips to three cigarette burns that formed an Orion's belt in the scratchy upholstery fabric. In the dark, she could hear women whispering behind the door to her old bedroom.

It might not be her room anymore, but she had re-entered another space almost as sacred, the greenhouse and Smith's hold.

When Kate woke up the next morning, Jackie's house was quiet and lit up with morning sun. Once she was up and dressed, Kate worked her way through dirty dishes in the kitchen sink. As she worked, she thought about Smith's greenhouse. A hundred and fifty plants were going to need a lot of water. Smith's bill was going to jump like crazy. Maybe if he started with rain barrels, soon he could keep the spike in flow invisible. But what about electricity?

She turned off the hot water tap. Kate pulled forks and spoons out of the pile on the counter. She submerged the silverware and wondered how Smith could move that many mature plants when Tammy tipped Lynette off before an inspection. More importantly, what would happen if Tammy didn't tip them off in time, or at all? Kate saw no way around that problem. Yet.

Kate had finished the dishes and was going through the cabinets in search of a coffeemaker, leaving cabinet doors ajar, when Maribel came through the back door weighed down with grocery bags. Yesterday, Maribel had been wearing the slaughterhouse uniform. She looked very different now. She was wearing makeup, eyeliner, and a gold-flecked eye shadow that accentuated her brown eyes. Her lips were glossed shiny pink. She wore gold hoop earrings that almost touched her shoulders, a white cotton sweater with a pair of khaki shorts and black strappy sandals with a kitten heel.

"Down there." Maribel pointed to the cabinet next to the one where Kate was standing. "You are looking for coffee?"

Kate reached down and found a vat of a pot, the kind that might be used at a church fellowship hour. She pulled it out and tried to fit the metal pieces together.

"Here," Maribel said coming to stand next to her.

Maribel set the metal parts inside one another. She stretched onto her toes, the backs of her sandals falling away from her heels as she reached for a giant filter the size of a plate from the top of the refrigerator. She handed it to Kate and returned to her grocery bags.

Maribel said, "You did dishes."

"There were so many."

The room just with the two of them was tense with mutual dislike.

While Kate made the coffee, Maribel began emptying the grocery bags, pulling out packages of chicken, stacking vegetables on the counter. Heads of lettuce, cabbage, tomatoes, a bag of potatoes, and a bag of red chilies created a colorful pile against the stained linoleum counter. Maribel took six cartons of eggs out of the last plastic bag and put them in the refrigerator.

If Jackie and Maribel were as close as it seemed, maybe Maribel knew something about Kate's daughter. Kate should try to be nicer, to make even a weak connection that might bring the information she needed.

The coffee pot gurgled and rattled as it percolated. "You work at the slaughterhouse?"

Maribel hesitated seeming to consider how to answer the question. "Sometimes I pick up shifts when I want to see what is happening somewhere, if it's a good place to have people go."

"My brother worked there right before he left."

"Hogs or turkeys?"

"Both." Kate remembered the smell on Luke, a mix of bleach and something else that turned your stomach.

Maribel opened a large Tupperware container with four stacks of corn tortillas. She took a glass cutting board from the counter where Kate had left it drying.

"You too?" Maribel laid the cutting board on the table and stood still. She looked at Kate and waited.

"Never the slaughterhouse. Turkey houses for a while."

Kate had worked for cash under the table with a farmer she met on Mrs. Newkirk's porch. The job had been checking the water and feed lines and picking up dead or dying birds. At first, Kate had trouble killing the weak ones. The farmer explained that if you left them there with a broken wing, a missing eye, an unspecified illness that made them weak, the flock would find them. They would start the pecking, a little bit here and there at first, pushing the sick one away from the feed lines, but then more aggressively, twenty to one, those hard, little beaks pecking, and the claws scratching until they killed the one that didn't belong.

After he explained that, Kate held them by their bony legs and killed them in one swing against the pressure treated beams.

"After I had a work permit, I worked at Tidewater with Smith."

Maribel tore open one of the packages of chicken, pulling off the plastic wrap. "Hogs are bigger, heavier, so it's worse when they get sick or die. And the smell. Much harder than turkeys."

"That's true," Kate said.

You didn't have to work hogs to know the smell. The smell was there most of the time now, but got stronger or receded depending on the direction of the wind.

Maribel pressed her fingers against the meat to get a better angle to cut around a bone. Kate didn't try to fill the silence. She didn't want this woman in her mother's kitchen, but she took a second cutting board from the counter. She wasn't going to ask if she could help the way she had with Lynette. Kate laid a cold chicken piece from the package on the cutting board and made a cut between the rib meat and breast bone. She and Maribel cut in silence for a while.

"The breeding house is the worst place." Maribel shook her head like she was trying to clear out something unwelcome and undesirable. "I tell people don't work there unless we cannot find something else."

Kate knew the breeding house. She had that job briefly when she came back after having the baby. She needed money then, a lot of it to get back out, to Massachusetts where Luke was. She took every shift of every job anyone would give her since she obviously couldn't go back and work at the greenhouse with Smith's family with him in prison and their child gone. That was about the time Lynette was threatening to charge Kate with kidnapping. Jackie wasn't happy either. Her mother kept asking about the paperwork she had signed, kept saying Kate was a minor and the agency shouldn't have let her sign anything without Jackie's consent.

When Kate took the job at the breeding house, she felt like she had fallen through a rotten subfloor into an empty space inside herself with no light. Kate was haunted then by the short time she had spent with the adoptive parents a few month before.

They called it an in-law apartment, but the bright, clean space she stayed was nearly the size of Jackie's house. Toni and Daniel made her meals with lots of greens and weird kinds of rice that were not rice, but she knew no other names for the coarse grains. They gave her a handful of vitamins to swallow every morning and took her to so many doctor's appointments she lost count. Then there was the horror of the labor and delivery, which the nurse called a "roller-coaster birth," so fast all you can do is hold on and scream. Then some confusion with the doctor who she could hear saying to Toni and Daniel in the hospital hallway, that in the state of Massachusetts, there was no grounds for a minor signing paperwork like this, that something seemed wrong with this arrangement, that they were taking advantage of things she did not know the definition of, *socio-economic status, evangelical organizations operating beyond regional boundaries*. Then the shift changed, and that concerned doctor was gone, and the paperwork, unlawful or not, prevailed.

Then the descending black hole of sadness after she let them take her bundle away. Kate's mind knew she couldn't keep that baby, but her body wanted nothing more. She regretted all of it, but maybe most of all, letting any of this happen in the first place. Then a sore, empty ride back with a volunteer from the service that arranged the adoption. The man who drove her home prayed randomly, loudly throughout the 15-hour ride. *Jesus, thank you for the sanctity of life. Heavenly Father, thank you for people who saved this girl from her mistakes and from eternal damnation. Jesus, let this young woman learn the lessons you have for her about recommitting her life to Christ and keeping her legs closed in the future, until a good Christian man is ready for her in marriage.*

Kate hadn't thought it could get worse after that, but it did.

When she took the job at the breeding house, she sat in a chair in the facility with other women collecting semen, holding the glass beaker under the AstroTurf-covered board sprayed with sow pheromones. The large male would be brought to the board and encouraged to do what was expected. Even with gloved hands, Kate hated this, the sounds, the smells, the entire idea of sitting and waiting to catch the specimen that would be used for in vitro fertilization later.

"It's disgusting." Kate finally managed to say her voice a little weak and shaky.

"It is the worst," Maribel said.

By the time they made their way through the rest of the chicken, Kate was surprised Jackie still wasn't awake. She took the dirty cutting boards and knives and put them back into the sink, turning on the hot water again. Maribel took a stick of butter from the refrigerator, peeled back the paper and greased a glass casserole dish.

"How long have you been here?" Kate asked.

"A while."

Kate saw the tense look on Maribel's face. "I know my mother has probably said horrible things about me, but—"

"She loves you."

Kate shrank back a bit. It reminded her of elementary school when people would say, "Jesus Loves You," a statement that confused Kate. What was that worth, the love of someone who was dead then came back to life but you could never see that somehow knew every sin you committed.

Kate opened her mouth to say something, to present the long list of proof that her mother did not love her, or at least did not love her enough or the way she should, but Maribel started in before she could.

"She has wanted to get you back here for a while. She was trying to figure out what would convince you."

Maribel took corn tortillas out one by one, layering them along the bottom of the greased casserole dish.

"I'm sorry I don't have a way to get your children," Kate said.

"She says you'll change your mind, but I don't think so." Kate could hear the bitterness in Maribel's voice. Maribel set a pot of water to boil on the stove.

"It's not about whether I want to or not. I don't have any way to get passports or any fake paperwork."

Maribel began chopping green chilies. She cut in neat little motions between the white seeds and the green flesh of the pepper. "I used to teach English. I went to college. I am a smart woman, but your government makes it impossible." Maribel rubbed a spot under her eye with the back of her wrist careful to not get the juice from the pepper on her face. She continued, "They change the laws, and they don't apply them the same way to everyone. They shut down the border, and all these people who have crossed back and forth to work for decades, now they have to pick a side and lose either way."

The coffee maker fell quiet, the orange light indicating it was ready. Kate opened the cabinet and took down the green mug her mother had slipped into her purse at a diner in Wallace when she didn't like the waitress. Kate pulled the tap forward to fill it. The mug was cheap, and the heat transferred quickly through the ceramic.

"My mother must want something from you."

"We are partners."

"I know about her partners." Kate took a sip of the coffee, weak in comparison to Charlie's French roast. "Has my mother ever mentioned anything about my daughter?"

Maribel shook her head. Kate didn't believe her. "Has she told you about my children? I have a daughter and two sons."

"She showed me a picture."

Maribel drew a deep breath, and took up the knife again. She dissected another chili down the middle. "My oldest is thirteen. Samuel. We email. I used to hear from him every week, sometimes more. He wrote about their school, what they were eating, whether his brother and sister were listening to my mother. Then… suddenly less emails. And the way he wrote changed."

Kate felt a tightening in her chest. She wanted to explain it again. She didn't have a way to help. "I'm sorry I can't help you. There must be someone that you can—"

"I wake up at night because I hear footsteps. I move over in the bed to make room for them, but there is no one there." Maribel's face was tense, her body stiff. "I have to get my children out before something happens to them."

Kate felt that familiar swell in her throat. "I would help you if I had a way to. Can they come the same way you did?"

Maribel scraped the chopped peppers into a bowl. "No. Not that way. No *coyotes* taking money then putting them in the back of a truck. No dehydration. No heat like that." Maribel looked up at Kate. "No watching people die around them."

Kate felt the hot anger coming from Maribel. "No. They are not coming that way."

"There has to be something else where—"

"*You* are the something else."

Both she and Maribel heard an incomprehensible shout come from Jackie's room. Maribel took a white paper pharmacy bag from one of the grocery bags on the counter.

Kate followed Maribel into her mother's room.

Jackie moved against the sheets, looking bird-like and bruised. Her eyes were open but unfocused.

"I'm here," Maribel said. "Jackie, you are dreaming."

When Jackie appeared to understand, to recognize where she was, she said, "Hand me my cigarettes."

"You need to eat something," Maribel said.

"Just give me the cigarettes."

"Just a little something with your medicine. Maybe some rice?"

"Just the cigarettes. Please, Bel." Jackie's voice was weak.

From the doorway where she stood, Kate watched Maribel rummage through the bedside table drawer, the crinkling of plastic, the flick of the lighter, her mother's rattling, grateful sigh.

Jackie asked, "Is she still here?"

"I'm here." Kate walked closer to the bed. Kate watched Maribel adjust Jackie's pillows and reach for a bottle of Jergens. Maribel pumped then smoothed the lotion onto Jackie's right hand. Kate could not figure out their relationship. It must be about money, but how much and which way was it flowing?

As Maribel leaned forward, rubbing the lotion into Jackie's papery skin, Kate noticed what she hadn't before. A necklace around Maribel's neck, the heart locket that Jackie had once given to her. Kate had left it on the top of her dresser before she left for Boston to find Luke, not wanting to bring anything of her mother with her in that escape.

She went to the window and opened the shade. The sky was bright blue. The barn swallows were gone. The window unit hummed. She could see the morning already waving under the weight of its own heat.

The necklace hadn't been worth anything to her then, but now seeing it on Maribel, she wanted it back.

TEN

WHEN HER MOTHER found her throwing up by the side of the house, Kate had been vomiting behind the packhouse for weeks. She couldn't make it that far that morning.

"Well, can't say I'm surprised," Jackie said, her hand against the clapboards, looking down at Kate.

Too nauseated and dizzy to muster the strength to claim the flu or food poisoning, Kate lifted her head and spat in the direction of her mother's feet.

"Watch it," Jackie said. "How far along are you?"

"I don't know," Kate said. "Five months maybe."

"I guess you hid it pretty good," Jackie said. "Does he know?"

"Luke?"

"No, the boy."

"He's happy."

Jackie sucked her teeth and shook her head. "That's because he doesn't know the first thing about it."

"He's going to help." Another wave of nausea washed over Kate.

"They always say that, but he won't."

She felt a flip in her stomach and wondered if it could be the baby. In a bookstore in Wilmington a week before, when Luke was a safe distance away in another aisle looking at SAT prep books, she had read that her baby was the size of an avocado. It seemed that one impossibility was building on another in her life lately, and now everything was being waged on something the size of a small fruit.

"Listen, you shouldn't keep it," Jackie said. "I can take you to a place. You have to be careful where you go. Most of them just try to save your soul and waste your time until it's too late."

"I can't do that."

"Katie, having a baby with what you have now means not having anything for longer than you can imagine."

"You had us."

"That's how I know."

It's not like Jackie's resentment was a secret, but her words still stung.

Jackie continued. "You have a chance to get out of something that you have no idea about."

"No."

"I know you're not like Luke, but you must want something. A baby will take the place of whatever that is."

Kate wasn't like Luke. Or Jackie. She didn't have a long-term plan or series of maneuvers that would bring her something bigger. She wanted Smith. She wanted to move out of Jackie's house. A baby seemed to serve those goals more than hinder them.

"No."

Her mother sighed. "Okay, then. You don't have much time to change your mind. Don't say later I didn't try to warn you." Jackie walked back toward the front of the house. "I'll go fix you a plate."

Kate held the house until the spinning subsided. When she went inside, Jackie was dropping pieces of Wonder Bread into the toaster. Luke sat at the kitchen table, clearly confused as their mother started to crack eggs into a pan. Kate had done most of the cooking since she was old enough to push the buttons on the microwave.

"Katie, do you have something to tell Luke?"

Luke was the last person she wanted to know. Telling Luke seemed like confirmation of something he had seen coming for a while. She told him anyway.

Luke looked unhappy but not surprised. Through him, she saw herself for what she was: seventeen and pregnant. "What am I supposed to say? Congratulations?"

"That would be a start," Jackie said.

"But now you'll never—" Luke looked at Jackie lighting a cigarette at the stove, her back to them.

Kate looked at her mother's bony shoulders under the thin robe. The nausea was subsiding, but dread was rushing in to take its place.

Jackie turned around and saw them looking at her. "What are you two staring at?"

"You shouldn't be smoking," Jackie said a few weeks later through the screen door. Kate was sitting on the back steps skipping eighth period.

Kate met her mother's eyes for a second before taking another drag. Jackie had been generally nicer ever since she found out Kate was pregnant. Mitchell had been away traveling to factories in other areas for inspections, and Jackie for once had not had any one else coming by. The house had grown quieter, calmer.

"I never could quit either." Jackie sat down next to Kate. "I know you don't give me any credit, but you'll see it's not easy. You just do what you have to do."

Kate felt gravity shift beneath her, a kind of leveling of angles with Jackie's comparison. Daughter to mother and back again. Kate ashed her cigarette against the brick step. Jackie reached into the pocket of her bathrobe and pulled out some squares of fabric. One was soft yellow with tiny brown and navy flowers, the other a deep turquoise with white buds. She held them out for Kate to see.

"I was thinking these for the main squares in a baby quilt. Unless you plan on finding out what it is."

Kate took the squares her mother held out. She ran her thumb over the frayed edge of one the pieces. It had been a long time since her mother had sewn anything. Kate had missed the sound of the machine, the concentration on her mother's face, brow often creased but eyes bright and focused.

"I got you something too," Jackie pulled a white cardboard box from the same pocket as the squares of fabric.

Kate stared at it.

"Well, are you going to open it or should I take it back?"

Kate took the box and lifted the top. Nestled in a puff of cotton was a gold, heart-shaped locket on a thin chain.

Kate didn't touch the necklace.

"You can put a picture of someone in there. You know, the baby or that boy." Jackie was busying herself pulling the plastic off a new pack of cigarettes.

"Thanks." She didn't wear jewelry, and she had no plan to wear anything that was heart-shaped or gold.

Jackie dropped her cigarettes and lighter in the pocket of her robe. She took the two pieces of fabric back from Kate. "I'm making Salisbury steak for dinner."

The thought of greasy meat with gravy on top almost made Kate gag, but she nodded. The more Jackie had taken up cooking meals like pork chops and chicken and dumplings, the less Kate wanted to eat. She couldn't help but think each of those animals had been a growing collection of cells inside of their own mothers. She'd never thought about weird things like that before, but now she couldn't stop.

Later that night, Smith and Kate were sitting out on the dock behind her house at the creek. A frost had hardened the grass on the path on the way down.

"You really want to do this?" she asked again pulling the hood of her sweatshirt up to keep her ears warm.

"Why do you keep asking me that?" Smith asked and flicked his cigarette into the black creek. It sizzled when it hit the water.

"Everything really is going to change," she said.

"Isn't that what you wanted?" He reached out and lifted the chain from beneath her sweatshirt. "Are you wearing heart things?"

"My mother gave it to me."

"Damn. I guess things *are* going to change."

Kate did not know it then, but she would understand it later: there are many seemingly meaningless moments before a thing becomes definite. For a while things shimmer and shift undefined, but there comes a point when everything is set in motion. Then it is done, irrevocable.

A couple months later, after Smith was arrested and received his sentence, all they had discussed, her leaving Jackie's house for his, the help Lynette said she would give with the baby, Kate felt all of that mirage beginning to fade. Was she really going to spend three years living in Lynette's house without Smith there? She could change plans and stay with Jackie, this new kinder Jackie. Smith would eventually come out, and by then she would have not a baby, but a child, a person that she would be completely responsible for in the next eighteen years of her life. Basically forever.

And Luke would be long gone by then, about to graduate into an entirely different world. And what would she be? What would be left for her? Luke had not finished saying it when she first told him she was pregnant, but what he almost spoke then stopped himself might be true.

You will never do anything.

She would end up like her mother.

In the adoption office, Kate was alone in the small waiting room where she was overwhelmed with all the checkboxes she had to address.

Ethnic background: Ashkenazi Jew, Eastern European, Western European, African, Asian, Hispanic.

Family health history: cancer, heart disease, epilepsy, blood disorders, ADHD, anxiety, depression, schizophrenia, bipolar, substance abuse. Check the box that most closely associates with your religion.

Then the short answer. What are your first memories? What were your childhood fears? Do you have a history of drug use? Of angry outbursts? Have you ever been charged with a crime?

She flipped forward to see how far they would go. On and on for ten pages.

When they called her name, the young woman, not much older than Kate, ushered her to a cubicle. Flipping through the papers from the clipboard, she absently pushed a box of tissues across the desk even though Kate wasn't crying. Kate stared at her auburn hair, short and fluffed around the sides of her face in a hairstyle that was much too old for her. It looked like it had been rolled up and then blown out the way Mrs. Newkirk had her hair done on Saturdays.

"As far as paternity goes, if you don't know who the father is—"

"I know who the father is," Kate said quickly, not wanting to seem like the kind of person who would be sitting where she was not knowing who the father was. "My boyfriend—"

"Wait," the woman said holding her hand out to stop Kate from saying anything else. "You might *think* you know who the father is, but unless you are completely, absolutely sure, you should mark unknown, because—"

"I know who the father is." Kate leaned back in her chair and crossed her arms across her chest. She was sick of this already.

"Listen to me. If you know who the father is, he will need to sign these papers too, so maybe you don't know who he is." The woman looked at Kate, widened her eyes and nodded her head forward to the paper where she circled in pencil the box marked: *unknown*.

Smith couldn't sign the papers from where he was locked up. He didn't even know what she was doing, so she checked the box.

"Also, I am just going to assume you are eighteen. You mentioned you don't have a driver's license, so there's no real way to know and that's fine, because I am sure you are eighteen, *right?*"

Kate nodded. She would turn eighteen in a couple months.

"Sign right here and here," the woman said. She watched Kate sign, then took another stack of papers from the side of her desk and slid them in front of Kate. "This is just preliminary paperwork. You sign the official adoption agreement after the baby is born."

Kate signed more open lines between passages of text.

The young woman then pulled out a binder. "Now for the fun part!" She clapped her hands together like they were going to pick out outfits from a catalogue. "These are our adoptive parents. There are so many wonderful families."

Kate turned the pages slowly and looked down at all of the couples in their posed shots—by trees, on beaches, some wedding photos, one couple dressed as cats at a Halloween party.

"Don't they look like fun?" the woman asked.

Tucson, San Francisco, Des Moines, Manassas, Orlando. They were from all over the country. Kate had not initially imagined her baby would be that far.

"Normally, we see girls earlier in their pregnancies, not at twenty-eight weeks. Normally, we would look through these together and decide who you might want to work with."

"So it's too late?" Kate asked feeling panicked.

"Actually, I'm so excited you came in today. I have a really special opportunity for you."

The woman said the agency didn't normally do this, except for the descriptions in the binder and some letters written back and forth between birth mothers and adoptive parents, they liked to keep distance. But there was a couple in Massachusetts with an attached apartment that wanted to take care of the mother, making sure she had proper nutrition and prenatal care before the baby was born.

"They had another girl staying with them but it fell through at the last minute," the woman said. "That was so, so hard on them, that I think they might be willing to reach an agreement with you even though you are really quite far along. They live outside of Boston."

Kate knew Luke was applying to schools there. Somehow she found that comforting even if the two paths had nothing to do with each other.

"This baby is white, right? Wait, you are white. Right?" The girl looked down at the paperwork.

Kate was feeling sicker and sicker. "Would I have to live with them?"

"Just until the baby is born."

Without a picture ID, the woman explained, Kate would have to take a bus instead of flying. Someone from the agency would drive her back after the baby was born. The woman smiled and took Kate's hands in hers. Kate tried to pull back, but the woman held on tight. "Let us pray." She bowed her head.

Kate stared at the top of the auburn dome and clenched her teeth. It was the first of many things she would do in the next couple months with her jaw so tight it seemed she might shatter bone.

A week had passed since she returned to Jackie's house. Smith still hadn't called her, even though his girls should be back with their mother by now. Kate also knew she needed to deal with what she had left behind in Boston. First, she needed to officially quit her job at the greenhouse. She still had time before Charlie would realize the car was gone from Cambridge. He just needed to stay on vacation, which was highly likely. She should have called Prendi, should have called to smooth things out with Luke. She did neither.

Kate knew the information she had come for was in that house somewhere, an address or phone number on a tucked-away slip of paper or back of a receipt. Jackie had always kept records and logs of the strangest things. Often, she had it all in her mind, but still she compulsively catalogued. Kate could go through the boxes. If she could find the information herself, she wouldn't have to be part of the odd plan Jackie had hatched that Kate believed would never work anyway.

While Jackie was awake, Kate had to stay busy. She put herself to work pulling weeds growing up against the front of the house. Once the weeds were piled in the dirt so they could dry out, she moved through the yard with a garbage bag, collecting the empty bottles and cans, the duct taped shoe. The next day, Kate took up a pair of blue rubber gloves, a can of Comet, and a scrub brush. She removed years of mildew from her mother's shower with a razor blade, careful not to cut too deeply into the grout. Kate took to the kitchen floor with a mop, washing and rinsing it until the water ran clear. When Valeria and Nina left for work, Kate swept under the bed, dusted the baseboards in the room, tidied small piles of clothes and shoes, made a stack of someone's dog-eared romance novels and scattered pre-paid phone cards. She glanced at a pocket-sized photo album with pages left splayed open to someone's wedding reception.

Kate's mind raced from the time she woke up to the moment she fell asleep on the hard green sofa.

Strip the beds. Change the towels. Anna. Smith surveying his crop, walking down the rows under the glass roof like his father. Dolomite lime to get a neutral pH of seven. A new layer of contact paper in the cabinet under the kitchen sink. Maybe collapsible solar panels, something under the glass that could swing out of the way, hide under more plastic. Money. Money. Money. The need for more money. Her name was Anna. Juan in the Fairmont, always coming or going, always with a passenger. Ask no questions. Get the kitchen floor clean and dry before anyone could walk across it. Anna. An almost empty bottle of Pine Sol. One hundred yards of greenhouse would take more than two hundred feet of PVC pipe, with intake and drainage. Would she recognize her child if she passed her on the street? The pulsing warmth of Smith's neck against her forehead when she rested her head against him in the greenhouse. A new box of contractor bags on the list.

In addition to cleaning the house to keep herself busy, Kate started helping Maribel in the kitchen. Kate woke up when she heard Maribel move through the dark house before sunrise on week days. By the time the house was filling with first light, the men arrived. Sometimes a dozen, sometimes more, they left their work boots on the front porch and their cash in the basket by the church-sized coffee pot. The men poured into the kitchen, talked fast in Spanish, and eyed Kate warily. She caught words here and there. Hot, brother, bitch. Money.

Maribel filled their paper plates from pans of chilaquiles and memelas cooling on the stove top. Kate passed out plates so heavy they curved like crescent moons in palms. Maribel smiled and teased the men about trying to stiff her wicker basket even though Kate saw how the bills accumulated, spilling over the sides. They ate fast, filled thermoses with coffee, took aluminum foil pouches full of the same food, and left more bills in the basket. Then they piled into the trucks and vans, some marked with company logos, others tricked out with shining aluminum built-in tool boxes and weather-proof pack racks. The vehicles all pulled up as the real light was breaking, and off they went to work sites. Kate didn't ask, but assumed many were staying at Mrs. Newkirk's house. The water and power were turned off to avoid detection, but at night she could see across the field the glow of candles and battery-powered lanterns creating warmth behind the papered windows.

Maribel often sounded happiest in the morning, her voice light and full of humor even if Kate couldn't understand the words. Kate could see Maribel played some kind of role in helping decide where the men went, leaning into van windows or translating for farmers and builders who drove up to find people to work for the day.

In the morning, the kitchen smelled like the men's shaving cream and soap. By the time they came back at night, it smelled like freshly broken open earth, bleach, paint and the solvents to remove it, mingling with the fragrant steam of Maribel's soups.

The men in the kitchen mostly worked the Registry Agriculture Inc. system of farms or on construction crews in Wilmington. The other people who passed through the back room of Jackie's house moved on quickly. Kate couldn't understand all the Spanish, but she knew the names of the towns Pinehurst. Tarboro. Kinston. She was learning the names of the crops that had to be hand-picked because the words were repeated so often: fresas, pimientos, tomates.

On her second Monday morning in the house, right after they had served breakfast, Kate heard Maribel arguing with someone outside. Kate looked out the front window to see the driver of a van with *P.T. Painting and Carpentry* slamming the door shut. "I should call ICE on this place."

When Kate walked out of the porch door, he spat in the dirt toward her. "Who the fuck are you?"

"You first, Tim. Who the fuck are you?" Kate had noted the embroidered letters on his work coveralls, but he seemed surprised she knew his name. She walked down to where Maribel was in the yard.

Maribel said, "How about we call on *you.*"

He stepped up toward Kate and Maribel, who were close enough together that their arms touched. Kate could smell the coffee and cigarettes on his breath.

Kate picked up on Maribel's line of defense. "We could, couldn't we, Tim? But you would be fine. You have W-2s on everyone who works for you, right? You're paying minimum wage, right?"

He spoke to Kate, not Maribel. "You tell her, that if she wants to keep collecting her cut, she better show me some respect."

"I don't need a translator. My English is better than yours," Maribel said breezily.

She sounded completely calm, but Kate could sense the tensing of Maribel's muscles, her rising anxiety strung tight between them.

"You better go, Tim," Kate said, then read out his license plate number.

"Stupid bitches. Think you run the world now. Don't you? They'll look the other way about my W-2s. But they'll ship your wetbacks right back down to where they came from. So you two better watch out." He backed away, leaving, but keeping his eyes on them. He put his van in reverse and flipped them off.

Kate turned and saw Maribel's face tight with worry. "Are you alright?"

Maribel shrugged. "He doesn't pay enough anyway."

Given what was happening in her mother's house, she wondered what would happen if Tim actually did call immigration to report undocumented workers. What would it mean for her? For Maribel? For the men at Mrs. Newkirk's? For her mother? She imagined the consequences would not be the same for all of them. She had a general idea of what was going on. It was a safe house, as far as Kate could tell. From what she had seen so far, the people who came through the back room roughly got what they needed. Hydration. Food. New clothes. But something was exchanged, and that made her skeptical. Her mother had not opened a shelter to serve the community. Things of value were changing hands, just as they always had under Jackie's roof.

Kate was sliding a paring knife between the glass and globbed-on latex paint on the trim on the bedroom window when her mother woke.

"What in the world are you doing over there?"

Kate turned to see Jackie's ice blue eyes. "Jesus, Mama. You scared me."

"Don't take the Lord's name in vain. Are you trying to improve the property value for when I die?"

"I don't want this house."

"Good, because you're not getting it." Jackie's voice was hoarse from smoking or dying, or both. That morning Jackie slept through the breakfast rush. Kate had noticed a pink plastic bed pan was now stored just under the bed. Jackie started another coughing fit holding the left side of her body. "Tell Maribel I need her."

"She left with some people. I can get your pills for you." Kate was spending more time at Jackie's bedside. She was holding the cups and tucking the sheets and administering the medicine as Maribel had.

"We're out of pills." Jackie pointed to the boxes on the nightstand. Kate walked across the room and looked closer to see one box with needles and one marked Duramorph. In smaller letters under the drug name, she read *morphine sulfate*.

"Where did you get this?" Kate asked, although Jackie didn't answer. Kate opened the needles beside the bed. "I don't know how to do this."

"Give it to me."

"If you go see a doctor, you know they can give you regular medicine."

"I have a doctor."

"Not the same one."

"Yes, the same one."

Kate remembered him and his dark Lincoln town car from when she was a child and Jackie made her call him. Her mother had come home holding her right arm tight to her body with her left. Jackie's head was cut and blood was running down into her eye.

"What happened, Mama?" Kate asked when Jackie came in.

Luke was out back in the packhouse working on a go-cart of some kind.

"I need you to call the doctor," Jackie said. "Look on the list of numbers in the cabinet. Call Dr. Reeves and tell him to come here."

When the doctor walked through the door he looked at Kate and said, "I delivered you and your brother. Doesn't seem like that long ago, but look at you now, all grown up."

She had shown him into the bedroom where Jackie was laying curled up, her bad arm still clutched to her chest. Kate had listened at the door.

"Jesus, who did this to you?" the doctor asked.

"I fell down the stairs." Jackie's voice was muffled.

"You don't have more than two stairs strung together in this entire house, Jacqueline."

Kate watched through the crack of the door as the doctor dabbed at the cut on her mother's head.

"This one needs stitches," he said.

"I don't want to go to the hospital."

"I can do it here," he said. "Setting that arm is going to be pretty bad."

"Can you give me something for the pain?" she asked. "Then we can do it here."

"That's the easy part. Stopping the cause is harder."

"You can stay if you want," Jackie said.

"For a little while."

After that first visit, the doctor avoided looking at them. Jackie spent a long time getting ready when he was coming. She did her hair and put on more mascara than usual, and made them clean the house.

"The doctor is coming over," Jackie said. "Luke, get the front yard cleaned up. Kate, do the bathroom, and I don't mean like you did last time. Really clean it. He's a doctor," Jackie said as if her guest might expect to scrub in.

Kate remembered seeing him in that nice car in their driveway talking into a tape recorder. She also remembered how the collection of pill bottles grew on her mother's bedside table for a while. Xanax, Percocet, Vicodin. Her mother lined them up in a neat little row on the side closest to her bed. Once the injuries healed, she didn't take the contents of the bottles anymore. She sold them, mostly to the men who visited her. When Kate was a teenager and started taking them herself and Jackie noticed the missing pills, they disappeared to some secret hiding place.

There were a few others like the doctor, in button-up shirts or suit blazers. These men tended to be in and out like they couldn't stay long. Most of the others spent the night, but they were truckers or in other jobs where they were often moving around.

No matter who they were, Kate heard them fight about money with her mother, who was always saying she needed more from them if they wanted to keep staying over, hiding from their wives or whatever they were avoiding. They could come, they could stay, but they needed to pay. She always put it terms of help. Help with the bills, help with her children's clothes, help with some of her debt. She would help them if they would help her. Kate still didn't know exactly what currency her mother traded in. Was she a professional or did she just sleep with anyone who would give her grocery money? Luke would say there was no difference.

Kate watched now as Jackie injected the drug into her thigh. After a minute or so, the creases in Jackie's forehead seemed to loosen, her breath slowed, although a sound like a rattlesnake was still in her chest.

Kate gathered up the wrapper from the dose of morphine and the syringe she took from her mother's loosened fingers. She let them fall into the waste basket lodged between the bed frame and nightstand. She noticed the bottom was lined with more of the same.

Jackie's eyelids fluttered slightly. As light as she was, Jackie looked somehow heavy, sinking into the pillows, still sinking deeper and deeper into herself. Kate thought it would be easier to watch someone die when you could mourn them fully, when you could love them because they had wholeheartedly loved you. Jackie was too complicated.

Jackie opened her mouth, but closed it again. She seemed to be trying to swallow. Kate reached for the Styrofoam cup with the straw and held it for her to drink from.

"Are you ready to help those children now?"

Kate could not hide the frustration in her voice. "Why are you so worried about her children?"

"Because I made a mess of things. A lot of things, but I can make up for it."

"But what do you want out of it?"

"Nothing."

Kate did not believe that.

Jackie's eyes were getting glassy, unfocused. "You're going to let them walk across the desert and die?"

"If you promised Maribel something that can't be done, that's on you, Mama."

Kate reached out to straighten the medical supplies along the bedside table. Saying no was getting harder for several reasons. The more time she spent with Maribel, the more she liked her, which made it increasingly hard to not help her. Maribel was smart. Maribel was the only person Kate ever heard out-argue Jackie and make her change her mind about a course of action. Maribel was also funny when she wanted to be. She did excellent impersonations of other people. She had a dead-on impersonation of Lynette that made Kate laugh out loud. So, the more Kate came to like Maribel, the angrier she became at Jackie. And while Maribel accepted Kate's help in the kitchen, it was clear she did not necessarily like Kate. Still, Kate felt increasingly worse that she hadn't agreed to get the children, even if it seemed like an impossible task.

Kate waited for Jackie's jaw to slacken and her eyelids to slowly close. Then she waited another minute until Jackie's breathing became steady and slow. Only then did Kate begin her search through the records of Jackie's life.

Kate held her breath as she slid out the boxes closest to her mother's sleeping body. She searched for some scrap of information that would lead her to Anna. But box after box, Kate only found receipts, so many receipts, some with the ink faded so she couldn't read them. There were old bills with men's names written in the bottom right corner and a handful of love letters. There were multiple requests from a trucker from Wake County begging Jackie to come cross-country with him. He assured her that the bed in the cab was very comfortable and that she could send her children to stay with his mother. There were poems in illegible writing from Ken Torrance, a farmer Kate remembered from Mrs. Newkirk's porch. There was one death threat. "Ill kil you hor" in large, disorderly letters. Despite the menacing message, Jackie had neatly written *Tom K. 2/15/91* at the bottom. Also in Jackie's neat lettering on the outside of an envelope was *Jimmy W. Kids' fall clothes.* On the back of a torn off part of a spelling test on which Luke got an A, Jackie wrote: *Riley T. 7/17/84-7/19, trip to Wrightsville Beach,*

Shoreside Motel, $68 accom., $250 for groceries and navy blue dress.

Kate even came across the doctor she remembered, *Gordon R.* *$125 for heat. Gordon R. $100 for car repair. Gordon R. $223 cash.*

Kate heard the back door open and then close a few seconds later. There was the sound of low voices talking back and forth in short phrases. Someone pushed a piece of furniture a few inches, most likely one of the beds, the vibration of it moving across the floor passed through the boards beneath Kate's feet. She didn't know how long the Duramorph would keep Jackie unconscious, but if there was anything worth finding, it would be closest to Jackie, heavily guarded. In a flat shirt box between her mother and the wall, Kate found a thin stack of photographs of a much younger Jackie. The photos were the same, except for the ages. Jackie standing alone, hands clasped in front of her in the dirt yard of the same house she still lived in. In the photo, though, the siding was bright white. In one photo, Jackie stood next to a man with the same piercing blue eyes, accentuated by the saturated color of photos of the early 70s like this one. Kate looked closely at the photo of the man who had to be her grandfather. He was tall, bent forward slightly. She had never seen a picture of him before. Jackie stood in each photo with the same clasped hands, the same blank expression. The man peered into the camera as if he didn't trust the person taking it to do it right.

Kate put the photos back in the shirt box and fit it into the same indention in the sheets so her mother wouldn't notice that anything had been moved.

She reached for a small flat box perhaps made to contain a necklace or piece of jewelry with *Thalhimers* embossed on the cardboard lid. She recognized the store name as one of the fancier department stores in Raleigh her mother sometimes talked about. She had never been but hoped to go one day. Inside, she found note-sized pieces of paper folded in half. Each was marked with *September 1979, V. Bianchi* in the top right corner. The ink on the dates was darker than the faded ink on the inside of the notes making Kate think Jackie had catalogued them more recently. As Kate opened the letters, some of them nearly fell apart, separating at the creases.

I saw you during the service. I know you have questions. Please come see me after the potluck tonight. –V.

J- God has given you a calling. I can help you hear it. –V.

J-I wasn't sure at first. You are different than the others. I am sure now. V.

J- This requires patience. Things will end soon, but that is just the beginning. –V.

Under all of the notes was a delicate gold cross on a chain with tiny meshed links. Kate pulled the necklace out and held it up to look closely for any engraving. There was a tiny heart as part of the design at the intersection of the cross. Letters so small they were barely readable gave no clues, only *14K*. She had never seen it before, definitely not on her mother's neck.

Jackie shifted in her sleep. Kate lowered the gold cross then reassembled the Thalhimer's box to seem untouched.

Kate was running out of places to search. She leaned over her mother reaching for a brown cardboard packing box with thin strips of blue calico fabric tied around it. On the top of the box, in Mrs. Newkirk's slanted, shaky script was a white piece of paper under clear packing tape. It was addressed to Kate but at Luke's address. Kate wondered how Mrs. Newkirk had gotten that. It likely meant that Jackie had figured out where Luke was, possibly because of his LLC designation for his restoration carpentry, registered at his home address as he did not yet have the workshop he dreamed of one day occupying. Kate had never told Jackie where she was, knowing an exact location might bring Jackie to Charlie's doorstep, if not in person, in some way that would be no less disruptive. She didn't want her mother finding out that property value.

With the box at the edge of Jackie's bed, Kate untied the fabric and pushed back the cardboard flaps. Mrs. Newkirk's silver teapot, unwrapped and tarnished. The other pieces of the set were triple-wrapped in bubble wrap, clear packing tape around each one, the way Mrs. Newkirk would have protected it for shipping. Tucked down one side of the box, Kate found a note written on one of the index cards Mrs. Newkirk used for her recipes.

September 28, 2005
Dear Katie,

This was supposed to be yours once you turned 18. But we weren't sure where you were. Your mother was able to find Luke's address on the computer at the library. Maybe you'll need this now, maybe you won't, but it's important to me that you have it. Lord, knows you polished it enough.

Yours, Mrs. Peter J. Newkirk
p.s. I know you are hiding right now, but keep up with your mother. She won't say so, but she needs you.

Kate touched the tarnish on the round base of the teapot. Her fingertip left a humid print. She wasn't sure how her mother had intercepted this package. Jackie must have planned to sell the set and had not gotten around to it.

Kate felt the sorrow of Mrs. Newkirk being gone, the guilt of not having stayed in touch, but then a wave of bitterness took hold. Mrs. Newkirk in her big house, or at least what had seemed like a big house then, up on her porch passing judgement on all the people who came through. Kate thought of all the hours Mrs. Newkirk spent teaching her about vegetable gardens and cooking, all the things she had passed down to her like a grandmother might. But for all that she must have known about how Jackie paid her bills, about how the men coming through the house were sometimes problematic for Kate. She must have known what Kate was avoiding, especially when the trucker from California was in town. He was the one who had broken Jackie's arm before she finally ran him off.

For all that Mrs. Newkirk must have seen across the field, she didn't *do* anything. She just kept imparting southern kitchen wisdom as if what constitutes a good pie crust or the most efficient angle for a blade between the peel and flesh of a peach could save you.

Jackie's head turned from side to side on her pillow. The morphine was losing its hold. Kate put the silver teapot back in the box. She didn't want the silver, it was too little a lot too late, but she also hated Jackie for keeping something not meant for her. Jackie believed everything was hers. People's promises and their time, children's whereabouts, antique silver sets. She thought they were hers for the taking, to catalogue and possess.

Kate carried the box out to the trunk of the Audi. She didn't want it, but she would take it, just so Jackie couldn't have it.

When Kate came back inside, she sat down again beside Jackie's bed. Jackie's breathing was ragged and uneven like an engine running out of gas, but she still wasn't awake.

Kate surveyed the boxes on the bed. She had been through every damn one of them, and none had contained Anna's address. Her mother grunted in some kind of pain, but still didn't wake. Kate saw that Jackie's nail polish was chipping on several fingers. Kate touched a nail tip lightly.

Kate tried to think where else Jackie would have hidden something of value. She had already gone through the nightstand drawer. She stood up and ran her fingers under the edge of the mattress. She turned to the low nightstand shelf with the box of syringes, container of alcohol wipes, and books.

Jackie had always moved through piles of library books, finishing the one on top quickly and moving it to the bottom. *Our Endangered Values* was still on top of the pile, the same as when Kate arrived. Kate reached for the book on the bottom, *Secrets of the Millionaire Mind*, and extracted it carefully so as not to send the others toppling.

When Kate and Luke were very small, Jackie had once shown them how to press flowers between the pages of her books in that pile. They put pansies and Queen Anne's Lace between wax paper and tucked it into the bottom book where it would be held under the most weight. Kate opened the front cover then thumbed through the pages from the back to the front of *Part II: The Wealth Files: Seventeen Ways Rich People Think and Act Differently from Poor and Middle-Class People*.

"You shouldn't meddle in other people's business."

Kate jumped at the sound of Jackie's voice. Jackie's breath caught on the rattle in her chest. She turned her head into her pillow and coughed so hard her face turned beet red and she struggled to catch her breath. Kate reached for the oxygen and helped secure it.

Kate tried to not look worried as Jackie coughed. When it finally subsided, Kate asked, "Do you want me to fix your nails?"

Jackie looked pale now with a yellow undertone. She was weak and out of breath. She held her hand up to examine her nails.

"Where's your polish?" Kate asked, opening the nightstand drawer.

Jackie shook her head. "Maribel can do it when she gets home. You couldn't paint a straight line if you tried. Not like me, I should have been a surgeon." Jackie held out her hand, fingers spread, perfectly still.

The dig was as old as the time when Jackie still made their clothes. Then, Luke would help their mother cut and pin fabric, but not Kate because Jackie said she was too imprecise.

Kate took out a travel size bottle of nail polish remover. "I'll at least take this off."

Jackie sighed. "Alright, but I'm going to have Maribel paint them."

Kate tipped the remover bottle into a folded square of tissue from the box on the bedside table. She took her mother's finger tips and began to wipe away the polish. The bluish tinge under her mother's nails didn't look right.

"You always had nice nails," Kate said.

"Thank you," Jackie said her voice hoarse. "That's one of the first things people notice about a woman. How she keeps herself up."

Kate held her mother's fingertip firmly while rubbing away the polish. Kate remembered when she was little the feel of Jackie's fingertips light and fast pinning the hem of a dress. In their work, light as butterfly wings, those fingertips had brushed Kate's shins and tickled the backs of her knees.

"People tend to see what they want to," Jackie said slowly, her eyes closed. "It's a lot of work to make them see what you want them to."

Jackie drifted off into sleep again. Kate removed the rest of the polish. When she was done, Kate used the kitchen phone, the same one with the rotary dial her mother had never bothered to replace. She couldn't press numbers to go directly to the voicemail boxes, so when someone answered, she asked for Prendi's voicemail. She hoped whoever it was would not offer to go find him. She had not planned out what she was going to say. She had just moved toward the phone instinctively after leaving her mother's room, to close a door for good.

She had been expecting to be transferred to Prendi's voicemail, but he answered his extension.

"Hi, it's me Kate."

"Are you alright? You just disappeared from your last shift. I didn't know if I should call the police or Professor—"

"I'm fine." Kate cut him off. She didn't want to think about Prendi calling Charlie like she was a missing child. "I've gone home to North Carolina. So I won't be back to work."

Prendi breathed deeply into the phone. She couldn't tell if the sigh was in exasperation or relief. She was thinking he was probably glad to be rid of her; she didn't fit in with the rest of the team.

"I will miss your expertise," Prendi said.

No one had acknowledged her ability in the time she had been at the greenhouse. She'd only ever heard, *Wait, you're not in a grad program?*

"Thank you for saying that."

"Good luck."

"You too."

Kate's heart pounded as she returned Jackie's phone to the receiver. The house was quiet all around her, both changed and familiar at the same time.

She needed to call her brother to tell him about their mother. Many people were estranged from their families, but they came together in the end, didn't they, at the very end before it was too late? At the very end, when someone was dying, you could say anything because there would be no time for what you admitted to be used against you.

She had to tell Luke, but the fact that since Maryland there was no call from him, plus the fact that he was likely still with Charlie somewhere on an island off the coast of Maine now, and most of all because Luke would continue to choose Charlie's family over her meant she could not call him back the way her mother had called her.

Three days later, Kate was running out of things to clean. She was on her hands and knees on her mother's front porch trying to scrub a green tinge of mildew off the floor. She was dizzy from the bleach fumes as she aggressively moved her bristle brush. Mostly, she had managed to stir up a greenish soup of dirt and gunk. She dunked the brush back into the bucket of water, her hands raw and red.

"Looks like you need a pressure washer," Smith said through the screen.

"Do you have one?" Kate asked, her heart pounding in her chest just from seeing him.

"No, but that don't change the fact you could use one." He moved to the top step.

"How are your girls?" Kate asked, trying to sound neutral.

"Good. Wild. I miss them when they're gone, but they are

capital L loud."

She nodded, but had nothing to add.

"I'm sorry about the timing. I've been thinking about you."

"That's okay," she said. "I've been busy."

"I can see that. Want to take a walk?"

Kate followed him through the brush onto the creek bank. She tried not to think about water moccasins and cottonmouths, or the alligators that wandered the banks. She remembered the first time Charlie told her there were almost no poisonous snakes in New England, she hadn't believed it possible. The thought that you could walk through the woods and not worry about a lethal snakebite had seemed so indulgent, so different from the place where she had grown up, where everything, especially at dusk, which was falling around them now, seethed with potentially lethal creatures that remained invisible until it was too late. She was getting used to tuning out the volume of the crickets and cicadas, but the sound came into focus all of a sudden. She was surprised again at just how loud they really were.

Smith's aluminum skiff was tied to the dock. Kate sat down and crossed her legs so they wouldn't hang over. Smith let his dangle over the black water.

The dock in the creek was on her mother's property, but other people had used it at one time or another. Jackie's boyfriend the shrimper had kept a little motor boat tied up and took it all the way down the Cape Fear to the deepwater marina in Wilmington sometimes. She had heard him talking with Jackie once about how generations of smugglers had used those waterways to avoid the British, to avoid law enforcement during prohibition. A lot could slip by without notice in a swamp.

"Remember how much we used to swim down here?" she asked him.

"Can't anymore. There's run-off from hog farms upstream."

"I can smell it."

She did not tell Smith she had once attended a fundraising event with Charlie for some environmental impact organization where they had projected aerial views of corporate hog operations while people shook their heads and sipped pinot grigio. In the audience, feeling a strange combination of shame and anger, Kate watched the speaker show with palpable disgust what happened when increasingly powerful tropical storm rains fell and broke the waste lagoons, flooding the waterways with pig sewage. She knew everything the organization was presenting that night was true, but the way they explained it didn't seem to tell the entire story. She could just barely remember when every tobacco farmer in their area had a few pens of pigs. No one in their right mind was going to put all their money into one crop. Living things had a tendency to die. It was just a matter of which species might tank in any given season. Granted, the farmers of her childhood had fifty hogs, not thousands as the industrial operations had now.

When the long silver livestock houses and the permanent-look-ing signs went up at the end of dirt drives indicating family farms were now funded by a system of agricultural corporations, Kate remembered people saying the system had saved them from bank-ruptcy. The yearly infusion of cash, even though it had to be paid back after the slaughter house, had given people the ability to stay on the land their families had inhabited for generations. It was just that the land was ruined now. The neighbors downwind of fumes so noxious sometimes fell ill.

Smith held out his pack of cigarettes. One of the cigarettes was upside down, a brown circle nestled in with the white filters. He still flipped over a lucky one that he would smoke last. Smith's brow furrowed as he lit his cigarette, then reached out to light hers. She leaned back as she took her first drag.

"Have you thought any more about what I said?" He kicked the tip of his work boot across the surface of the water, sending out an arc of ripples. A mosquito landed on her knee, but before she could brush it away, Smith's hand smacked down on top of it, leaving a smear of grey and blood.

"About helping you?"

"Working with me."

"That's about all I've thought about." She took another drag. "Is the boiler room still there?"

He nodded then reached back and slapped at his neck.

"You could move everything down there, out of sight, but then you'd need lights. That would definitely mean less plants but would be much more secure."

"I could put in solar panels if I did that." He stood up and walked to the side of the dock where his boat was.

"I thought about panels too. You would need to be able to explain why you need solar power in a glass house. It's a red flag." She watched him step down onto the boat, then added, "I've been thinking something you're not going to like."

He laughed, shaking his head as he flipped the plastic top back on the little engine. "Wouldn't be the first time."

"You should go more slowly." She turned and moved to the other side of the dock hanging her feet over the side of his boat. "With more plants, you need more space, then with more soil, you've got more humidity, which you have to be careful about in old green-houses like yours."

"I got vents and fans moving the air all the time." He checked the oil, pulling the dip stick out slowly.

"Pretty much everything you put in the soil is going to come back out. You know that."

"I haven't had any mildew at all." He put the dip stick back in.

"You have to think about it before it happens. You get powder on a couple plants, and it's too late to stop it. You could get an industrial dehumidifier, something that could pull maybe a hundred and fifty, two hundred pints out of the air a day.

"How much would that run me?" He came back and sat down next to her just past the stern of the boat.

"I don't know."

"Can you find out? Ask the people at that greenhouse up there?"

"I quit my job, so they're not real likely to help me price equipment."

He considered this. "Alright, I can look it up online."

"Smith, you can't just look things up." Kate had listened enough to Charlie and his friends talk about data mining and NSA surveillance. "You can't leave a trail."

"I do own a legitimate greenhouse. I could be looking up that kind of thing."

He had said he wanted her help, but now he wasn't listening to her. The frustration was a feeling she was familiar with at the greenhouse in Boston, with Charlie's family, and more recently with Luke. It seemed a certain degree of vocabulary or level of self-assuredness was needed to get people to believe her. Normally, she just checked out when it seemed like no one would listen, but she cared about this place. She had loved his greenhouse and Smith's family for a long time, so she would try to make him hear her.

"What kind of fertilizer are you using?" she asked, but didn't wait for him to answer. "That's another thing you have to think about before you go bigger. How much food and fertilizer do you need? How often do you use it? You're better off with soil that is undernourished than over fertilized. It's like being hungry compared to being poisoned."

"You think I don't know that?"

"And where do you buy it from that no one notices? You absolutely have to use cash. Every single time."

"You sound like Juan." Smith flicked the butt of his cigarette into the river where it landed with a sizzle.

She didn't like to think about Juan's role in any of this. Adding in unknown players and networks, not to mention firearms like the one Juan carried, forced her to face that this was not just a horticultural challenge, not just re-entering a long standing relationship.

"Then Juan knows what he's talking about," Kate said.

"He doesn't know more about growing that I do."

"I didn't say he did, but if he's your partner, you should listen to him about—"

"He's not my partner."

She saw how tense his shoulders were next to her. He lit another cigarette. He was slightly hunched forward like he was protecting himself, like he was pulling into himself.

"You asked me to help you," Kate said. "I know you know how dangerous this is."

"Katie, I've got my entire life staked on this crop," Smith said.

"Spoken like a true farmer." She brushed a mosquito away from his arm. He caught her wrist gently in the warm circle of his fingers. She could feel his pulse in his fingertips, or maybe it was hers. He put his arm around her, and she let him pull her in. She felt the warmth of his chest through his thin T-shirt.

"This crop has to work out, or I'm gone. I'm fucked."

"That's not a good position to be in," Kate said. "You'll be taking unnecessary risks."

"It doesn't matter. This crop has to come in."

Kate understood this kind of need, but she realized she had forgotten about it for the last few years. She had been living in Charlie's world where everything was optional. Everything could be considered. There was no *must* or *have to*. If she was not living in his house, not living on his accounts, his gas card, his groceries…without an actual job, without a way to generate revenue, Kate would return to an existence of being weighted by *paying rent, counting days to the next paycheck, owing twice what was being brought in.*

Smith waved his hand in front of his face, swatting away another mosquito. "I'm thinking long term too. You know this creek runs to another that runs to the river."

"Yeah."

"Well, that river is access to the port. In a small boat you can go almost undetected."

Kate's concern was rising. She had mostly been thinking about the growing, since that was the part she loved. She was not thinking about the web of people needed to move product. The more involved she became, the more she would have to be connected to that part too.

"A quarter ounce is still a felony charge, right?"

"Far as I know." Smith brushed something away from her arm. "Anyway, I heard you are getting Maribel's kids."

Kate pulled away from Smith. "I have not agreed to that. Mama's asking me to do it for some reason I can't figure out yet. I'm not doing anything until I know why. I'd think it was about money somehow, but she hasn't got much longer to spend it."

"Old habits are hard to change. She's always hustled like that."

"But there's no real money in getting kids across a border. So I don't get it."

"Well. Maybe your mama has changed. She has helped a lot of people. She's trying to help you."

"How is she helping me?"

He turned slowly and looked at her. "The baby. You're stuck there, and Jackie knows it."

She hated how he said it. Almost like he felt sorry for her. The baby was their baby. Maybe that didn't matter to him anymore since he had two more. "Then why won't she tell me where she is? Why does she hold it over my head?"

"Look, Katie. You know you can find the same information if you want it."

"No, I've tried."

And she had. Earlier that week, she'd driven all the way into the library in Wilmington. At one of the computers, Kate tried to use every variation of information on the folded birth and adoption certificates she removed from her pocket. She couldn't find anything. After that she drove to the adoption office where she had signed the papers, her hands sweating into the steering wheel. Kate had pulled into the parking lot and felt frozen in the driver seat of the Audi as she looked at the building. The shape of it was the same, the entrance in the same place, but it was a yoga studio now. Kate watched a woman get out of her white Blazer and run toward the front of the building, a blue yoga mat under her arm. She had tried to find Anna's address on her own, but so far it was a secret blown into dust. That left her with Jackie.

Kate didn't want to talk about this with Smith. She watched the edge of the creek catch the fading light. "Do you ever think about leaving this place?"

"That's the kind of question that means something else." He took a drag, lighting his face in an orange glow as the cherry burned brighter. "Are you back here for good now?"

"I don't know. I don't have a job. I'm going to need money."

Kate was starting to think she could stay in her mother's house. Maybe. Coming back had seemed like a terrifying prospect. Now here with Smith though, it was harder to remember why she had left in the first place. She wondered what would have happened, if he had never gone to prison. If she had not gotten pregnant. If she had not followed Luke when she should have waited for Smith. If. If. If.

Smith looked down into the darkening water for a while before he said, "Katie, if this crop comes in…it would be worth somewhere around a quarter million. And you would have a share."

She could stay here with him. She could probably build his business better than he could. She might be able to keep him out of prison for a second time. Kate was not analytical or overly cautious like Luke, but she *was* more careful than Smith. Her throat swelled with all of this, the fact that she was on the edge of telling him that she loved him, that she had all but forgotten what this feeling was, this pull. She stopped herself. She was still afraid to voice that truth. He was the person she could trust most, but even then, some part of her, a part she inherited from Jackie, said there is no one you can trust.

"You have to be really focused, really serious about it."

"I've got my entire life staked on it."

"That's not the same as being careful, Smith."

He reached into his pocket and took out a small wooden box. He flipped a panel on the top of the box and took out a metal tube.

He pressed it into the well with the weed. He took a hit and handed it to her. They hit the box again and again, the smoke merging with the humid air into a fog that hung over the water before it was carried off. They laid back on the splintering wood of the dock.

"I'm not going to fuck it up," he said.

"Okay, then."

After a couple of minutes, a man emerged from the bend in the creek on a new-looking Carolina Skiff. His greasy dark hair was swept back from his sunburned forehead. Kate propped herself up on her elbows and watched him pass by. He and Smith nodded at each other but didn't say anything as he moved through slowly. Now that he was close, Kate saw that he wore a black T-shirt that read "Ammo-sexual" in big letters across his chest with the image of gold-colored casings across his heavy belly. He had a massive five-foot catfish laid across the bottom of the boat, the head up against one side and the tail arching up the other.

Once the boat was out of earshot, Kate asked, "Who comes up this far?"

"All sorts of people now. That development put in a slip upstream."

"If you want to use the creek for what you are planning, that subdivision is a problem."

She lay back down on the dock, feeling a rocking motion like she was on a raft past the breakers, rising and falling with her breath. She looked up into the limbs that moved gently back and forth the way a mother's hands might move across a child's back to encourage sleep. The smell of the boat's exhaust mixed with their smoke and she swallowed the chemical taste of both.

She reached up and placed her hand on Smith's lower back. She looked at the line of Smith's shoulders, the familiar tense silhouette, his left shoulder slightly higher than his right. She moved her hand up and traced that sloping line. Under her touch was a tattoo that matched her own. That was one of the last things they did together before he got caught. They had traced the roots of each other into their skin forever. For a while, that saturated ink was all that was left of them. She felt now they were growing back from that dormant season.

ELEVEN

AT FIRST, KATE thought it was Maribel's children crying. She was dreaming about them, or at least in her dream there were three children trapped in the cab of a pickup truck. Kate couldn't find the keys to get them out.

When she sat up on the green couch, she realized the sound was coming from the back room. A woman cried out, louder this time. Kate pushed off the quilt and pulled on her cut-off shorts, another score from her old closet. Her skin was damp with sweat.

In the back room, Kate saw Juan with his arm wrapped around the waist of a woman wilting into his side. Maribel was there too. She helped the woman to sit on the edge of the bed. Kate smelled the scent of unbathed bodies and something else, maybe gasoline. The only light in the room came from the bathroom where a man in a white undershirt stood at the sink cupping water in his hands then splashing it on his face. Maribel knelt in front of the woman where she now sat on the bed.

"What happened?" Kate asked.

Even in the dim light Kate could see an impression on Juan's forehead where his hat left a mark. He and Maribel exchanged a look. Maribel shook her head gently at him as if to say, don't worry about her.

"Get her something to drink." Maribel said to Kate. "The Gatorade."

In the refrigerator, Kate found the bottles stacked in the produce drawers. When she returned to the back room, Juan was gone. Kate unscrewed the cap and handed Maribel the bottle. The woman on the bed looked right through them as if her eyes couldn't focus. Maribel held the drink to the woman's lips.

"What happened?" Kate asked again.

"A very long ride," Maribel answered.

Jackie called out from her bedroom. Maribel handed Kate the Gatorade. "Stay with her. Get her to drink this."

"She won't be able to understand me."

"They can't understand me either. They speak Tzotzil. Or Ch'ol. It's hard for me to tell sometimes."

Maribel left the room. The man closed the bathroom door, making the room even darker.

"It's okay. Here." Kate held the bottle out to the woman. When she took it, Kate saw the backs of her hands were blistered in places, her skin reddened, raw.

Kate had been home two weeks now. She often overheard the sounds of people coming and going in the night. The opening and closing of doors, cardboard boxes' flaps scraping as they were opened for supplies. The sound of the shower running for one person, then another, then another. The back room was often empty again by the time Kate was up in the morning, although not always. For the most part, the doors stayed closed inside the house to separate all that was happening. The back room door stayed shut because people were coming and going. Jackie's door stayed shut to keep the air conditioning in. The front bedroom, Kate and Luke's old room, stayed shut unless Valeria, Nina, or Maribel were coming in and out of it.

Kate understood that something had gone wrong with this arrival. Juan had forgotten to shut doors on his way out. Maribel hadn't closed Jackie's door behind her, so Kate could hear everything.

Jackie's voice was hoarse but strong. "This is half of what it should be."

"They were robbed," Maribel said.

"How?"

"In Mississippi."

"We can't just collect half. They have to pay."

"No pueden," Maribel said sternly. "They don't have more."

"Bien. Then they can stay and work." Jackie started coughing, a deep rattle that sounded raw and painful.

"They can't stay. I have a place for them in Harrells."

"We can't run at a loss like this."

"Well, you can't always gain from people with nothing."

Kate sat on the top step on the low back porch. The washing machine whirled behind her, the spin cycle cleaning the clothes the couple were wearing when they arrived along with the few other items they had carried with them in a single plastic bag. Kate could hear the couple inside when the washing machine slowed before the final rinse. She thought at first it was the woman crying. She couldn't be sure it wasn't the man.

When Maribel stepped from the house, she looked tired.

"Did they come from Mexico?" Kate asked looking up to where Maribel stood on the step above her.

"Chiapas." She sat down next to Kate. Her shoulders hunched forward. Her hair was loose and fell around her face. "So, yes.

Mexico, very far south."

Kate held her cigarette package out, but Maribel shook her head and pushed her hair back. She took a deep breath then put her elbows on her knees and rested her chin on her upturned palms. The air was wet and still warm, making Kate sweat through all she wore. Her back was wet. She was getting used to that again, even appreciating that wet clothes cooled you off, even if just a little.

"My husband's parents were from there."

Kate blushed with a flash of guilt. Of course Maribel's children had a father. She had just never thought to ask about him. She was suddenly embarrassed at how she had been so focused on herself, on what she could and could not do, which surely Maribel had noticed.

"Where is he now?"

Maribel lifted her chin from her hands and sat up straight again. "He's with God."

"I'm sorry."

Maribel looked directly at Kate. "What are you doing here?"

They locked eyes for a moment. It was the same back porch steps where her mother had given her the locket, the one still around Maribel's neck, the chain visible, but the heart under her shirt. Kate lit her cigarette but held it out to the side to keep the smoke from blowing the wrong way. "It's kind of a long story."

"I know about those."

A bullfrog croaked somewhere, cutting the whirring hum of all the crickets and cicadas.

Maribel asked, "Has your mother told you the entire story?"

"Which one? She has a lot of stories."

"The story of why we need your help."

"I don't believe my mama's stories."

"Then maybe you will believe mine."

"Maybe. More likely I'd believe you than her."

"I'll tell it, and we will see what you believe."

Kate could sense Maribel's anger. "You don't have to tell me anything. I didn't ask."

Maribel was quiet for a moment before she finally continued. "I'm going to tell you. Because I think you are going to have to hear it all the way to the end to understand."

"If that's what you want."

"What I want has nothing to do with it. It's what's necessary to get you to understand."

Kate felt her own anger rising. She didn't claim to know everything. That was one of the main advantages of keeping to herself. The smoke kept floating toward Maribel. Kate put her cigarette out on the step and tucked the butt in the grass. "I'll listen. But I think you and my mama are not hearing what I am saying. I don't have some magical ability to do what you want."

Maribel nodded slightly. "I just want you to understand this is urgent. I want to tell you why."

"Okay. Fine. I'm listening."

Maribel rubbed her hands against her face, her fingertips in her hairline, like she was trying to wipe away a shadow of bad memory before she continued. "I never wanted to leave my city. Even when I was studying in El Paso, I never planned on moving permanently to the U.S."

Maribel stared straight ahead into the dark. "It's hard to explain how it is. We live under the weight of you. You are always sending your soldiers and college boys to tear things apart. You leave your trash in our streets. You put your maquiladoras on our side, while El Paso keeps itself clean. No dust. No debris."

"You know, I'm not responsible for my entire country."

"No, but you benefit." Maribel took a deep breath, the kind Kate recognized as someone trying to keep from losing their temper. She reached out her hand and pointed at the pack on the brick step next to Kate and said, "I will take one of those."

Maribel's smoke floated away from Kate. She only took a couple drags. Kate could tell she did not smoke often.

"At least Juárez is honest with itself. It's a place that knows what it is, the good and the bad. And we love it.

"When I was younger, we crossed back and forth all the time. It was stressful because you never knew the mood of the guards. You had to be ready to prove that you were good enough and following the laws. Still, we went over whenever we wanted.

"For years, my husband worked as an electrician in El Paso. The money was better. I was an English teacher until Rodrigo was born. Then I started doing translation in Juárez. The schedule was more flexible. I worked for the state sometimes but mostly factories. American managers came down a lot to oversee things. Sometimes they needed translators, and there was always paperwork that needed translating.

"Then 9/11 happened. The border closed down. My husband lost his job in El Paso. Not too long after that, he passed away."

"What happened?" She felt intrusive for asking. Then again, Maribel said she wanted to tell the entire story.

"He was in a car accident. Our friend was driving them back from a job in Los Trios, but he fell asleep at the wheel." Maribel put out the half smoked cigarette and let it drop.

"I'm so sorry," Kate said.

Maribel cleared her throat to keep her voice from breaking. "We moved in with my mother. I was in a fog for a couple years.

I looked up one day and realized things were worse. There were suddenly more cartels, more drugs, more problems with the police. Girls started going missing at one of the factories where I worked. I was looking at the time cards and the paperwork in the main office, and I could see the last time they had clocked in. I could see their hometowns, most outside of the city. I had information I thought could help the police, or if they ignored it, which they probably would, I wanted to tell the families looking for them."

As they sat on the step, Maribel had her knees pulled up towards her. Her arms wrapped around the front of her legs where her fingers interlocked. Kate noticed that one of her thumbs was rubbing against the other.

"I should have been more careful, but I was still angry about my husband being gone. I wanted to save someone, I guess. But I asked too many questions. I asked too much about a manager who had ties high up with the police. He was seen with each of the girls in the days before they disappeared."

The more Maribel told, the more one thumb moved against the other, almost like she was striking a flint to start a flame.

"They came and ransacked our house. They took all our paper-work. My children's birth certificates. My passport. My husband's border control card, which of course he no longer needed. They took all of that but not some gold jewelry my mother and I had. I knew then they weren't just looking for things to sell."

Kate was going to ask, *who is "they,"* but thought better of it.

"We were out shopping and came home to find it all gone. I don't want to think about what would have happened if we had been there. The next day, a neighbor said the police were coming to look for me. I had to leave quickly."

Kate saw a new level of pain cross in the shadows of Maribel's face. "I cannot go back there. I need to get my children out. My mother will not go. She says nothing bad has happened since I left. She doesn't want my children to leave, but I want them with me."

The sky behind the packhouse was lightening into a blue, the pines silhouetted black against the dawn beyond the building. The kitchen would fill soon with men looking for breakfast. Maribel had made lunch to go as well, tamales that were easy to eat on job sites. They needed to be sectioned out and packaged. The piles of laundry in the living room needed to be cleared out.

Maribel straightened her legs out in front of her so they reached the bottom step. "We should go check on them. See if they need anything else."

Back inside, Maribel leaned over the woman where she rested. Her husband was lying on his stomach, his face turned toward the wall.

They left the couple to sleep, pulling the door between the kitchen and the back room closed. Kate measured the coffee into the filter while Maribel pulled trays out of the refrigerator and preheated the oven. She kept her voice quiet as she said, "I lied to your mother. I said they were robbed, but really they didn't have enough money."

Kate looked toward her mother's door, which was closed.

Maribel said, "I gave her the next dose. She's asleep."

"Money is all she cares about."

"In some ways."

"In every way. Believe me. You can't trust her."

"I think you don't know her anymore."

She looked over at Maribel, a stranger to Kate. A new daughter to her mother. Hadn't Jackie made that clear? Hadn't Maribel been at Jackie's bedside, their heads bent low and close, planning? Kate had left, giving up her right to that seat. She didn't want it, didn't want to be a part of the business they were running, but she was still struggling to watch someone else in what would have been her place in a different version of reality. After all, this was her grandfather's land, the house he built. It was her family's place, no matter how low, swampy, inhabited by mosquitoes and copperheads.

Kate knew she had to face that home was no longer yours when you left it. Not in the same way. Maybe she and Maribel both had that in common, although Kate understood the exodus was different. They no longer belonged in the places they left.

"I've been dealing with my mother for my entire life. You've known her for a couple years. There were people before you, usually men, that she had grand schemes with. Big plans. There is always something she is working on."

Maribel walked into the living room and took up a laundry basket that was by the kerosene heater used in winter. Kate followed her. Maribel sat down on the armchair by the heater and tossed a clean shirt to Kate. She caught it. She dragged the other laundry basket toward her and took her place on the green sofa.

"Maybe we know her in different ways," Maribel said.

"Maybe so." Kate riffled through the white T-shirts and pairs of men's pale blue boxers. This week they had started washing the clothes of the men were staying at Mrs. Newkirk's house. Maribel had received a tip that officers from ICE were watching laundromats catching people to deport. Kate folded a T-shirt making a quarter of the half moon collar. Maribel matched bright white crew socks, the kind that Kate saw in the boxes when she first arrived in the back room.

"Your mother helped me."

"Her 'helping' usually means taking something for payment."

"You don't know anything about this story." Maribel tossed the coupled socks into the pile forming next to her bare feet on the floor. "This is different than anything that could happen to you. You don't understand real borders. You aren't listening."

Kate clenched her teeth and folded another T-shirt. She was still irritated being told what was true, what she understood or didn't. It reminded her of Charlie or Luke, the way Maribel was so sure about what Kate knew. She did have to admit that while she had crossed state lines and the Mason-Dixon, while she had crossed class lines from the bottom to the very top, no, she had not crossed a dangerous border with her life on the line. Perhaps her quality of life was up for grabs every time she had to risk a crossing, but not her actual beating heart.

"It really is possible my mother is using you to get what she wants."

"What she wants is what I want. I told you. I'm telling you this for a reason. And I'm not to the end of the story."

Kate saw that Maribel's eyes were becoming wet, not full blown tears, but her frustration was causing a glistening like the moment before the voice breaks and someone actually cries.

Kate steadied herself, remembered the people in the back room, how Maribel was with them. She reminded herself she didn't really know, had not known at all until she had returned here to see some of what was happening. "Okay, go ahead then. I am trying to listen."

Maribel swallowed and regained a steady voice as she told the rest of it.

"There are so many bad things that happen when people cross, but they didn't happen to me. I left quickly, with a coyote. We went twenty miles east of Juárez and walked right across. No problems.

"The entire time we walked, I kept thinking it made no sense.

I had travelled across the bridge over the border so many times. To go shopping. To go to restaurants. I went to UTEP for the same as Texas in-state tuition. I graduated magna cum laude, but now, I was in the desert crossing with people I had nothing in common with. I just couldn't make sense of how I had gotten there. Then across the border, things went bad."

By the time they reached the bottom of the next laundry basket, Maribel had told Kate the rest. Kate felt sick. She felt lightheaded, but she understood why Maribel was telling her the entire story. She was telling it because it ended with Jackie.

Maribel explained how after they made it across, they were divided into the backs of waiting trucks. She thought she was going to stay in Texas and figure out how to get her children across as quickly and safely as possible. But they drove and drove in the heat with no water, what felt like no air. And when they arrived wherever it was they were many hours later, they were divided again by more men. In the weeks to come, they learned the smell of some of those men's necks, sour and sweaty. The fighting. The losing.

"I was on a farm in Alabama for a while," Maribel said. "They said we owed money. They charged us for what we ate, for water to drink and wash. They locked our trailers from the outside. I ran from a strawberry field one day. I tried to get some others to come with me, but they said, 'where is there to go?' I couldn't answer that, but I ran anyway.

"Then I met Juan. Then I met your mother. They needed someone to translate. But by then, I realized I was pregnant. Your mother, she took me to end it. She told me what I really wanted was my own children, not the one that had been forced on me, not this way. She promised to help me get mine back."

Kate felt a knot in her own throat seeing the pain on Maribel's face but made herself keep folding. There was no real comfort she could offer, but she said it anyway. "I'm so sorry." Kate watched as Maribel connected the last pair of loose socks. Then she took the stack and returned them to the laundry basket now ready for redistribution. "I had no idea. My mother never said anything about you."

Maribel shrugged. "You were not here. And we were busy. I worked as many places as I could to make connections to place people. Jackie started to think about getting bigger. She wanted to buy Mrs. Newkirk's house, but we would need more money. So she started using it anyway. Then she got sick. So she called you.

"Listen to me." Maribel moved to the green couch to sit by Kate. "In the last two years, I have seen so many things. I have heard the stories."

Maribel listed some of the horrors of the desert crossings of people she had seen on the other end. Searing pain of snake bites. Fevers. Plastic jugs carried and rationed down to a few swallows. People lost to dehydration. People left behind because they were a liability. Water promised at designated points, but then gallons found slashed open and dry. Burnt skin from the inescapable sun. Airless, hot cavities in trucks and trains. Tears in the skin from climbing under corrugated metal fences or over barbed wire. La Migra. A drunk officer on duty alone, swinging his military-grade weapon, popping off a few shots.

"He lined the group up, made the men kneel with their hands behind their heads," Maribel's voice was calm and flat, almost cold as she told it. "He counted them off then sent half back toward the border to Mexico. He told the other half to keep walking into the U.S. Then he shot the ones who crossed. Their bodies were sent back with reports that they were smuggling."

"That's awful," Kate said. "I'm sorry." Kate's apology felt feather light against the weight of what had actually happened. Useless.

Maribel was still for a moment on the couch next to Kate. Then she said calmly, clearly, "My children will not cross the border that way. In the desert, it's too dangerous. Sometimes, they let the groups of young men through because the patrols know businesses need them for labor. But children have trouble keeping up. They get left behind. That is not happening to mine." Maribel paused and looked intently at Kate. "And if we tried to get them new paperwork officially, new birth certificates to replace what was stolen, I'm worried someone will notice. I'm worried someone in a city office would tip off the people I made angry and something could happen to them."

"I'm sorry."

"Don't keep saying that. Say you will do something."

Kate thought again about Anna. She had held onto her baby for only forty-eight hours and could still feel her.

Maribel sat up straighter. "I don't have time for whatever is between you and Jackie. I need my children back."

They heard the sound of the tires outside in the grass as the first truck arrived.

Kate said, "I don't know a way right now, but let me keep thinking."

Maribel stood up from the couch. "That's the kind of luxury you have...to think about it."

Maribel went into the kitchen to check the trays in the oven. They were now running behind on breakfast, which might make people late for their shifts, which could endanger their employment, which could mean exposure and deportation, which could mean being forced to return empty-handed to families who depended on them or worse, deliver them to murder and retaliation from those they fled.

Kate didn't know if she could deal with the weight of all of this, but Maribel was right. It was a form of privilege to have time for doubt. Still, she could not see past the doubt. Jackie said the border was nothing. Maribel's story proved the opposite.

TWELVE

THREE DAYS LATER, Kate woke up on a Tuesday after the sun was high in the sky. She was wondering how she could have slept through men coming through for breakfast when Maribel came out of the bathroom in her blue terrycloth robe.

"Where is everyone?" Kate asked.

"We're closed today."

They both turned when they heard someone come through the back door. Juan entered the kitchen with several cases of Mason jars stacked in his arms.

"You should get ready for a long day." Maribel passed into the front bedroom.

Kate headed toward the bathroom. In the back room, she saw four new men, two in the double bed and one per bunk. Each of them was turned away from the center of the room, facing their closest wall except one man. He was lying on his back, moving a rosary through his fingers. He looked up when Kate came in then quickly back down.

Juan was gone when Kate came back to the kitchen, her damp hair twisted into a bun. The smell hit her immediately, familiar and powerful. Maribel opened one of the three brown paper grocery bags stuffed full with marijuana stalks.

Valeria came out of the front bedroom and stood at the table. She wore a loose pink sun dress and let her long curly hair fall down around her shoulders all the way to her elbows. She had a large tattoo of a dream catcher with feathers floating in an eternal breeze on her arm. "You want to make some real money today, gringa? This is the fun part." Valeria smiled and picked a stalk out of the bag.

Maribel shook her head. "There is nothing fun about this."

"Tener dinero es divertido." Valeria flipped her hair back over her shoulder.

Maribel lined up the Mason jars in a row in the center of the kitchen table. "El dinero es necesario. By the end of the day, your fingers are falling off."

Maribel explained the idea was to move through the crop as fast as possible, trim, weigh, and seal it into airtight Mason jars. Her voice was flat and distant. Kate saw how tired she looked and realized she did not like this.

Kate knew this must be Smith's last harvest. She liked seeing it all, realizing that this was the end product of what she and Smith would have if they got their growing right and nothing disastrous happened.

Six hours later, they were still trimming. There were five of them holding small pruning shears, cutting with delicate movements. Valeria and Nina, who sat directly across the kitchen table from Kate and Maribel, were younger, barely out of their teens. Nina wore a blue and white gingham jumper with short shorts, her liquid eyeliner drawn heavy and black in an expert point up from the corner of her eye.

A woman named Carla was at the head of the table across

from Maribel. Carla was older, silver streaks running through her thick black hair coiled in a bun at the base of her neck. She wore a hooded sweatshirt despite the warm kitchen and peered through silver-rimmed bifocals that sat on the end of her nose. She had a small lamp clipped onto the table to give her extra light. Her wrist flicked as she snipped around the edges of buds where she was cutting back the leaves. Carla kept an unlit cigarette between her lips. She talked through the side of her mouth and cut faster than the rest of them. She would point out every so often that Valeria had stems in her hair or someone had done a sloppy job.

They moved the ends of the shears like little beaks to cut away the buds. Kate watched their piles grow, the stems and leaves that were cut away, the stalks of flowers that were good. When they had one that was especially beautiful, they would hold it out to the others. They sorted them into piles according to quality. They deposited the stems and leaves in another pile on the table.

Just as they finished trimming the plants from the third paper bag, Juan arrived with five more. The smell in the kitchen was overwhelming. The plants were so pungent that the air itself felt sticky with the residue.

The women at the table had to rub their fingers clean with baby oil when they got up to stretch or use the bathroom or whatever they touched would stick to them.

"You getting better, pinche gringa," Nina said with a strong accent. "But too slow. More trim, more money."

"She's fine," Maribel said.

"Lenta, lenta, lenta," Valeria said. "We are paid by weight. You are slow...we are slow."

Juan came inside every few hours to weigh the contents of the trimmed bud on a kitchen scale and put it in Mason jars. He wrote down numbers in a book. Kate noticed the women talked less when he was there, but then picked up again when he left, interrupting each other, talking over each other. When he wasn't inside, he sat in the Fairmont parked in the side yard where he could watch both the front and back of the house.

"If we're in such a hurry, how come he doesn't help?" Kate asked.

"Los hombres no pueden hacer esto." Valeria said. "Hands too big."

Kate's hands were stiff and her back hurt from sitting in the chair for hours. She squeezed and extended her fingers to try to loosen them.

Carla noticed this and started talking to Kate in Spanish. Maribel translated while keeping her scissors moving fast and steady through the green. "She says, this harvest is nothing. She said she worked one once that took two weeks nearly around the clock with ten girls."

As they trimmed, Nina and Valeria argued with Carla over the music coming from a boom box. Kate recognized it as the one Luke bought in the spring of ninth grade with the money he made picking strawberries. Maribel flipped back and forth between the pop station that came in from Wilmington, which the younger two wanted, and the country station Carla wanted.

Nina complained about the music again, so Maribel switched the radio to a Latin music station. Nina murmured in approval before they fell silent, moving the scissors fast and precise like masterful surgeons making tiny stitches and incisions, cutting away at what wasn't needed.

Sometime before dawn, after they each took at two-hour break to sleep, Kate heard Juan come through the back door. Although Juan had closed the door between the kitchen and the back room,

Kate could hear a child's voice mixed in with Juan and another man's. The men were arguing. It was escalating, the voices getting louder and louder.

Maribel spoke in a hushed string of whispers to the other women at the table, but Kate couldn't understand. Nina and Valeria shook their heads. The child in the back room started crying amidst the heated discussion between the men.

Maribel stood from their table and went into the back room. Soon her voice joined the fray, the child crying louder.

Valeria stopped cutting and listened. Nina cut so fast she accidentally nipped herself with her scissors. She moved her finger to her mouth and held the cut to her lips.

Carla just kept trimming. "Todo estará bien," she said with one eye squeezed shut as she made a careful cut around a stem. "¡Qué Dios nos bendiga!"

Kate knew *dios* meant talk of God. She could see that Valeria was in doubt about whatever Carla had said, although she and Nina both crossed themselves in response. In the back room, the voices grew quieter. Kate picked up another stem and cut through it. She thought about Maribel's children. Kate swallowed back the rising knot in her throat and set down her tiny shears. She could not bear the sound of that child crying. She could not.

Since Maribel had shared the story of all she had lost, Kate thought nonstop about how she could get the paperwork and IDs she needed. She could try Luke, even Prendi. Charlie had mentioned Anton made fake licenses in undergrad, but she didn't know if Anton would help her. She guessed by now, Charlie might have returned to find her clothes and his car missing. The window of being able to help was closing. There was a reckoning coming, surely, where she would have to deal with what she had left behind.

When Maribel returned to the table, Kate's voice shook as she said, "I can get your children for you."

Each woman's head snapped up from her cutting. Except for Carla who hummed to herself. Maribel stared at her but did not speak.

"I've been thinking about it. There is someone I know who can make fake IDs. I don't think he has done passports, but he might be able to help."

"¿Qué pasó? ¿Qué sucedió?" Carla asked, noticing something had changed in the conversation. No one answered. "¿Qué?" Carla asked again more insistent.

"Ella dice que va a ayudar a Maribel," Valeria said.

All of their eyes were on Kate.

"¿Qué es lo quequiere?" Carla asked.

Before anyone could translate it for her, Kate said, "I don't want anything. Not from you, anyway."

Kate could see the pain of renewed hope in Maribel's eyes. "You can do this?"

"I can try," Kate said. "I will really, really try to figure it out. If we can't get passports, we'll just figure out something else. Most American kids don't have passports anyway."

"But if you could get them, it would mean less trouble at the border. I want no problems."

"I understand."

Jackie's bedroom door creaked open. The women all turned to see Jackie moving gingerly from her room. Jackie wore a sage green velour track suit that hung baggy on her skeletal frame. When she stopped behind Nina's chair, she held to the vinyl seat back for support. "Katie. I need you to take me to Walmart."

"What?"

"Walmart. I need a ride."

Maribel stood and went to Jackie. "I can get what you need from the store. You should be in bed."

"It's not something you can help with. Come on, Katie. Let's go."

Kate had not been sure Jackie could get out of bed ever again, much less leave the house. She wasn't sure what to do next. Maribel handed Kate the baby oil to clean her hands. Kate looked at her as she took the plastic bottle. She nodded to reassure Maribel. She didn't want to say anything in front of her mother, but she tried to say it with her eyes.

I will get them.

Kate followed Jackie through the Walmart past the children's clothes and towering displays of toilet paper and paper towels to the sporting goods section where they stood at the firearms counter.

"You want a gun?"

"It's a God-given American right," Jackie said leaning against the glass counter. Kate realized her mother could barely hold up her own weight.

"What are you going to do with it?"

"It's for protection," Jackie said. She looked awful, but still maybe a little better than she had a few days ago. There were two other customers in the section, one who was looking at deer stands, the other examining a tray of knives the salesperson had put on top of the case for him.

"But why do you want it now?" Kate asked.

"Because you're here."

"I don't understand."

"I could explain it to you, Katie, but I can't understand it for you. So maybe it's best if you don't ask."

"Can I help you?" the salesman behind the counter asked. He had a combover of blondish brown hair and a fluorescent name tag that read "BOB" pinned crooked to his blue vest.

"We would like to purchase some handguns," Jackie said.

"I'm sorry ma'am. We haven't stocked those since the 90s. We do carry ammunition for handguns."

Jackie itched her elbow. Her skin was unnaturally yellow-grey, like a bruise. "That won't help me."

"You need a permit for anything other than a shotgun or rifle. That you've got to file with the Sheriff's office in the county you live in. They run a background check, then they'll get you all set up."

"Well, then I guess I want one of whatever you can sell me now," Jackie said.

"I have what you see here in the showcase." He waved his hand at the rotating cylinder of rifles and shotguns on display at the end of the counter. "What do you want it for?"

"Not sure that's any of your business," Jackie said.

"It might help me know what to sell you." His face grew harder, unfriendly.

"Home protection," Kate jumped in, smiling at him.

"You have any experience with guns?"

"Yes," Kate said. "We are registered for the gun safety class at the range across town. The one right off 40," She hoped the firing range was still there and in business.

"Do you have your registration for the class?" Bob moved forward to unlock the case. "Because I could work out a discount."

Kate smiled at him again. She doubted a corporation like Walmart would give a local discount, but she was used to men like Bob trying to offer up something she would be indebted for. "I don't have it with me."

Bob looked Kate up and down. "I'll take your word for it." He unlocked then reached into the case where the long guns were vertically arranged on the carousel, butts down, barrels up. "You might like the Remington 870 tactical, 12 gauge." He relocked the cabinet then laid the weapon on the glass in front of him.

"How many can we buy?" Jackie asked. She was opening up a small piece of paper, unfolding it to see something written inside.

"You can buy however many you want, but if you buy two or more in a five-day period, I have to report it to the ATF. Some people don't want the federal government involved."

Jackie looked up from whatever she was reading. "Do you have anything called a Bushmaster?"

"Yes ma'am, we do. A few models of ARs. I like the Colt we carry better than the Bushmaster. Y'all, excuse me for just a minute." Bob walked down the case to the hunter who was taking out his wallet.

"What are you doing?" Kate tried to keep her voice down. "What's this for?"

"I need you to put one of these under your name."

Kate picked up the shotgun.

"God, I love a woman with a gun," said the man looking at the deer stands. "That piece looks good on you, honey."

Kate ignored him at first, but then thought it better to say, "Thank you." She broke the barrel open then closed it again.

"Where'd you learn to do that?" Jackie looked surprised.

"Mitchell," Kate said. "He used to take Luke and me out back and let us shoot into the field."

Kate remembered how Mitchell would chain smoke and watch her and Luke shoot. He would let them shoot out empty beer bottles, shattering them into the edge of the tobacco until her wrist and shoulder were sore and her hands shook.

"Uh-uh, Baby Girl," Mitchell had said. "You don't want to be shooting with a shaky hand. And neither does anyone near you."

Even when she knew it was coming, the recoil got her every time. No matter how hard Kate tried to hold steady, the pull of the trigger shoved her back with a shattering jolt. Luke was better at it. Even with Mitchell's .44 Magnum, he didn't lose his aim to the recoil. With a look of determination, he barely flinched as he pulled the trigger.

Bob came back to them. Kate laid the shotgun back down for him to take. He rotated the rifles and shotguns in the case half way around. He unlocked then replaced the Remington and took out what Jackie asked for.

"Here's the most powerful Bushmaster we sell. It'll give you thirty-rounds."

He laid out what looked to Kate like a military weapon. Kate did not touch this one.

"We'll take two," Jackie said. "One for each of us. What about that discount?"

"Well, now that's not available on this particular model. Six days from now you can each get another without the report to the ATF," Bob said.

Jackie took a stack of cash out of her purse. Slowly, she counted seventeen one hundred dollar bills and laid them on the counter.

"I'll need both your licenses."

Jackie looked at Kate and sighed like a parent who was disappointed with a report card.

"Never mind. Put them both under my name. Report it all you want to the ATF."

Driving back from Walmart, Kate kept missing the lights by a few seconds. Every time the car came to a full stop, her mother winced.

"Mitchell took you out shooting?"

"All the time."

"Where was I?" Jackie's eyes opened and closed slowly.

"I have no idea." The anger in Kate's voice just surfaced like a fin before she pushed it back down. Kate felt her throat tighten and spread into an ache in her chest as she missed another light. She would have run this one, but the white Buick in front of her slowed abruptly as soon as it turned yellow. Jackie whimpered and held her hand tight to her rib cage.

"I should have got a gun a long time ago," Jackie said. "I could have run off that line cook who wouldn't leave. Where was he from?"

"Savannah. No. Charleston," Kate said. "His feet smelled up the entire house."

"I remember that. And that truck driver. The one from Fresno or somewhere. If I had a gun, I would have blown a hole right through that son of a you know what."

When the light turned green, they drove for a while, away from the area that had been spreading out faster and wider with development since Kate left. Kate flicked her right turn signal for the ramp to I-40. "All of this is a bit late, don't you think, Mama?"

Jackie started to cough, a low gravelly cough that shook her entire body. Kate felt a flash of panic that she should have brought the oxygen with them. Jackie bent forward in her seat with her shoulders hunched. The coughing fit lasted for a couple minutes as Kate gripped the steering wheel with her left hand and held her right against her mother's bony back, support that couldn't change the trajectory of anything already set in motion.

When Jackie finally stopped coughing, Kate asked if she was

OK.

Jackie didn't answer.

"Really. What are you up to, Mama?" Kate knew they were long past the point of questions that had actual answers.

"I'm helping people," Jackie said and leaned her head back, face drained of color. Jackie looked so fragile Kate almost made the mistake of seeing her mother as harmless, as someone needing protection. Then she remembered. Her mother was like a comet. Fascinating. Potentially destructive. Impossible to look away from. Kate could never know what she was up to, not really.

THIRTEEN

KATE WAS DRIVING over to Smith's house when Anton finally answered his phone. It had taken some effort to find his number. She remembered his address from visiting Brooklyn and that he mentioned he was a property manager in the building he lived in, among others. She had spent almost an hour on a terminal at the public library before she found it.

"I'm sorry, what are you asking for exactly?"

Anton listened to her explain it again.

"Passports. Or papers. Something to get me across a border with three children I'm pretending are mine."

He was quiet for so long that she looked down at her phone's screen to make sure the call was still connected. She waited, careful to not push too hard.

"This is kind of out of nowhere. Where are you again?"

"Home," she said. "Also, I need a driver's license."

Anton owed her nothing. He had no reason to do her this favor.

"I haven't made IDs for a while. That was more of an undergrad initiative."

"I understand. I know it's illegal, it's just…this would help some people in desperate circumstances. People with no other options."

219

He laughed. "I don't care it's illegal. I just don't know if I could make anything convincing. For one, I don't have access to the kind of commercial printers I used to. And it would be really hard to get the kind of holographic overlays they use now."

Kate bit into her lip, her eyes closed. She was glad he couldn't see the expression on her face. She did not say *please* out loud, but she felt the desperation in her entire body.

Finally, Anton said, "I would need passport photos. Maybe avoid the post office. Take the kids to a drug store, and get photos."

"They aren't in this country."

He was quiet a moment before saying, "Do you have any photos of them? From straight on?"

"I can try to get a hold of some."

"I heard you and Charlie are through."

Her stomach flipped. "Who told you that?"

"Everyone," Anton said. "See what you can find for photos, then call me back."

When she went back to Jackie's, she would tell Maribel they needed to figure out photos. Maribel had been on the phone a lot, Kate assumed with her mother in Juárez who was with the children. Jackie had been back in bed since the outing for guns, but had been providing instructions when she wasn't asleep. *Make sure you use cash. Make sure you keep your gas above a quarter tank. Quit taking clothes for a teenager out of that box in the closet and make sure you wear what you came here in.*

When Kate pulled up to the greenhouse, Smith was unloading bags of fertilizer from the bed of his truck and stacking them under the light outside of Lynette's florist shop. Above his head, moths swarmed the bulb.

"Did they have the one with the calcium like I said?" she asked.

"They had a few. I just bought them all. And some with less nitrogen. I don't know, a bunch of shit." He waved his hand at a moth that floated around his head.

"What's wrong?" she asked.

"Nothing." He wouldn't look her in the eye.

"Something's wrong."

"I just don't like how things have changed. My father didn't have to go around asking for help, asking every last person what they thought he should do before he did it. He just grew things, on his own, but now that's not enough somehow."

"Well, yes, things change."

"Now everyone else wants a cut and everyone knows your business."

"Are you talking about me?" She had not formalized a cut, but he had offered it to her. She planned to take it.

"No, not you," he said, but she didn't believe him. He continued, "All these people who aren't even from here are involved now. They're making it more dangerous."

"This is all really risky whether you involve anyone else or not," Kate said. "That's what I have been trying to tell you."

He turned his back on her to pick up another bag. "I'm just working to take back what's mine, what's been in my family for generations. You don't know what it's like to be standing in your own place, your own land, only now you're the only one speaking English. You're the only one from here. Nothing that was ours is ours anymore."

Kate heard this in Boston too. Everyone thought that their people were the ones who worked the hardest, who deserved the most, who were being cheated out of something by someone else. It didn't matter that Smith was focusing on the wrong grievances. If he didn't listen to Juan, or her for that matter, he would likely be putting himself and everything he believed he was protecting in danger.

Smith had always blamed other people for his own problems, even the ones of his own making. Kate knew the way he operated, the way he could not see a bigger picture was a problem. The truth was, he was not the grower his father was. He was not the grower she was for that matter. If she continued to let him drive, she would have to consider that he might drive them right off the road into a ditch.

She held the cart steady while he placed the last bag on top of the rest. "Let's just think about the plants for now. Let's see how they're doing."

They were growing. What had been tiny fingers held close together were now outstretched palms intent on spreading. Kate pulled the cart behind her as they moved down the aisles. She suggested they divide the rows up and try different fertilizers by row. They were marking the tables with chalked numbers so they could track where they were putting each kind. In the humidity of the houses with the sounds of the fans, she felt truly in her element. When she came back from helping Maribel, she would be here every day, moving through these aisles, working with the plants, making sure Smith didn't let things get out of control.

Before that, she and Maribel would drive together south. Maribel wanted her children back the second they crossed over the drawn line of the border. Although they had less tension between them than when Kate had first returned home, it was clear Maribel did not trust Kate. Not that Kate totally trusted Maribel. They needed each other to get what they wanted out of the plan that

Jackie had engineered. They didn't need to be best friends. They would be gone for at least a week, maybe longer depending on how long they decided to wait before Kate crossed the border for the children.

"I'm going to Mexico," Kate said.

Smith nodded and placed his finger inside one of the pots to check the soil. "I know. Juan said so."

"No secrets in this town."

"Not with those people." There was a hardness in Smith's voice as he wiped his finger against his pant leg to get the dirt off. "This should be wet enough to fertilize."

Kate cut through the top of the bag marked with a 3 in Sharpie on the plastic to match the chalked number on the row. Kate knew Smith had never liked outsiders, which was pretty much everyone who hadn't grown up there. It annoyed her that he could use people's labor and expertise then lump them together to complain about them.

"If Juan bothers you so much, why do you work with him?"

"I don't have a choice," Smith said.

The smell of the fertilizer was sharp in her nose. Whether Smith liked it or not, all of their lives were intertwined because people like her and Luke had left and never planned to work that hard again. The region needed a new labor force.

They worked for a while in silence. Measuring fertilizer into big plastic beakers, mixing then pouring just the right amount into the plants. They worked their way through the row until they were standing next to each other again, then they moved their equipment to the next.

"You need a better system for tracking all of this," Kate said.

"I need more money.

"You need better security."

"Like I said, I need real money."

They stood and surveyed the crop. She wondered how many farmers had stood in that county over the centuries, arms crossed over their chests the way hers and Smith's were while they considered all that was at stake. All those generations wondering what would happen when the cotton broke through the pod or if the tobacco leaves would make it to maturity on the stalk.

There was a difference of course between those who had the land deeded to them and those who didn't. The landowners believed they had it worse because they could lose all they believed they had earned. The sharecroppers, like Kate's ancestors, knew there was nothing but losing at the end of just about every season no matter how high the yields. Then there were the people who had never even been asked what they were owed. Everything of calculable value was already taken from them and many of their ancestors.

For a couple centuries, that combination of people had watched their fortunes rise and fall in various ways. Deeply separated from each other, they had still looked upon the same swaths of land considering every variable, making endless calculations on the soil, seeds, and sun, though they would yield unequal rewards.

Every single time, they came up with different equations from each other. They could not use the same math.

The truth was that even the most devout farmers knew whatever God the preacher promised existed seemed to play it fast and loose with the seasons, doling out a different set of tribulations every year. Early frosts or late. An influx of rodents or insects. A drought, followed by a deluge that drowned the life out of everything.

"Don't change anything while I'm gone," Kate said. "Track the acidity levels and do not over water them."

Smith nodded. "I might have to use some lamps."

"Don't use lamps."

"Might have to. There's a tropical storm coming up from the Bahamas. It's supposed to rain for a week." Smith looked up through the glass ceiling. The stars shone clearly through.

"Don't. Wait on it. Trust the climate you created."

Kate walked in front of him through the dark. She was glad he couldn't see her face. She was worried. He had such a clear way of seeing himself, never doubting that he was right. In that way, he was like Charlie and Luke, even Jackie. But unlike them, Smith was reckless and often, very often, although Kate did not like to admit it because it made teenage Luke right, he calculated things incorrectly. Jackie almost never miscalculated.

Jackie had a hawk-like view on all the moving parts of any situation she was tipping to her advantage. Charlie had money and an immovable position no matter what mistakes he made. Luke had brilliance and drive. Smith had none of those things. It occurred to Kate that the line that tied her to Smith might also be what would pull her down to the sandy ocean bottom with him if he sank.

As they moved through Lynette's florist shop, the smell of lilies and roses was almost sickening. Kate felt how deeply she had always been tied to him, even when Luke told her Smith was a bad idea, even after she gave up their daughter. Still, Kate had to face the fact that she did not trust his judgement. When they went outside, there were even more moths throwing themselves against the glass of the light fixture. Smith reached inside the door for the switch to turn it off. With the light gone, Kate looked up and saw how thick the stars looked, almost three dimensional, when there was no glass in front of them.

He walked her to her car and asked, "You're driving this

tomorrow, right?"

"Yeah."

"I'll get it ready, change the oil and all that."

"You don't need to do that."

"I'm pretty sure I've got the right size filter. Remember when I used to do nice things for you."

"No, I don't," she teased.

"Well, I did. Come on, I'll give you a ride back to your house."

Parked in Jackie's dirt front yard, Kate handed Smith the keys to the Audi. He took them but didn't let go of her hand.

"You should be careful down there. If I thought I could get across the border with those kids without raising questions, I would do it," Smith said. "But it will take someone like you."

Their hands still both wrapped around the keys, she said, "I'll be back in less than a week. Don't use lamps. Someone will catch you if you start blazing electricity."

Smith pointed above Jackie's house. "Something else is blazing right now."

Kate got out of the car and Smith followed her toward the plume of smoke drifting straight up from the back yard. They found Jackie sitting in an old nylon lawn chair.

In a patch of yard a few feet in front of her, Kate saw that Jackie was burning things.

"I guess you're too old for me to say anything about you traipsing around with my daughter," Jackie said to Smith, tossing the top of a shoebox onto the fire.

"You usually say whatever you want, Ms. Jessup." Smith walked forward cautiously. "You doing alright out here?"

"Just cleaning house."

Kate walked slowly just past Smith. She saw a singed receipt at the black edge of where the fire burned in the grass while the grey ash of burnt paper wafted up like broken apart ghosts.

"Do you want me to stay?" Smith whispered.

Kate shook her head. All she could think of was whether or not Jackie had burned Anna's address.

"I'll bring the car back later," he said and left.

Kate walked forward like she was approaching a sick animal. "You're up two days in a row." She could see Jackie lean forward in the lawn chair, adjusting against some pain. She sat down in the grass next to her mother.

"I thought you and Maribel were going to get an early start."

"We are." Kate watched the flames lick at the blackened, shrinking paper. She stole a quick look at her mother. The light from the fire deepened the hollows in Jackie's face, under her cheek bones and eyes. Her mother knew she was going but still wouldn't give her the information on Anna until she returned with three children in tow.

"Mama, what are you doing with all of this?"

"I'm having a funeral pyre."

Jackie handed Kate a thin stack of envelopes. "Toss those in there, would you?"

They watched the fire for another minute before Jackie pointed to a plastic grocery bag full of paper halfway between her chair and the edge of the fire. "Add that. That's the last of it."

Kate took the last bag that contained many of the papers she had already combed through. She'd turned up nothing; another loss, another start without a finish.

"It's not like you're any better than me," Jackie said from her lawn chair.

"What are you talking about? I never said I was." Kate held the empty plastic bag in her hand and looked down at her mother in her ragged lawn chair.

"But you tried to go off and be something else."

If Kate didn't know better, she would have thought Jackie might be about to cry.

"You better get some rest tonight," Jackie said. "Y'all should be on the road before six. Early bird gets the worm, Baby."

"Baby?"

Jackie pushed back a lock of dry hair from her forehead like it took all her strength. "You were. Once."

Later that night, Kate was talking to Anton on the phone in Jackie's kitchen. "I'll do a registration too in your name. What's the make and model?"

"A 2004 Audi A6."

Kate was spelling the children's names for Anton from a piece of paper Maribel had given her, "S-A-M-U-E-L," when she heard something scatter across her mother's floor, followed by a loud thump. Kate hung up and went into Jackie's room. She wasn't in the bed. She finally saw Jackie in the darkness, lying on the floor in front of the door that connected Jackie's room to Kate and Luke's old bedroom. She had pulled down her sewing box from the dresser, scattering its contents across the floor. Clear plastic bobbins, a couple silver thimbles, spools of thread in endless colors rolled across the floor.

Jackie's eyes were open and moving, but the left side of her body was limp. The left side of her face was slack while the right side was tight, the fine muscles seized up and twitching around her eye.

"Mama?"

Kate rushed forward and lifted Jackie from underneath her

arms. She was impossibly light as Kate pulled her back toward the bed. As she let Jackie slip down onto the mattress, Kate felt the tension fighting in Jackie's right side, whereas the left fell loose, dead weight against the sheets.

Jackie's eyes were open, wide with fear. She opened her mouth at an odd angle and then closed it over and over. Air moved out over her lolling tongue in a coarse whisper.

"It's Okay, Mama." Kate's voice broke. "You're alright."

Jackie's eyes seemed to try to focus on Kate but couldn't.

"I'm going to call an ambulance," Kate said.

Jackie's right hand reached Kate's arm. The fingernails in her flesh weren't painful as much as they were strong and clear. "I know you hate hospitals, but this is serious."

From Jackie's course whisper, Kate could make out a clear *no*.

"Mama," she said her voice breaking. She did not know what to do.

Kate noticed Jackie glancing at her right arm then back at Kate, over and over. Over and over. Finally, Kate understood and looked down at Jackie's clasped right hand. Kate uncurled her mother's tight fingers. In the space between Jackie's thumb and the pointer finger, Kate saw the edge of a piece of paper. In the dim light coming in from the kitchen, Kate opened it and read an address in Lake Forest, Illinois.

Kate sat on the bed next to Jackie until she finally closed her eyes. She was still breathing shallow breaths, but Kate understood that something had broken inside of her. Her heart pounded as she stood up from the bed where her mother lay. The answer to what she believed she wanted was in her palm. She backed across the room until the vertebrae in her spine met with the door that separated their bedrooms. As Kate closed her palm around Anna's address, it occurred to her for the first time that all those years as she and Luke had listened for their mother through the door that separated them, Jackie was right on the other side listening back.

FOURTEEN

BEFORE THE SUN was up, Kate was washing her face in the bathroom, trying not to splash her white tank top. It seemed fitting in the arc of Kate's life that, after eight years, now that she finally knew her daughter was up in Lake Forest, Illinois, where Toni and Daniel had apparently moved after the adoption, Kate was driving south instead. The paper Jackie had clutched in her hand was pressed into the top of Kate's bra against her heart. It was not the same as holding that baby, but it was not unlike it either, Anna's location, held close to Kate's damp skin, where her head had once rested so briefly. She had checked the address a couple times, unfolding the paper, seeing the ink of her mother's handwriting smudging, but it didn't matter. Kate had memorized it anyway. When Kate was done helping Maribel, she would drive north to this address outside of Chicago. That would delay her return to Smith and the crop, but she had waited long enough to figure out where Anna was. Toni and Daniel wouldn't like it, but she would take everything she had learned in Boston; she would be that version of herself, the one that seemed sophisticated and elevated. She would just say she wanted to meet her. To say, hi. To just find out what she liked, what she didn't like. Her hair color. Her favorite kind of cake. Kate would tell

Anna she had not come out of nowhere. She had two grandmothers and two half-sisters. A biological father and mother. And although by giving her up, Kate had given Anna a much better life by nearly every definition, she wished it could have been different. A person deserved to know their beginning.

As she dried her face, through the door between the bathroom and Jackie's room, Kate heard hushed voices. Kate pushed the door open part way and saw Maribel and Valeria standing by Jackie's bed. Valeria set a small green cosmetics bag and a new box of needles on the bedside table. Jackie was still unconscious, unmoving, her mouth slack and open.

"¿Será suficiente?" Maribel asked as Valeria opened the green cosmetic bag.

Valeria extracted a small plastic baggie of brown powder tied off at the top. "Sí, será."

They looked up and saw Kate. She pushed the door to the bedroom all the way open. A man had once kicked that same door in when Kate was a kid. She couldn't even remember the circumstances now, except she and Luke were in the bathroom getting ready for school when the door flew off its hinges behind them. She remembered the way it looked, ripped off at the top but still hanging on its bottom hinge, looking wrong like a dislocated shoulder. Luke and Kate stood silent at the sink, staring into their mother's room where the man now seemed surprised by his own action.

Jackie was calm, standing in her underwear and bra, one hand on her hip, a cigarette in the other. "Beau, you are going to buy me a new door," Jackie said. "And not a cheap one either."

Kate walked over and sat at the end of the bed near where her mother's feet made a small mound under the sheet. Jackie laid so still, her breathing barely perceptible. Kate laid her hand heavily on her mother's upturned wrist. Kate felt for Jackie's slow, weak pulse.

Maribel asked, "Maybe it's time to take her to the hospital? She can't argue about it anymore."

Kate shook her head. "She hates hospitals." She held her open palm out to Valeria.

Maribel sat down next to Kate on the bed. Valeria handed her the bag of brown powder.

"Is this all we can get her? We are out of the prescriptions?"

Maribel nodded. "Unless she goes to the hospital."

Kate struggled to speak. "If she gets really bad, I mean worse than she is…"

"Entiendo," Valeria said. "If she needs it, I will."

"She wouldn't want to be like this," Kate said. "I'm not saying that you should…I just don't want her to be…I don't want her to…I know we didn't get along—"

"She is your mother," Maribel interrupted.

Kate felt the warmth of Maribel's arm touching hers where they sat together. "Yes."

They missed the worst of rush hour in Atlanta. Flying down I-85 through the middle of the city, the cars moved like links of the same chain, frighteningly close together to be moving as fast as they were. Kate tried to keep the Audi in sync with the other traffic as the cars moved together under and over the tall concrete overpasses, flickering tail lights flashing alongside the lights of video billboards.

"Don't speed." Maribel knitted her fingers together nervously in the passenger seat. A paper atlas of the fifty states laid open in her lap to the two-page, full-country view.

"This is the speed limit." Kate let up from seventy to sixty-five. "This guy is right on me."

Maribel leaned to look in the mirror on her side of the car. "We cannot get pulled over."

As they moved through the long state of Alabama, the highway was surrounded by fields. The reduction in traffic made Kate feel like she had more room to breathe, but Maribel was getting more and more agitated in the passenger seat, shifting and readjusting.

"You can drive faster now."

"You said not to get pulled over."

"I know, but I hate this place. I hate it so much."

"I'll do ten over. No one will stop me for that."

Kate and Charlie had watched the Hurricane Katrina coverage together the previous summer. He pointed out that the most historic places in the city like the French Quarter had been spared. Now as Kate followed Maribel's directions, off the exit ramp, she knew they were not in that part. What she and Maribel drove through now was destroyed. Most houses were missing a roof here, front porches and the lower part of the siding ripped off there. Even the intact houses were boarded up. FEMA trailers dotted the muddy landscape. They were parked next to foundations missing their houses completely.

Wreckage was everywhere. Tires, refrigerators, lawnmowers tipped upside down and covered in dried mud. Occasionally a dog would cross the road with no regard for moving vehicles. There were hardly any other cars, hardly any people in the houses as far as Kate could tell.

Maribel pointed to an intersection in the road where a couch tipped onto its back, sun bleached, served as a strange roundabout.

"Turn right." Maribel reached into her purse and rubbed a floral smelling lotion into her skin, then pressed the back of her hand to her nose, trying to block out the smell that was seeping in through the Audi's vents.

Kate knew the smell of rot. Hydroponic systems that needed to be flushed. Vases full of stagnant water that need to be dumped. The smell in turkey and hog houses carried several levels of stench, one acidic and sharp that burned the nose and another more pungent, both the smell of the excrement of living things. She had not experienced a smell worse than any of those until now. She cut the AC so the vents wouldn't blow in the reeking scent. She held her hand to her nose, which smelled like soap from a gas station in Mobile.

For a few blocks, Maribel and Kate were behind a pickup truck driving with a group of workers seated around the rim of the truck bed. The road was rippled and broken in places, and as they hit bumps, the men gripped the metal sides to keep from falling off.

Kate looked down to the piece of paper that contained the directions Maribel was using. Kate recognized Smith's neat block letters. Maribel directed Kate to pull into a driveway, or at least what Kate thought used to be a driveway. In front of them, one house was still standing although the two others next door had fallen down into themselves.

"You stay here."

"What are we doing?"

"Open the trunk."

In the rearview mirror, Kate watched as Maribel lifted out the extra-long pink duffle bag against which Kate had nestled her own when they loaded the trunk back at Jackie's house. As Maribel struggled to lift the bag, Kate heard the unmistakable sound of metal against metal. Kate watched as Maribel walked up to the sagging front porch, the duffle bag's weight forcing her into a lean.

"Fuck," Kate said out loud in the quiet tomb of the car. She realized it was probably guns, some of which were likely the ones she and her mother had purchased at Walmart.

Maribel knocked and waited. Finally, the metal screen door, which was nearly rusted through at the bottom, swung out. Kate couldn't see the person who opened it. Maribel said something, then waited as the door swung back shut.

A few minutes later Maribel finally went inside with the pink bag. A girl, maybe in her early teens, with a flowing yellow cotton skirt and tiny white halter top opened the screen door. She walked to the edge of the porch and stared directly at Kate. She twirled a handful of snarled blonde hair around her fingers.

There were more guns in that heavy bag than what Kate and Jackie had purchased. Jackie had no need of money anymore, so maybe this was the desire to pull off one last con. It was Smith who would be looking for the influx of cash from selling that many firearms. Then there was Maribel who might have no choice. Then again, maybe it was all about money. Surely Maribel needed it too, and Jackie could just be operating out of force of habit for wanting profit. If Jackie, Maribel, and Smith were behind selling firearms, it could all be for different reasons.

When Maribel got back in the car, Kate saw the tears forming at the edges of Maribel's eyes. "Are you okay?"

"Let's just drive."

Kate put the car in reverse and backed out of the dried mud yard. She looked in the rearview mirror. The girl stood on the porch, following them with her eyes.

By Lafayette, Louisiana, Kate couldn't drive anymore. The wet shine of the streets shimmered under the traffic lights after a heavy rain storm that had slowed them down as they tried to find a motel. Inside the La Quinta's lobby, Kate worried about what would happen when she tried to use Charlie's credit card. There had to be an end point. Maribel placed cash on the desk for the clerk before Kate had to find out.

The next day, Maribel and Kate were up early, hitting the road again before anyone was even at the front desk of the motel to check them out, or at least the night clerk was asleep in a back room somewhere. Kate could feel them sinking down deeper into a part of what she knew was her country but felt completely foreign to her. In Shreveport, the swampy grasslands that lined the bodies of water they flew by rose up so high, seeming to threaten to flood over into the highway.

In Eastern Texas, among the tall trees and fields alongside the ribbon of grey asphalt they followed, Kate had not expected such a bright, vivid green. She had to wipe away the smears of insects with the washer fluid until it ran dry, clouds of them thunking against the windshield. East of Dallas, still surrounded by the green, Maribel started talking more freely now that Atlanta, Alabama, and the drop in New Orleans were behind them. She talked about her children, what they had been like as babies. The girl was the best sleeper. The oldest the best eater. The youngest boy had a tendency to crawl right out of the house if you weren't watching him.

Kate listened and felt a pulsing against her skin where she still kept the piece of paper with Anna's address. Something about hearing these details of Maribel's children made Kate feel empty and unsettled. She knew no information like this about someone she felt was hers.

By the time Texas started to dry out, the sky growing large and vacuous, the vegetation losing its green for shades of tan and red-brown, Kate felt like a desert herself.

They stopped in San Antonio only six hours from Lafayette, earlier than they expected because Kate wasn't feeling all that well.

In the motel parking lot, a chain link fence surrounded an empty, stained concrete basin. A blue tarp had come untied and blown halfway back across the empty pool making a rustling noise when the hot breeze picked up. A haggard looking couple sat on the ground, backs up against the chain link fence. They watched Kate and Maribel with hollow stares, but their eyes eventually came to rest on the Audi and stayed there. After she got the room key from the front office, Kate saw the couple against the fence was actually younger than she thought at first, maybe even teenagers.

"I need a shower, but do you want to go first?" Kate asked once they were in the room.

"No, you go ahead," Maribel turned the dials on the window unit.

In the bathroom, Kate looked at herself in the mirror. Her hair was dirty, her skin oily. The white tank top she was wearing was yellowed under the arms. Kate turned the cold water on. The Audi might look out of place here, but she was standing out less and less since coming south from Cambridge a few weeks ago. Before her shower, she took the piece of paper with Anna's address and laid it carefully on the edge of the sink, first making sure the surface wasn't wet.

When Kate came out of the bathroom, Maribel was kneeling down beside one of the beds praying. She held a small pewter crucifix and mouthed words, rocking back and forth slightly.

Kate slipped under the sheet in her bed as quietly as possible.

When Maribel stood, she said, "I can't get the AC to work. Do you want to ask for another room?"

That would probably make her feel better, but being out of the car was already helping. Kate welcomed the feeling of being flat after being in the car so long. "No. It's okay."

Maribel flipped on the TV and found a Spanish channel. She watched some kind of dating show for a while before going into the bathroom, leaving the door open behind her. Kate watched through the bathroom door as Maribel ran the hand towels and washcloths under cold water. She handed Kate half of the supply.

"This is what we did on hot nights."

"We did this too, me and my brother," said Kate. "We used to freeze them."

Maribel looked around the room. "It would be better if we had a fan."

Kate watched Maribel take her hair down from the tight bun she had kept it in all day. They could not have even passed as sisters. Kate felt the flimsiness of the story she was supposed to tell at the border. *These kids who look nothing like me, who look at me like I am a complete stranger, yes, officer they are mine.*

"Maribel, are you sure this is going to work?"

"If you want air conditioning, we have to change rooms."

"That's not what I meant."

Maribel was quiet for a moment. "It will work."

Kate pulled up the bottom of her shirt and put a wet towel across her stomach. "How do you know?"

Maribel turned and searched Kate's face. Kate saw in that moment again what she held over Maribel. It wasn't intentional, but it was woven into what Kate was able to do that Maribel could not. It was buried in what Kate could just as easily decide to not do. Kate had all the power standing between Maribel and the thing she wanted most.

"I can't think about it not working." Maribel turned off the TV. The room was completely dark. "I think about my children. That is all I think about."

FIFTEEN

IN EL PASO, they waited. The takeout boxes piled up as Maribel had requested no cleaning services. She did not want people coming in and out of the room. Kate swam in her black underwear and bra in the motel's overly warm kidney bean-shaped pool, floating on her back, looking up into the cloudless sky. She felt suspended and immobile even outside of the pool.

Finally, on their third morning, the package they had been waiting for arrived. As Kate opened the FedEx envelope, Maribel sat next to her at the rickety dinette set by the motel room's window. Kate removed her first ever Massachusetts driver's license with the photo she had taken at the Walmart photo lab. She found the fake registration in her name for the Audi. Also inside were four plastic passes the same size as the driver's licenses except SENTRI was printed across the top. Last out of the envelope was a small electronic square with instructions to affix it to the vehicle's windshield.

"I asked him for passports," Kate said.

"These are fine. SENTRI passes get you through faster anyway." Maribel took the cards and looked down at the pictures of the children. The genders and ages were right, but that was about it.

"Do they look enough like your kids?" Kate asked.

Maribel had reached out to a woman she once placed on the crew at a cleaning company that specialized in office parks in town. Her children were with her, roughly similar ages to Maribel's, so she could get official passport photos made.

Maribel nodded although Kate thought she looked unsure. "Tomorrow is Sunday. Less traffic so less border guards working. That is the day to go."

Maribel took out a map she had drawn herself with straight black lines of marker. "There are a few bridges, but someone like you would go Bridge of the Americas. No toll and safer."

Kate watched as Maribel underlined different words in her step-by-step written directions below the map.

"You are not going very far into the city. Just a few exits, then it's not far from the highway. You go to this address." She underlined it three times. "This is my mother's house."

She took a plastic sandwich bag out from her purse. It was filled with cash "Please give her this."

Kate pulled the plastic bag toward her on the table. "I will."

Maribel continued, "At the border on the way back, you say your husband is Mexican, that they have been visiting their abuela. They know they have to pretend that you are their mother until they see me."

Maribel took a diamond ring and wedding band out of her pocket and slid them across the table.

"And they speak English?"

Maribel looked at Kate like she was trying to decide something. "Maybe my oldest remembers some."

"My mother said they did." Kate felt heat rising up in her cheeks.

Maribel looked down and circled an exit number with her pen. "Samuel is still taking English in school. I think."

"What happens if the guard speaks Spanish and I don't understand?"

"Then the kids will answer."

"What if the question is for me?"

"Just answer everything in English, and they will switch."

"What if they keep talking in Spanish though?"

"They won't."

"But they might."

"I don't know! I don't know what will happen. You have an expensive car, and you are American. You have SENTRI passes, so probably they won't even question you." Maribel pushed the papers back away from her. "Do you think I want you to be the one?"

Kate felt her body pulling away from the table, a desire to move away from all of this completely. "What does that mean?"

"It means you have what those guards are looking for. But it's not like you did anything. You aren't smarter. You didn't work harder. You just get away with more."

Kate was losing her patience. Her worry and fear about what she was about to do was morphing into anger. "Do you want me to save them or not?"

Maribel slammed her fist down on the table causing the fake engagement ring to jump. "They didn't need saving until your country built an impassable border."

"I said before, I'm not responsible for what the government decides to do."

"We don't have time for a lesson on the political system." Maribel's voice was hot with rage.

Kate shook her head and looked around the motel room. All of it was sad and worn, the two double beds with the intricately patterned chintz bedspreads intended to hide stains, the beige wallpaper that brightened up the room somewhat but had an orange smear in a place near the entrance to the bathroom. "All of this is weak. I've been saying that since the beginning. We don't even look like each other."

"Yes, that's the point. We both have dark hair and dark eyes, but you are a bit lighter with the right face. And that makes all the difference in what they will let you do that I cannot."

Kate picked up the ring from where it sat on the table. It was too light to be real. "I will get them. I told you I would, and I will. I'm just trying to think through what could go wrong before it does."

Maribel took a deep breath. "Just don't change your mind."

That night, lying in the hotel bed, Kate watched a reality show about fishermen off the coast of Gloucester. She could hear Maribel on the phone in the bathroom. Kate guessed she must be talking to her mother. Maribel's voice was softer, sweeter than Kate had heard it before, so maybe it was one of her children. She heard the moment when Maribel started crying.

Kate took out her phone and texted Anton. *Thx* was all she sent.

Kate put her cell phone down on the box with Mrs. Newkirk's silver set. When they arrived in El Paso, Maribel had told her not to leave anything of value in the car. So the cardboard box tied with fabric strips, which she had taken from her mother's bed out of spite, was set on the floor beside the hotel bedside table.

Kate returned her attention to the fishermen pulling in a cod catch. She wondered if the longer they stayed out at sea, the harder it was to come back in. Or maybe, they were so homesick, they gunned it full throttle all the way into the shore, hull packed with ice and fish. The fishermen on the screen were fighting about their fuel levels and how long they should stay out at sea.

Kate's phone vibrated on top of the box. She saw it was Luke. She had not heard from him since the Maryland gas station. He called two more times. She didn't touch the phone until she saw the notification for the voicemail.

When she listened to the message, she heard Luke sounding tired, his voice far away. "Katie, call me. Charlie reported his car stolen. Please call me."

She switched off the television. Maribel had turned on the shower. Through the thin wall, Kate listened to the sound of the water splash. She pulled the cotton blanket over her and put her head under the pillow. She felt suspended for a moment.

Instead of responding to Luke, she texted Anton.

I could have used some license plates.

Almost immediately he replied, *I only work in paper.* Then a few minutes later, *there are plates everywhere*

She thought about it, but that seemed to carry its own risk, going out in the parking lot and unscrewing someone else's plates. Who knew what was behind those plates, who knew if someone would see her.

If she had more time, she could figure it out. If she had more time, she could have figured out how to get clean plates. If she had more time. For a while there she had so much time it had spread out endless in front of her. Now, everything was compressing.

At first, this return home was about getting the information she wanted, a negotiation with Jackie. But in what was likely her last moment of consciousness, Jackie had willingly turned over to Kate what she wanted.

She now knew where Anna was, but somehow Kate increasingly felt worse. Now that she had the information she'd tried so hard to obtain, Kate felt reuniting with Anna might be part of a dream, not something good for anyone in reality, especially her child. Seeping in with this rising worry was the grating bedrock of another realization. Despite the fact she was getting to know and like Maribel, Kate doubted she liked anyone enough to drive a stolen vehicle across an international border where guards looked for any excuse to pull you out of line at the checkpoint.

SIXTEEN

AT THE MOMENT Jackie took her last, jagged breath, she held in the shape of her open mouth the final word in a long argument. It was her apology for Kate, although no one would ever expect such a thing from Jackie. Kate was not there to hear it, but her brother was.

Luke had come home to stop his sister, to bring her back from the edge. He was too late to find Kate, but he did find Jackie. She could no longer speak. He bent forward toward her sunken form, his mother a broken body aged far beyond her years, barely breathing. He tried to make sense of what she was struggling to say, but he could make no meaning from the hissing sound that was like the deflating of a raft.

At that very moment, Kate drove the stolen Audi across the arching curve of the overpass as she eased toward the Bridge of the Americas. The arches were smooth and rounded and contrasted with what was further in the distance, the angled and craggy back of the desert mountains. From the overpasses, she could see the two cities, starkly different, but running into each other. El Paso was taller with more varied building heights, office towers and hotels, most the color of sandstone in the midday sun. Juárez's buildings were closer together, not varying much in height but different in color: pale blue and pink and faded green.

She read sign after sign that offered options for exiting before the border. She kept following the straight white arrows pointing to Juárez. She noticed other signs. Signs that warned about bringing produce across the border. A sign only in Spanish with an icon of a bee. A picture of a gun with a red line through it.

As she approached the first set of gates for customs, an arrow illuminated green and let the car two in front of her through. If it turned red, you were inspected. Maribel had explained this was the stop that you would be checked to see if you had anything you had to declare.

Kate watched as a delivery truck in front of her slowed. A red arrow. An official came out of the booth and pointed the truck to the right lane to be inspected.

When Kate pulled toward the lowering arm of the gate, a man in a neon yellow vest held his hand out to slow her before the light blinked green and the gate lifted again.

Maribel said the second stop was the more nerve wracking one, a military checkpoint that routinely pulled people looking for drugs, weapons, cash. She said they were most likely to stop vans and SUVs with tinted windows. She said it would be much worse going back north. Off to the side of the gate was a building where a few cars were lined up, men in black uniforms opening trunks and leaning inside the vehicles. Kate was careful to keep the muscles in her face loose, so she would not look anxious. They waved her through, and she drove into Mexico.

Immediately across the border, people selling goods crossed between medians forcing the cars to slow down. Mobile phone cases, mops, newspapers. Kate jumped when a woman in the lane reached out and knocked on the hood of her car, a child in tow behind her and a baby wrapped and tied around her chest. The woman held her hand out to Kate, cupped and empty. Kate didn't unroll her window.

Maribel had not been in her city for two years, but the directions were clear. Kate drove first through a commercial area with a Santander bank, restaurants, auto body shops and other businesses she couldn't identify from the signs. There were some empty lots closed off behind chain link fences where bushy green bunches of weeds grew. Most everywhere else seemed busy, men up on ladders making repairs, people walking along the sidewalks. Music pulsed from a storefront then was eventually replaced with the sound of another song pumping from the windows of a truck heading the opposite direction.

Soon she was navigating wide residential streets with stucco buildings. There were fewer people here, although it wasn't deserted. A woman pulling a wire shopping trolley loaded with groceries waited at a corner for Kate to pass so she could cross. A man a block ahead bicycled by with his shirttail floating behind him. Wrought iron fences connected walls painted lime green, aqua blue, bright pink, along with more subdued tans and beiges. Iron grates, many with varying, intricate designs, covered most of the windows. Cars were parked along the road, some of their windshields coated in a fine layer of dust. At the end of most blocks where signs read *alto*, she slowed to stop. Trees grew near the buildings, sometimes reaching across the street to touch a partner's branches arching from the other side.

Within ten minutes, Kate passed a grey cinderblock building with three red metal garage doors, a landmark in Maribel's directions. She saw graffiti of a red and black snake twisting up the cinderblock between the closed doors along with tagged letters so curled and stylized in their script, she couldn't make them out. Right after that was the address she was looking for, a single-story square house in a row with two others that looked similar in size and shape.

Kate parked on the other side of the street. In front of her, three men played cards at a folding table in the shade of a large umbrella-shaped tree growing from a space in the sidewalk. They stared at her, still protecting their hands from each other, curling their cards toward themselves. One of the men wore a white tracksuit and mopped sweat from his forehead with his free hand. Even in the heat, his tracksuit jacket was zipped up under his chin. A second man wore black jeans and a black T-shirt with highlighter yellow Adidas. The third person was a teenage boy in a baggy white basketball shorts and a grey tank top, his hair buzzed close to his scalp.

As Kate got out of the Audi then reached back in for the small backpack containing the cash Maribel had asked her to carry, the men continued to watch her. Kate walked toward the house, not looking at them but still feeling their eyes. She reached the iron gate at the front. She pulled on the latch, but it was locked. Kate felt pulsing adrenaline like sharp, shooting arrows pumping through her as she looked into the courtyard on the other side of the gate. It was littered with abandoned things, a broken broom, some browning aloe plants growing in plastic buckets, a rusty pink bike, a faded plastic Big Wheel tricycle, a deflated rubber ball. Surveying the courtyard here reminded her of only a few weeks ago, although it seemed like much longer, when she first arrived in Jackie's yard, how she had tried to understand what was happening in the house based on what was strewn outside.

Metal clattered against metal when she pulled again on the gate. Kate turned to see the teenager coming toward her from the card table. She stepped back as he reached through the metal bars and found a latch at the top of the gate and swung it open. She nodded in thanks, but worried when he walked through the courtyard in front of her. He motioned for her to follow him. She saw now a thin scar running across the back of his scalp, a line where the hair no longer grew. He pushed the front door of the house open. As they entered the cooler, more humid air inside, Kate recognized the earthy, buttery smell of fried cornmeal. She was sun blind, everything burnt blue in the relative darkness, but managed to see a big German shepherd that slept motionless in a narrow front hall. She put her hand against the plaster wall to steady herself as she stepped around the dog.

The teenager turned back to Kate. "That's Felix. Don't worry. He's nice."

Kate felt relief that the kid spoke her language. The imagined variables of disaster that came from her not being able to communicate in the right words at the right time worried her the most about all of this.

Once inside an open square-shaped room, the teenager called out, "Señora, ella está aquí buscándola!"

Kate heard a woman call out in acknowledgement from behind the only closed door Kate saw leading from the main room. A stove was against the far wall next to a vintage-looking refrigerator. A table similar to the Formica one Jackie had in her kitchen was positioned near the wall with the appliances. Under the table was a red and white soccer ball. The teenager walked over to the stove and lifted the lid off one of the pots. A plume of steam escaped as he leaned in closer to smell what was simmering.

When the woman emerged from the bedroom rolling a black suitcase, Kate saw the resemblance immediately. She was the same height with the same body shape as Maribel. She wore a long skirt, with a form fitting blouse that showed the curve at her waist. Her hair was almost like her daughter's, but salt and pepper, grey spun against black, twisted into a fat knot at the base of her neck. Just like the three grandchildren who followed her, Maribel's mother had the same beautiful, nearly black eyes. The oldest boy followed first. Tall and thin for thirteen, Kate recognized him as Samuel. He held the hand of the smallest one, Rodrigo. The middle girl, Sofia, followed them holding a black puppy. The puppy playfully nipped at her long hair, which was the same wavy texture as her mother.

The children stood stiffly, hanging back behind their grandmother as she approached Kate. Maribel's mother held out her hand.

Kate took the Ziploc bag of cash from her backpack. She handed it to Maribel's mother.

"Gracias," Maribel's mother said. As she took the bag, she then pointed to herself. "Dolores."

"Kate."

Dolores nodded. Her eyes were filling with tears. She wiped them away before they could fall.

Kate wanted to say something about how well Maribel was doing, but Kate stopped herself. She didn't know how to say anything she wanted to in Spanish, but even if the teenager still at the stove could translate for her, Kate also knew that knowing your daughter is "better off" doesn't make the loss any less. Kate chose to say nothing because she knew that's what she could offer this woman who had not wanted Maribel to leave in the first place, who was now losing the grandchildren she had been raising.

Kate turned to the children and smiled while pointing to name each of them. "Samuel. Sofia. Rodrigo."

Only Rodrigo met her with a smile. "Ese soy yo!"

Dolores stepped forward and held Kate's hand. Her hands were warm but dry. "¿Tienes hambre? ¿Quieres comer?"

Kate shook her head. She didn't want to be rude, but she wanted the crossing over as soon as possible. "Thank you, but we need to go." Maribel had told Kate this was the time of day with the least amount of border officers, a double win with it being Sunday.

Dolores reached out and took hold of Kate's hands. Her large eyes narrowed as she began talking faster. Kate didn't understand, so both she and Dolores looked over to the teenager who was helping himself to whatever was in the pot on the stove.

Without turning around from serving himself, the teenager said, "She says, 'Tell my daughter that if anything happens to them, I will never forgive her.'"

Kate swallowed hard and squeezed back against Dolores's warm hands. "Tell her, I promise I will make sure they are safe."

The boy translated, but Dolores did not look relieved. She slipped her hands away from Kate's and turned to the children. She tried to take the puppy from Sofia. The girl started crying, which made Rodrigo cry. The only thing Kate could understand of what their grandmother was saying to them was how many times she said "Mama." Sofia shook her head and cried even harder.

Dolores wiped at her own cheeks. Samuel leaned down in front of Sofia and held her by the shoulder. He spoke softly to his sister, looking her directly in the eyes. Sofia, although she kept sniffling, handed the puppy to her grandmother who turned it loose on the floor. The puppy skittered away, its claws clicking against the shiny ceramic tiles as it ran over to the boy at the stove.

Samuel unzipped the side of the black suitcase. He handed a white teddy bear to Rodrigo, then pulled out a rag doll with long, black yarn braids and handed it to the girl. Sofia would not take it at first. Kate guessed it was a poor substitute for the puppy. Samuel spoke in hushed tones for a moment. Finally, Sofia took the doll and both of the younger children clutched the toys to their chests.

Dolores walked toward Kate and tipped the handle of the roller suitcase toward her. Then she held all three of her grandchildren against her for just a moment, pressing them so hard the littlest one made a squeaking sound like a mouse. "Dios está con ustedes," she said into them before letting them go, disappearing back through the door into the other room.

Kate's chest felt as if it might break open leaving Dolores behind in the house, but she made herself move forward. She pulled the black roller suitcase as she followed the teenager back out through the courtyard. Maribel's three children trailed behind her. Outside in the bright sunlight, she saw across the street where her car was parked that the two men in the striped tracksuits who had been sitting with the teenager when she arrived were now leaning inside the Audi's trunk.

"What are you doing?" Kate asked as the gate shut behind her. No one answered her. She stopped in the middle of the street, putting her arms out to hold the children behind her.

Two black handguns were on the pavement just under the bumper of the Audi. At first, Kate thought the two men were putting the guns into the car, but she quickly realized they were taking things out. Kate didn't know what to do as she watched them pull up the felt flooring that covered the spare tire. They removed the spare tire and then used a drill to unbolt the metal panel that housed it. They placed the metal frame from her trunk on the ground behind them. They pulled out a heavy black duffel bag from that space, which made a metal clinking sound.

The teenager walked over to the car and opened the front door. "Hey, what are you doing?" Kate asked him again.

"Don't worry about it. We're lightening your load. Just wait there." He crouched down between the open door and the driver's seat. He felt along the plastic interior panel of the door. He slid his finger under an indention at the very bottom of the door panel. He pulled gently at first then harder until the panel popped off. He crouched down and put his arm far inside the door. He yanked hard on something and eventually pulled out a bundle wrapped in plastic grocery bags. He pulled back the layers of plastic, checking the package, and Kate saw more black metal.

It had to be Smith. Her body felt like it was filling with concrete. In her statue stillness in the street, the children behind her, Kate understood in a flash of fear what he had done. He must have loaded the Audi with the guns when he took the car to change the oil the night before she left. Smith knowingly saddled Kate with cargo that, if discovered, would send her to prison for longer than he ever served.

It wasn't that Smith had broken the law that was tearing through her. She shared her mother's ambivalence toward what was allowed or not allowed. What was making her feel like her knees might buckle, like she might never get off that side street in Juárez, was that Smith had used her. She might well have driven those weapons right across the border herself for the right price or even more likely, the right reason. Instead, he kept her in the dark. He kept telling her how smart she was, how he needed her, but she had been nothing but stupid.

When the men had what they wanted, they put the panels back in place. One of them held the back door for the children as they climbed in.

The teenager came up to Kate and placed his hand lightly on her shoulder. He could only be a couple years older than Samuel who was buckling his little brother into the middle of the back seat. "You remind Maribel, if she wants to be free, she has to finish the job. We can always find them if we need to."

Kate moved out from under the teenager's bony hand. She started the car and pulled away as fast as she could.

A few minutes later, she stopped at an intersection, about to leave the quiet neighborhood for the busier road that would take them back to the border. As she waited for a good moment to turn left across the traffic, she glanced in the rearview mirror. She only caught it for a second, so briefly that she could have convinced herself she imagined it, Rodrigo with his hand under his little T-shirt scratching at something. Samuel reached over and gently pulled his brother's hand back down to rest, which revealed briefly a corner of a plastic bag against the boy's skin, affixed there with the edge of matte silver duct tape. She could have willed herself to unsee it, except there was Samuel looking at her in the rearview, eyes steady, not revealing any emotion, not exactly a challenge but holding a silent gaze that said, "We have to keep going."

Prickly heat, dry heat, radiant heat, scorching heat. Waving-up-from-the-asphalt-like-a-mirage heat. White heat. Crackling heat. Hotter-than-Hades heat. Kate had known heat her entire life, but she had never felt heat like this. As she approached the DCL lane for SENTRI pass users, her heart pounded. The children in the back seat stayed nearly motionless for the half mile of traffic that inched forward to the border. Street vendors walked back and forth slowing down the traffic to a standstill. A man sold a wooden ball-catching game, demonstrating while he wore a board attached to his back displaying bright colored yo-yos. A boy about Rodrigo's age offered varied colors of carnations in cellophane. A woman held a flat box of digital alarm clocks in front of her. On either side of the lane where they inched forward, a girl and a boy sold chicles. Each child held a box containing colorful packages of the gum. Kate could not tell if the two children were competitors or a coordinated sales team as they moved past the cars. Rodrigo pointed and expressed an interest. His older brother told him no.

When they were at a complete stop in the traffic, Kate tried to take a deep breath and looked in the rearview mirror at herself. The children watched her from the backseat. She ran her fingers through her hair. "Estará bien," she said.

She was losing track of time as they waited, not because it was going by quickly, but because her heart rate was distracting her, her inability to breathe fully. As they made their way to the front of the line, the entry gate was flanked by a large silver booth with a dark black window that was reflecting the sun. The gate swung up, and the guard sitting inside waved her through. Now they were on a bridge. To Kate's left she saw the quarter mile of stopped cars not in the DCL lane.

"Estará bien," Kate said again. The children did not respond.

Finally, they reached American customs. The guard raised his hand to slow her as she approached. She took a deep breath and thought of all the lies she had told in her life, most of them without saying a word, just letting people believe something about her. She unrolled the Audi's window.

"Hello." She smiled wide, the way she knew usually worked and tipped her sunglasses up on her head.

"Hello, Miss." "He glanced at the kids in the back seat and corrected himself. "Ma'am. How long have you been in Mexico?"

"Just a few hours. I was picking up my kids from their abuela's house."

"Where does she live?"

Kate gave the address Maribel had told her to give. Not where Dolores lived, but a different place in the nicest parts of Juárez. Maribel said the false address was in one of the elite neighborhoods where those who had not left for El Paso or safer towns still lived behind guarded locked iron gates.

"Is this your car?"

"Yes."

"Can I please see your license and registration?"

"Sure," she said. She didn't know what happened when a vehicle was reported stolen, if they would somehow automatically know. Maybe all the security cameras bolted into the infrastructure of the gates could send images of the license plate numbers to be run through a system. She reached for the glove compartment and pulled the latch to let it drop open. Inside was an owner's manual and a flat piece of white paper, the fake registration for the Audi which put the car in Kate's name.

She held out the white paper trying to keep her hand steady, tipped at an angle so he could see the large engagement ring and wedding band.

The guard glanced at her registration then handed it back.

"These are you children?" he asked.

"Yes."

"Do you have IDs?"

"Yes, sir, I do."

She handed him the SENTRI passes and her fake license. The officer looked carefully at each one. He stooped to see into the back seat. Kate tried to not turn around like she was worried. In the mirror, she saw Samuel wave at the officer and say, "Hello!"

The officer came back to her window and said, "If you're from Massachusetts, why do you have SENTRI passes?"

"My husband teaches in the summer at UTEP. He's from Juárez and the children stay with my mother-in-law sometimes on the weekends." Kate kept her voice calm, slightly bored, devoid of the fear she actually felt pounding inside her chest.

She and Maribel had even looked up the name of a sociology professor at the University, but the officer didn't ask for her husband's name.

"Ma'am, please open your trunk."

As Kate reached down to find the latch, the officer walked behind the car. She heard him lift the felt lining to check the spare tire compartment. She choked on something that wasn't there and tried to catch her breath.

The guard finally shut the trunk and walked back to the driver's side window. He was pulling the black suitcase behind him.

"Don't worry. A lot of people with the SENTRI pass forget they have to have an empty trunk."

He placed it on the hood of the Audi and unzipped the bag. She watched as he pushed through what looked mostly like clothes. Through the windshield in front them, Kate and the children watched as he searched. He zipped it up and walked it around to the empty passenger seat.

"You're good to go ma'am. Drive safe."

Kate waited for the last gate to lift between Juárez and El Paso. As she followed the signs back to the highway that would lead her to the pink stucco motel with its kidney bean swimming pool and Maribel, Kate could feel the surge which came with being allowed to cross that border. She had been born on the wrong side of many things, but on the right side of an invisible line that allowed her a certain kind of wealth she never even realized she possessed.

Until that moment, Kate had never really thought about freedom, had never really felt it in her bones. She never thought what it really meant, being able to move from one building to another, to travel between towns, across highways, to stop at any restaurant or gas station you wanted. To make purchases, to have a conversation, an argument with a clerk, all out in the open. Those with citizenship held fistfuls of options as valuable and malleable as gold.

Kate had miscalculated many things. She had lost more than she had gained in the sum total of her twenty-six-years, but she could choose who she wanted to be with, choose where to return, choose who she would become from here on out. Everything felt infinite and possible, as she looked in the rearview mirror at the three children who were not hers, but she had brought them with her across that infamous line anyway.

"Welcome to America," she said to them.

SEVENTEEN

KATE WATCHED AS Maribel took a pair of sharp scissors and lined her children up in front of where she sat on her hotel bed. She spoke softly in Spanish, quickly, almost like she was singing a song. Starting with the oldest, one by one, she lifted up her children's shirts and cut through the duct tape. After Maribel unraveled four flat packages of brown powder from Samuel's abdomen, she stacked each one in a flowered, canvas shoulder bag.

Her tongue as dry as cotton in her mouth, Kate asked, "Did my mother know about this?"

Maribel didn't respond as she began to work on the packages taped to her daughter.

"Smith too?" Kate sat down on her bed, the mattress sagging under her weight. Kate pressed her hands to her hot forehead. She thought she might throw up.

"Yes, everyone knew." Maribel said, her eyes focused on the scissors, making sure not to graze her Sofia's skin. "It was safer if you didn't know."

Rodrigo reached out to pull the end of a lock of his sister's hair. Maribel caught the little boy's hand and placed it gently back at his side.

"What if they caught us?"

"They wouldn't search someone like you," Maribel said. She removed the final package from Sofia and placed it in the bag. Released, Sofia jumped on to the bed next to her brother Samuel though he made no acknowledgment of her. He reached for the remote control and started flipping through channels.

"What if there had been dogs?"

Maribel did not respond as she drew Rodrigo closer to her.

"Who's idea was it? My mother or Smith?"

"What does it matter?"

"It matters."

Maribel kissed Rodrigo on the forehead, pressing her lips for a long time to the boy's skin. "They both made it happen."

They were silent, except for the television until Maribel was done with Rodrigo. Then Samuel put down the remote, walked over to the other bed and picked up the teddy bear and the rag doll with the braids, and brought them to his mother.

"You wouldn't let your kids go with a coyote, but you let them cross the border loaded with heroin? What kind of mother does that?" Kate's rage pounded in her head and threatened to close up her throat.

Maribel's eyes welled with tears, but her voice was steady and full of hate when she said, "You are not a mother. You don't know what I would do."

Maribel cut with slow precision through the bear's abdomen. She shushed the little cry that came from Rodrigo who was still near his mother watching. She pushed aside the filling revealing a gleaming, taped up bag of white powder tucked inside. Maribel looked over her shoulder to where Kate sat bewildered on the bed.

"Do you think this was what I wanted? I didn't have a choice.

I had to get them out before things got even worse. You don't understand the kind of people we are dealing with."

"But what if the border control found it? They would have taken them." Kate gestured at the children, the older two whose faces looked guarded understanding an argument was unfolding.

"Then they still would have gotten out. There are people I am much more scared of than the guards at the border."

"There had to be some other way."

"There wasn't. There was no time. You don't know. Once they decided they wanted you to come across with this, there were other people involved. People you have to give what they want."

Kate understood you often acted to quell the demands of your most dangerous enemy. She just hadn't realized until a minute before that the people she had finally accepted were "home" for her were still this kind of threat.

"So I didn't get to decide anything," Maribel said. "People like you decided this would happen. People like you carry most of the drugs over the border. The rest of us just try to stay alive. So don't ever forget it. You made this happen. And the people in my mother's house, the people getting involved with my son, the reason they have that power is because of the demand from people like you. So don't talk to me about what kind of mother does something. You would not know."

Before Maribel even finished putting away all the plastic bags Kate carried across the border, Kate left the motel room. She walked a few buildings down the busy road to a taqueria.

Luke had eradicated Mexican early on in his research of foods that might lead to their father. She welcomed the burn on the roof of her mouth. It tasted like revenge.

Let them rot, she thought. Let the mildew and humidity and kudzu come and cover Jackie's house, let it block out the light on Smith's greenhouses, let the weeds strangle his plants. Let them drown and sink down into the black creek. Smith. Maribel. Jackie. Luke. All of them could sink down into the darkness together for all she cared.

Kate had known it her entire life that people couldn't be trusted, but somehow, she kept losing the sharp focus of that fact. She needed to make herself remember that truth. People will lie to you. They will not tell you who your father is. They will bring a river of dangerous men through your house. They will take your baby across state lines and give her away. They might load your car with firearms to move them over a border to make more money when the crop can't produce enough income. They will ask you to break the law. While you sleep, they will riffle through your paperwork, the records which are the only way you can account for all you have gained, all you have lost. Sometimes, your mother will make you a drug mule in order to bring you home to her. Sometimes, your mother gives you up before she can even know you.

She felt herself flush, embarrassed that her mother and Smith had watched her delude herself about how she could walk back into the life of her eight-year-old daughter. Kate realized just how much she had been lying to herself since her mother had called her home. Anna's legal parents weren't going to let Kate get close to that child, not now when she was only eight. Probably not ever. If she went there, if she followed the lines on a map, they wouldn't let her in the door. It didn't matter that something had been off about the entire thing, that as a minor she couldn't sign that paperwork. That organization bent the rules, served its mission above all else: stop girls from having abortions and take big money from people who can pay the fees. Jackie, if she was herself, could have helped Kate cut through all of that, figure out how to pull the bottom out of what had been agreed to but not handled properly under the eyes of the law.

Her mind was spinning, thinking like her mother. Kate stopped herself thinking of her daughter. Part of the reason she had given her baby up in the first place was because she knew she could not protect her from what someone with more resources could. Anna's parents had the ability to protect her from everything. Strangers were just for starters. It was heartbreaking to consider, but probably true that Kate could be a better mother by not being any kind of mother at all. Maribel was right. She wasn't one.

Kate was relieved her daughter was safe. She was also broken apart. She was going to have to live with the opposing weight of both.

Like so many times before in her life, Kate returned to a place she wasn't sure she should be because there was nowhere else to go. Kate had been betrayed, but Maribel was right about a lot. Kate sat in the taqueria for hours, until they were closing. She thought things through long enough to accept how far down this path they already were, at least accept it enough to go back to the motel.

Inside the room, Maribel sat on her bed, her face swollen and red from crying. Kate's stomach sunk. The room was too quiet. The children were gone. After all of this, someone had taken the kids, exacting his price for something.

"Where are they?" Kate asked.

"In the bathtub."

Kate heard then the splashing of the water in the bathroom where an argument erupted between Rodrigo and Sofia.

"And here," Maribel wiped under her eyes with the heel of her palm and pointed behind her in the bed. The oldest, Samuel, was asleep. Only his hair, still wet from his shower, was visible from under the covers. Kate hadn't noticed his shape when she came in. He was the quietest, even when Maribel touched him or seemed to be asking him something, he said very little.

"Then what's wrong?" Kate asked.

"Juan called," Maribel said. "Your mother died."

For a moment Kate stood motionless, confused. Then she felt a pain spread through her chest like a crack in a sheet of ice.

"I'm sorry. You should call your brother. Juan said he was there when she died."

"That can't be right."

"Juan said he was there."

Kate sat down on the bed next to Maribel, careful to avoid sitting on Samuel's feet. The hard mattress gave slightly, making them shift toward each other until their shoulders touched. Maribel laid her hand on top of Kate's where it rested at the edge of the bed. "I am sorry about what I said before. You *are* a mother. I know you have a child."

Kate felt dizzy, dehydrated, the heat from her walk from the restaurant back along the busy road still making her body pulse with heat. "No. I am sorry. I would have done the same thing you did to bring them back. If they were mine."

"Listen," Maribel said. She pointed at the flowered bag on the floor of the open motel closet full of heroin and cocaine. "I know some people in Memphis who can take that. It's supposed to go back to North Carolina, but I am not going to take my children back there. What comes next there is not good."

Kate shook her head. "You can't disappear with that. Won't they find you?"

"It's not disappearing, just going to a different person in the same chain. It's what the people you saw yesterday want."

Kate realized that meant Smith was getting cut out. He had used her, but she still felt the weight of what he might lose without the infusion of money he expected. Then she felt it fall away. The loyalty to him, the compensation she felt she owed him since leaving when he had been in prison, all of it slipped away. It was time to admit that Luke had been right all along. She and Smith were more likely to destroy than save each other.

"When I go to Memphis, I need you to keep my children," Maribel said.

"They're not going to like being separated from you again."

"It will only take a few days. Take them to a different hotel, maybe go north to Albuquerque, just in case. I have to keep them as safe as possible," Maribel said and squeezed Kate's hand. "I cannot risk taking them with me. I need you to do this one last thing."

Kate could see in Maribel's face that this was still hard. They still didn't trust each other fully, perhaps they had both seen too much to ever completely trust anyone, but Maribel was being forced to pick the person she distrusted the least.

"You know what I said to your mother when she first wanted to ask you to be the one to cross the border?" Maribel asked. "I told her it was better if it was someone else. That it could really be any attractive white-enough woman who also had a nice car. I said we could just rent a car, a Mercedes or something. Your mother kept insisting it had to be you."

"Because she wanted to get me arrested?"

"No. I told you. She wanted you back. She wanted you to come home. She just didn't know how to do that in the right way." Maribel moved her hand from Kate's arm and said, "It doesn't always look like love, but it is. It always is. I'm sorry she is gone."

She reached her hands into the back of the collar of her shirt. Her fingers stayed there for a moment working on something. Then she brought forward the gold heart locket. She reached down and took Kate's hand in hers, turning it to open the palm. She laid the heart in the center and let the thin chain pool around it.

Maribel went back into the bathroom to check on her younger children.

Kate thought about that for a while. How few people she had loved and how it did not look like what she thought it would. She called Luke and was shocked when he confirmed that what Maribel said was true. As soon as Charlie had reported the car stolen, Luke had come to Jackie's house to stop Kate before she did something irrevocable. He was too late for that, but he found Jackie just before she died.

Luke sounded tired but calm. "There are a lot of Mexicans here. I thought she hated Mexicans."

"I guess she changed," said Kate, clearing her throat.

"She gave me letters. From this guy named Bianchi. I mean she didn't give them to me, but they were marked with my name. I found them on her nightstand."

Luke was quiet for a moment and Kate could hear people in the background, dishes clanking. She imagined Luke standing in the kitchen, the landline phone against his ear. Who would be there with him? The men who relied on Jackie's kitchen for their daily meals? Smith, Lynette, Juan, Valeria, Nina, and maybe Carla, along with whoever else had come to pay their respects.

Luke continued, "I looked him up. He was an evangelical preacher. Travelled through where she was at college before she dropped out. From Atlantic City. He was Italian." He paused.

"I don't even like Italian food that much."

They were both quiet on the line for a moment before Luke said, "I don't think I'm going to be welcome with them anymore. I think I'm going to get cut out."

Kate knew Luke meant with Charlie's family. That was what she had sensed all along. Their place was impermanent, contingent on her playing a certain role and Luke playing another, and if they told the truth about who they really were, the invitations and access would be quickly removed.

"You don't need them," she said.

"But it was nice for a while."

"But it wasn't real."

"I know, but I liked it anyway."

Kate knew then her brother would be OK. He was home, if only for a bit. Her mother was gone. Her daughter was found but could never really be hers. Her heart ached because she and Smith were broken beyond repair. Also, she could kill him. If he was in front of her, she *would* kill him for putting her in that kind of danger.

She was truly on her own. She had nowhere to go. She was alive though. She was free, which she now understood was priceless. Maribel was right; it was too dangerous to go back to North Carolina. Besides, there was nothing left for her there. Again. From El Paso, Kate could go north. Or west. First, she would help Maribel with what she needed. Because for all their differences, Kate thought what they might have in common was being swept down river into rapids you weren't sure you could navigate through no particular fault of your own.

Kate's power might be limited, but she would do what she could to keep Maribel from going down under the surface.

EIGHTEEN

MARIBEL SUGGESTED THEY abandon the stolen Audi by the airport or at a scrap yard. Instead, Kate drove it to a used car lot with strings of red, white, and blue plastic triangles sagging in the heat. She hoped the forged registration from Anton would work, and it did. She negotiated for $14,000, much less than it was worth, but she also knew it was stolen. She didn't want the man who looked too old to still be working the lot, sweating in his green blazer, to run it through a database.

It was a risk, but she left the auto lot with the thick fold of one-hundred-dollar bills tucked in her backpack. She walked to the motel along the side of the road, which was a state highway lined with car lots and fast food restaurants. The packed dry soil was littered with broken metal and plastic headlights, bits of burnt out rubber, and discarded trash, soda bottles, tin cans empty of their once-sticky dip, crushed French fry boxes, all the labels faded from the same sun that beat down on Kate's bare shoulders and the top of her head. The traffic moved fast alongside her, sending her hair flying. Once, an expensive looking pickup truck slowed down beside her. The driver unrolled his window. She flipped him off. He shouted something then sped off.

When Kate came back into the motel room, Maribel was standing in front of the mirror at the sink outside of the bathroom cutting off locks of wet hair. Kate shut the hotel door behind her.

They looked at each other in the mirror.

"It looks nice on you," Kate said. "I can even it up for you in the back."

Maribel handed her the scissors. Kate smoothed her hand down the back of Maribel's head. Maribel looked very different in a pixie cut. It would help hide her well. From what exactly, Kate did not know. She held pieces between her middle and pointer fingers and used the scissor's points to blend the layers at the base of Maribel's skull.

"Thank you," Maribel said, her head still down so Kate could cut.

"I used to cut Luke's hair."

"No. I never said thank you for bringing my children. Thank you."

Kate and Maribel stood in the motel parking lot behind the trunk of the rental car Kate had picked up. Kate hugged Maribel, pressing her cheek against her short damp hair that smelled like the hotel shampoo. Maribel held Rodrigo like the toddler he was when she left. He was five now and long, pressed between them in their embrace. The other two were inside watching TV. Samuel had barely looked at Maribel when she held his head to her chest and kissed it.

"I'll sell the silver set today," Kate said. "I saw a pawn shop when I was walking back from the car lot."

"As much cash as possible," Maribel said and handed Rodrigo over to Kate. "Take care of them. Especially Samuel."

Kate took the weight of the boy and touched Maribel's arm.

"He'll come around."

She noticed that Maribel could not look back at them as she walked to the driver's side. To Rodrigo she said, "When your mom comes back we will have ice cream." She wasn't sure if he understood, but he seemed relatively at ease.

Back inside the hotel room, Samuel flipped through the channels on the TV. Kate put Rodrigo down on the bed next to his brother. Sofia started to get up off Kate's bed.

"Está bien," Kate said and patted the mattress. Sofia sunk back against the pillows.

Kate sat down next to the girl and pulled the box with the tied calico strips closer. She pushed the fabric off the edge and opened the cardboard flaps to see the silver set. Kate removed the teapot and set it on the bed. Sofia reached out and touched the engraved handle.

"Pretty, isn't it?" Kate said. "Bonita?"

Sofia nodded.

Kate pulled back the packing tape and many layers of bubble wrap. Underneath the plastic, the silver tray, creamer, and sugar bowl were each wrapped with muslin cloth. Kate laid each piece out on the bed in front of her. Except for the tarnished teapot that had been unwrapped longer by Jackie, the silver gleamed like stars against the motel sheet.

Kate touched the delicate, grooved handle on the lid of the sugar dish. If Mrs. Newkirk had polished all of this herself, it would have taken forever with her arthritis. It would have been painful. Even the inside of the sugar dish gleamed. Kate noticed something taped on the underside of the lid. She peeled back the corner of the piece of tape with her fingernail and pulled a folded piece of pink paper away. As she unfolded the pink piece of paper, a silver key fell out and clanked against the tray. Kate recognized Mrs. Newkirk's handwriting.

Box # 15674, Mountain Valley Bank, 125 Main Street, Walden, Colorado.

Kate did not know if it was her own voice or her mother's or Mrs. Newkirk expressing surprise in the words that came out of her mouth. "Well, I'll be."

In a way it was all three of them, and each saying the same thing: you never really know what's coming. Kate had underestimated Mrs. Newkirk's desire to have the last word, even from the grave.

NINETEEN

EVERY DAY SINCE they arrived, she and the children walked the land in Northern Colorado until the light was almost gone. Kate never realized before that sky like this existed. She had not known that mountains, even though they were miles away, could tower so high they scraped against the endless blue of an eternal sky.

Two of Mr. Newkirk's trucks that had come in to carry the timber away decades ago were still on the property, rusted out, and unusable. There were troughs cut into the earth, hard as fossils, at the entrance of the road.

Every night, she let the children climb up on the roof of the forest green 1997 Dodge Caravan bought from a different used auto lot in El Paso than where she sold the Audi. They huddled together on the metal roof and watched the sun set across Kate's land.

On their first night, sitting up on the minivan's roof, Kate heard the shivery sound of a rattlesnake. She looked down to the red dirt and saw it curl and uncurl in s-shapes, moving fast. Samuel saw it too. They looked at each other but didn't say anything to his younger siblings.

The four of them slept across the van's seats under sleeping bags and comforters, which Kate bought at a thrift store in Albuquerque on their way to the address written on the piece of paper Kate had found in the tea set. She slept surprisingly well.

When Kate had called Maribel from the El Paso motel to tell her about what she found in the silver, they both agreed it was a good idea to get out of El Paso anyway. They would meet in Colorado after Maribel unloaded in Memphis. By then Kate would know what the piece of paper from Mrs. Newkirk's silver set meant.

The first day Kate and the children had arrived at the Walden branch of the Mountain Valley Bank, she told the banker, "I'm just passing through." She handed him the little silver key that had been taped into the sugar dish.

"Your children look just like you." He wore a beige suit and cowboy hat and had smiled a lot, shaking her hand vigorously like they were old friends when he told her, "I'm Lyle. I have a boy about his age." He pointed to Rodrigo and held out a box of plastic wrapped lollipops. Kate did not correct him about the children because she didn't want to raise any kind of alarm.

Twenty minutes later, Kate still sat mostly speechless across the desk from Lyle who was trying to make her understand. The key taped to the lid of the sugar dish was for a safety deposit box. The box contained a deed to a hundred and sixty acres of land.

"It's an old timber parcel," he said again. He pulled up a map on his computer and turned the screen to show her the boundary lines of the property. "It's up there just about all the way to Wyoming."

The kids were on their third round of lollipops. Kate asked him to explain it one more time. He smiled patiently adjusting the leather strings connected by a piece of turquoise at the top button of his shirt. He read her the account information from his computer screen. The deeds had been changed to Kate's name ten months before, in September 2005. The land originally belonged to a Mr. Peter J. Newkirk who had left it to his wife, Mrs. Newkirk, upon his death. The land was to be passed to her two sons when she died. But then last September, Mrs. Peter J. Newkirk had changed the ownership to one Kathryn Robyn Jessup.

"You don't usually see someone change ownership while they're still living," Lyle said. "Maybe they arrange it for after their death, but not usually before."

Rodrigo had crawled up into Kate's lap, looking to see where the banker put the box of lollipops.

"I know where this is," Lyle said. "It's not too far from my people's reservation land. Sort of near Independence Mountain. Lots of the acreage over that way was stripped clean for timber, but some of it might have a good view of the mountain. Depending on what's between it and the peak."

Kate swallowed hard and adjusted Rodrigo in her lap. She wrapped her arms tighter around the boy's rib cage and cleared her throat. "What do people grow out here?"

"Grow? It's mostly livestock up that way. Some white retirees will try to live out there, yurts or trailers, one man with one of those communes with the mud houses that are off the grid. But that's further south from this." Lyle handed Rodrigo another lollipop. He tapped the drawing of the parcel's boundary lines on his computer screen again. His fingernail on the glass made tinny clicking sounds. "The land is just about valueless when it's remote as yours. Then again, that means you can do whatever you want."

They had already been on the land a few days, but Kate knew

Samuel was still not sleeping much at night. Kate woke up to find the reclined passenger seat empty. She saw through the windshield he was sitting on the minivan's hood.

She pulled herself up next to him as the metal of the hood gave a bit. The night sounded different here. There was not the sound of insects, not in the same volume or at the same pitch anyway. It was quieter overall, except for the coyotes yipping and howling at each other or at something bigger in the distance.

"What is it?" Kate asked.

Samuel shook his head.

They sat and watched the darkness in front of them. Something, maybe a small deer or a coyote, moved behind the abandoned trailer in the distance near where a stream ran.

"She'll be back for you," Kate said.

He stared straight ahead. Maybe he wasn't worried his mother wasn't coming back. Maybe it was something else.

Kate could understand how Samuel saw the situation. He might not trust Maribel. She had left them for years, then returned for a few days, and now she was gone again. Kate knew Samuel was old enough to know what his mother had cut from him and his siblings, what she had tucked in her bags to take somewhere else. She told Kate not to say to the kids it was Memphis. It was safer the less they knew.

Kate put her arm around him. He didn't lean into her, but he didn't move away from her either.

"Tu madres amores."

Samuel corrected her, "Tu madre te ama."

"I know. My Spanish is bad." Kate jumped down from the hood and got a blanket out of the car where Sofia and Rodrigo still slept soundly. She wrapped the blanket around Samuel's shoulders.

"I called your mother yesterday after we went to the bank," Kate said, not knowing how much Samuel understood, but he nodded slightly. "She will be here soon, just a few more days."

They sat still for a while, the darkness around them so complete she felt both absorbed and protected by it.

"My mother," Kate said and pointed at herself. "She was bad."

"Bad?" Samuel asked.

Kate knew it was more complicated than that, but she couldn't explain it in English, much less Spanish. "Bad. But she loved me. And your mother is good. She is a good person. She loves you. Do you understand?"

Samuel nodded.

"When your mother comes back this time, she won't leave you again."

That was not a promise she could make, but she also knew just how much Samuel needed to hear it. The tiniest glow of light broke above the horizon to their right. Kate and Samuel waited and watched the sun slowly rise.

As they watched the sky lighten in shades of deep purple then vivid coral pink, Kate began to see some new options. She accepted she could not just show up and see her daughter. But maybe she could start with a letter sent to Toni and Daniel before they moved again. She could give them her own contact information in case they would let Anna reach out to her someday. She had an address of her own now. She knew that daughters did seek their mothers in time, even if they didn't like them, even if they did not forgive them, even if they were worlds apart.

The next morning, Kate was ready to get to work. She took the children back into Walden. The small town was organized on a main street with a diner, two liquor stores, and a feed supply/hardware store. At the farm supply store, Kate bought every heavy-duty cleaner she could find. TSP, ammonia, bleach. She bought buckets, scrub brushes, sand paper, a long fluorescent lightbulb, contractor bags, cans of white latex paint, and a case of snap traps for mice.

"Do you sell peanut butter?" she asked while the three children looked at the candy in the racks by the register.

The kid behind the register shook his head as he put all that she had bought in empty cardboard boxes instead of bags. "No, but the liquor store does."

She thanked him but didn't bother asking which one as she put a handful of candy bars on the counter with the cleaning supplies.

When she went inside the diner, the tables were full of men wearing work shirts studded with silver rivets on the breast pockets and cowboy hats tipped down over leathery faces. They stared at her in the baggy Broncos sweatshirts she bought at a gas station along their way. She had not brought all her things from Jackie's, just a couple days of clothes. They all needed more to wear to keep warm at night.

"Coffee?" the waitress asked. Kate looked up to see a heavy woman carrying a glass coffee pitcher with a brown plastic rim and handle.

"Coffee would be great."

Sofia and Rodrigo were stacking up the creamers in precarious towers. Samuel looked at the menu, his lips moving slightly as he sounded out the words in English.

The waitress flipped the cup that was resting upside down on the paper placemat. She looked uncomfortable as if she was plagued by arthritis or some other pain. Her face was puffy and sallow.

"You Apache?" she asked as she poured the coffee.

"No," Kate said.

"Ute?" The waitress tried to size Kate up again, searching her face, her hair, which was down, heavy against her back.

"No."

"I haven't seen you around before."

"I'm moving out here. Some land out toward Cowdrey." Kate wrapped her hands around the heat of the ceramic mug.

The waitress took out her green note pad. "Not sure if I should say welcome or sorry. What can I get you all?"

Kate spread the butter and poured the syrup before cutting the pancakes. Rodrigo and Sofia watched intently while Samuel cut his own. Kate ate a piece of bacon Sofia had pushed away and listened to the men at the next table over talk. They were farmers, talking about rainfall and some new regulation on a pesticide one of them had sworn by. It didn't work worth a damn anyway, nothing did, another of them said.

Kate told the kids she would be right back. When she approached the table, the men stopped arguing. "Excuse me. I'm just wondering if any of you could recommend a place to get a good small-scale irrigation system."

The men looked at each other across coffee mugs and greasy plates. She knew they wouldn't take her seriously, but if Mrs. Newkirk had taught her anything, it was how to win people over by listening to their advice.

"For livestock? Fowl or bovine?" The man who had answered her immediately glanced back at the men at his table.

"For crops," Kate said.

The oldest looking man at the table crossed his arms over his chest and said, "Crops? I guess that depends on what you're trying to grow. What you need depends on what you're trying to do."

"I want to start a big garden for now," Kate said. "Later, I might be in the market for plate glass. A lot of it, but we'll see how the garden goes first."

She made one more stop at the post office. Kate bought a small padded envelope and included the short note to Toni and Daniel she had written in the van that morning. She included the full address for the P.O. box she set up with the clerk behind the counter. Inside the envelope, she also tucked a folded piece of newsprint from a free community newspaper in a rack by the door. Inside the page of listed land and farm equipment for sale was the gold heart locket Jackie had given Kate when she was pregnant with Anna. It had been a poor choice in that it was not Kate's style or something she thought she wanted. Now, it would serve the purpose of drawing lines between the three stars in a constellation of women linked by blood and troubled love. Kate would keep that P.O. Box open for as long as it took. She hoped they would reach out to her. If they didn't though, someday, when her daughter was no longer a child, when Anna was the age Kate knew girls try to figure out who their mothers are, Kate would find her.

When they returned from town, Kate sent the kids out to play, telling Samuel to keep an eye on them while she cleaned out the trailer. It was currently uninhabitable, parked on the far side of her land near a deep stream with a decent current. The trailer was painted matte white with a red stripe at the middle and bottom, except for where the metal was rusted out. Kate pulled on the broken doorknob that didn't actually latch.

Inside, the aluminum pinged around her, metal contracting as it warmed up under the intensifying sun. She set out her bucket, the bleach, and two scrub brushes. She put in a new florescent lightbulb above the sink with no running water. She pulled the pull chain. Nothing. She had figured she probably needed a new generator, but it was worth a shot.

At the back of the trailer was a double bed. It was clear from the holes in the mattress, not to mention the droppings, animals had been living in it. Kate pushed open the windows along the backside of the trailer that faced the stream. She pulled down a panel of laminate on hinges that folded out from the wall that served as a kitchen table.

All day Kate dragged out everything that wasn't bolted down, and some things that were. She would set a lot of it on fire that night in the clearing she had made: the mattress, a broken cabinet, three wooden doors that didn't seem to go with anything. She and the children would sit around it like a campfire and let everything go up in flames.

Her nasal passages burned from the disinfectants she had used to clean the surfaces in the kitchen, the walls, and the floors. Her head pounded and ached. She stripped off her bleach-stained clothes and changed into a clean tank top and underwear. She carried the dirty clothes into the stream with her. After a week on her land, she didn't even look over her shoulder anymore. She knew no one, besides the kids, was there to see her.

Kate walked into the stream at the place where she had found the flattest, smoothest rocks. The water was cold, but she was getting used to it. She held her clothes under the flowing current and rubbed the fabric together, letting the water numb her skin where the bleach had irritated it.

The next day, they drove back to town for more supplies, more pancakes, and for Kate to call Maribel from a pay phone. Charlie had cut her cell phone, although there was no signal anywhere on her land anyway. She left the kids in the car while she called Maribel.

"It's done," Maribel had said. "How are they?"

"They're good."

"Samuel too?"

"He's okay. He'll be better when you get here. They all miss you."

Maribel cleared her throat. "I got a puppy. They were selling them out of the back of a truck at this gas station somewhere. Jonesboro? I think it might have been a mistake. She peed through her box twice already."

Kate laughed.

"I think it's a pitbull mix. She's so cute. Don't tell them. I want it to be a surprise."

Kate had not told Maribel about the puppy Sofia cried about leaving in Juárez. Maybe the girl had told her mother herself.

"They will love that," Kate said. "You're a good mother."

Maribel was silent on the other end for a moment. Kate thought maybe the signal had dropped.

"We aren't going to stay there," Maribel said. "We'll move on after a few days."

Kate swallowed hard. She looked back at the children, but with the way the light was hitting the windshield, she couldn't see them.

"I understand."

Kate had hoped Maribel would start over out here with her, that maybe they would do things the way they wanted to. Kate knew what kind of fertilizer she would use, how she would rotate the soil. She and Maribel would be smarter, more careful than Smith. They were women who inherently knew the value of things, what was worth risk and what wasn't.

Kate understood now that she was expecting too much. Maribel had a network of people out there, somewhere. Kate didn't have that, but she did have this land now. They had trusted each other long enough to help each other out of a dangerous place, and that was a lot. Kate had the love of horticulture. Maribel, after all, was an English teacher.

Kate could call Luke. She was ready to grow. She would do it alone if she had to, but she suspected he would not be able to resist the idea of building something like this. Even without Charlie's family, Luke would find plenty of work in Boston. She bet he could find time, a few weeks, a month or two, to come out and help her build the kind of structures she needed. She needed a house for growing. She needed a building for drying and packaging. She needed somewhere to live, a house, something simple, but something that was hers. Mrs. Newkirk had provided the land. She would have to find a way to sustain life on it.

No matter what, Kate would not go backwards. She had a place to stay.

Every one of them needed a bath. The light was fading as the two younger children sat on the bank of the creek in their underwear. Samuel was up to his waist in his shorts trying to coax in his brother and sister. Kate had already washed their change of clothes. They hung along with hers in the low branches of a straggly tree to dry.

Kate floated in her tank top and jean shorts out to the farthest bend of the creek where the water was deepest. When Samuel finally coaxed Rodrigo in the water, Kate swam up next to Sofia on the bank.

Kate stretched out her arms and took the girl's warm body against her chest, drawing her into the water. Sofia sucked in her breath, her arms wrapped tightly around Kate's neck. Kate inhaled the sweet smell of little girl sweat and grass and dirt in the warmth of Sofia's skin.

"Hold your breath," Kate said. She breathed in deeply and puffed out her cheeks to show Sofia what she meant. Sofia held herself against Kate's chest, her eyes clenched, her breath held ready to go under. Kate dropped backwards into the water, taking Sofia with her.

Ruby Newkirk had once said to Kate, "Don't expect anything to last in the freezer unless you blanch it."

They were in Mrs. Newkirk's kitchen putting up summer squash. Kate lifted the strainer basket with the yellow slices out of the boiling water.

"Alright, now hurry over here to the sink," Mrs. Newkirk stepped out of the way and gestured to the big bowl of ice water she had waiting. "Get them in quick and hold them down there under the surface to stop the cooking."

Kate caught the floating squash under her fingers and palms and held them to the bottom of the bowl until her hands hurt.

"How much longer?"

Mrs. Newkirk wiped her hands on the bottom of her apron. "As long as you can stand."

Kate brought Sofia back up from under the surface of the creek. The child laughed and shrieked in her arms. The girl did not know it yet, but Kate hoped she would see it clearly in the women who loved her, on all sides of the different borders and barriers she would cross in her life, whatever is in front of you, whatever is behind, it is possible to start over. Kate would keep that truth too, whatever is above you, whatever is below, it is possible to spread new roots into something that is finally all your own.

ACKNOWLEDGEMENTS

I was having one the worst days of my professional life when I received word that an early version of this manuscript had won the Marianne Russo Award for a novel-in-progress from the Key West Literary Seminar. That support and experience in Key West with Dantiel Moniz, Michael Lee, Katya Apekina, Leila Chatti, and Naomi Jackson among others in January 2018 was a critical turning point in surviving the fifteen years it took to finish this book.

Other writing communities provided vital support and inspiration along the way starting with Emerson College's MFA community and Maria Flook who told me to stop trying to transfer and to start writing. Thank you to the Stockholm First Pages Prize and especially to Sarah Fuchs, Sandra Jensen, and Lizzie Harwood and to the women of the L'ATELIER Writers community. So many conversations, exchanges, and long, glorious dinners shaped my outlook and writing.

I have been lucky to benefit from an artistic grant from the Elizabeth George Foundation and from fellowships from MacDowell. There is nowhere else I have learned so much in such a short period of time as I did in Peterborough. The fellows I met had a significant impact on how I see art and its place in the world. Picture me in various department meetings or in front of sinks full of dirty dishes drawing deep on those experiences to get me through. Because I have. Frequently.

I am grateful to two, wildly talented writers Alena Dillon and Karen Nadu Ologoudou, who never let me get away with my favorite avoidance tactic of complaining. You women accept no excuses.

Thank you to early readers including Jenny Bridgers, Caitlin McGillicuddy, Mike Elvin, Arielle Gronner, and Suzy Hooker. Your response to those messy, searching drafts helped the work find its footing.

Another thanks that can be traced back to the beginning goes to Michelle Bailat-Jones who pulled me out of a bookstore in Lausanne when I was pregnant with my first child and said I was not allowed to stop writing, which I was actively trying to do. Thank you for your friendship, editing, and endless, brilliant literary perspective and passion for craft. You have sustained me.

Special thanks to my friends Ana Laguarda, Yadira Ibarra-Dackert, and Chris Blagg, who read at the very end of this process with an eye to the complexities of language and the places I was trying to bring to life. It's hard to express just how much you helped change the work for the better. Thank you to Alejandra Oliva who provided feedback on timing, immigration policies, and perspectives of people who are in situations similar to some of the characters in this book.

I am eternally grateful to both Jenni Ferrari-Adler of Union Literary and Diane Goettel of Black Lawrence Press. They recognized the potential in this book at different points in the process. Quite simply, their belief in the story, editing, and advice brought this work into the world. Many thanks also to Zoe-Aline Howard and Cassie Mannes Murray at Pine State Publicity who worked their magic to give me such meaningful opportunities to talk about this work and share it more widely.

Thank you to my father whose faith must have wavered at points, although he never, ever showed it. Forgive him for how he is going to carry on at the coffee shop. Deep gratitude goes to my mother who paid me twenty-five cents a page as a child to write in a journal, who drove me to Iowa to try to break off the waitlist, who listened to lots of self-pitying phone calls over the years and weathered my silence in between. She read more versions of this thing that anyone else. She is a smart, observant critic and talented writer herself. Without her, there would be no book.

Thanks to my own children who have dealt with my hiding away in bedrooms, attics, various offices, hotel lobbies, and writing residencies. Watching you all now forge your own creative paths has been the greatest honor of my life.

And for David, who is the most patient person I know. He never once discouraged me, never once told me to wait until later. He cleared up time, space, and money when all were in short supply to make this possible. I am forever grateful, forever in debt. Put it on my tab.

SARA JOHNSON ALLEN was raised (mostly) in North Carolina. *Down Here We Come Up*, winner of the Big Moose Prize from Black Lawrence Press, is her debut novel.

A recipient of the Marianne Russo Award for Emerging Writers by the Key West Literary Seminar, the Stockholm Writers Festival First Pages Prize, an artistic grant from the Elizabeth George Foundation, and MacDowell fellowships, her work has appeared in *PANK Magazine*, *SmokeLong Quarterly*, and *Reckon Review* among others.

When she is not teaching or trying to keep up with her three kids, she writes about 'place' and how it shapes us.